FALLING

BOOK THREE AFTER THE THAW

TAMAR SLOAN
HEIDI CATHERINE

SEQUEL HOUSE

For Connor and Ash

NOVA

The Outlands were in sight when the storm hit.

Thom had kept his gaze on the sliver of land the moment they saw it, reporting each detail as it came into view.

Nothing but burnt trees.

No sign of life.

Whoa, it's much bigger than we thought.

Flick, on the other hand, kept her gaze skyward the moment they realized a storm was approaching.

It'll probably be one of the small ones like we've had recently.

We might be able to out-paddle it.

Sweet Terra that's coming fast.

Nova had just gritted her teeth and drawn her oar through the water, over and over and over. One sentence became her mantra. Her heartfelt wish.

Get me and my baby to shore.

Get me and my baby to shore.

Get me and my baby to shore.

When the first drops of rain hit, heavy and hard and punishing, it became a prayer.

Please let us get to shore.

1

Please, please, please let me and my baby make it to shore.

It turns out Flick's final observation was right.

The storm comes in fast, growing quickly. The swell multiplying below as the rain pummels from above. Any semblance of day is swallowed by the black clouds.

"I'm going to bring the sail down," Thom shouts over the wind. He scrabbles to the center of the raft, yanking down the length of sheet that was tied to the metal pole jutting up through the middle.

His addition to the raft had been the vital component that got them to the Outlands so fast. Flick had danced with such glee Nova wasn't sure her curls were going to stay intact when they'd shown it to her. Thank Terra the sail got them this close before the storm hit.

A blast of wind yanks at the raft, pushing it backward. Nova wipes the spray from her face, her eyes already stinging. "We can't afford to lose the ground we've made," she calls out.

"We need to row hard!" Thom shouts, water slicking down his face.

Nova's arms scream with the strain of having rowed for so long, but she doesn't let up. Their only chance of survival is to get to the Outlands.

Beside her, Flick doesn't stop repeating the same words as she rows. "It came so fast. Only the big ones come this fast."

Gritting her teeth, Nova pours all her energy into helping them move forward. She hasn't come this far to end up dissolving in the ocean. The wind buffets again, droplets splashing them, trying to draw the raft away from the promise of shore. Nova digs the oar in deeper, seeing Thom and Flick do the same, fighting to regain the lost ground.

But in the sleeting rain and growing waves, she can no longer tell if they're making progress.

In fact, it feels like they're still going backward.

Lightning strikes, splintering through the sky that's become drenched in night. Flick screams, curling into herself, Thom diving to protect her. Nova's hands clench around her oar as a boom of thunder instantly follows it, the sound feeling like it's rattling her bones.

The raft is thrown high before bottoming out, the world around them a wall of sea and Flick screams again. Hands trembling, she looks around as if she's not sure how she got here. "I can't die! My baby!" she shrieks.

Nova squints through the rain to see the bag of what little food and water they'd packed is gone. What's more, Flick's lost her oar. Her eyes stinging from more than just the acid seawater, Nova knows she can't give in to the fear exploding within her. Their only chance is to row for as long as they can.

She turns to Thom. "We have to try."

Thom nods, his hair and clothes plastered to his body as he picks up his oar. Together, they spear them into the angry sea, desperately trying to gain some control and move the raft forward.

But as the raft is tossed like a leaf, Nova realizes two things —they're powerless against the rage Mother Nature is throwing at them...and she has no idea which direction the Outlands are anymore.

The next wave doesn't lift them, it crashes over them. Nova crumples beneath the force, clinging to the raft with one hand as she clasps the oar to her. Without it, they're nothing but a piece of driftwood on this seething sea.

As the water ebbs away, lightning forks through the sky again and Nova looks up, rain pelting her face. When she sees the violence above, her hand clamps to her chest, her heart feeling like it's going to crash right through her ribs.

Sweet Terra, the danger isn't just beneath them as the ocean tries to swallow them. The skies are alive with electricity.

Lightning illuminates the world again, the sound deafening,

the glare blinding. Fear is all Nova has left. But it's enough. It's what she'll use to fight for her baby's life.

"There!" shouts Flick, pointing ahead. "Land!"

"Row!" Thom shouts back, his voice laced with determination. "Row, Nova!"

Her arms trembling, Nova scoops her oar through the water. This time, when a wave douses them, it propels them in the direction they're heading. It's enough to spark a small ray of hope.

Please let us get to shore.

On the other side of the raft, Thom roars with each pull of the oar. Panting, Nova times her stroke with each bellow, her muscles exhausted and powered by nothing but adrenalin. They just need to get close to shore. Swimming is going to be inevitable, but the less they have to do it, the higher their chance of survival will be.

She sees the next bolt of lightning arc across the sky, this one splitting then splitting again. It lights up the black clouds, piercing them with shades of bruise and blood.

Nova's heart jackknifes to her throat. "The lightning! It's getting closer!"

She glances at the pole rising up from the center of the raft. What was their savior has now become a beacon for death.

When she sees the beginning of the next strike, Nova knows millions of volts are about to come at them.

"Jump!" she screams as she dives for the water, hoping Flick and Thom are doing the same.

The warm ocean engulfs her, feeling no safer than the world she just left. The violent waves push her down, the pressure just as suffocating as the absence of air.

She goes limp, the current tugging at her as she waits to watch any bubbles rise to the surface. Finding the fragile globules of air, she follows them, kicking hard as her lungs shriek desperately for air.

She surfaces, water filling her gasping mouth, the world smelling like electrocuted air. Frantically, she looks one way then the other. "Flick! Thom!"

But everywhere is nothing but angry water and black terror.

She spots the raft a few feet away, a flicker of fire like a beacon where the lightning struck. Knowing she can't go back, Nova treads water, already tiring at trying to keep her head above water.

"Flick. Thom." This time, it's a struggle to shout their names.

It seems so useless. The roar of the waves. The clamor in the sky. They won't hear her.

She's never felt so small in her life. So insignificant. So vulnerable.

Everything the raft was protecting them from is now a reality.

Leatherskins.

Acid eroding their bodies.

Drowning.

Fighting what feels inevitable, Nova tries once more. "Thom. Flick. Please, answer me."

Lightning strikes again, as if Mother Nature is mocking her with exactly how defenseless she is. A sob escapes her throat. They came so close.

"We're here."

Nova spins around. The words were weak but unmistakable. "Thom! Where are you?" She turns again, eyes squinting in the low visibility. Water tugs at her body as it pours down from above. Please don't let that have been her imagination.

As the sea peaks on a wave, Nova sees them. Thom is bobbing in the water, holding Flick, not far from the raft. "Nova! Here!" he calls.

A burst of energy slices through Nova as she battles the water to reach them. Breathing heavily, she discovers why they didn't make the same effort to reach her.

Flick is unconscious.

Thom is half-floating on his back, holding Flick to him, face up. "The waves... She was under too long..." Thom pants.

Swimming over, Nova presses her fingers to Flick's throat. Relief has her eyes closing for precious seconds. "She's still alive."

Thom's face looks like Nova just gave him the most precious of gifts. "Thank Terra."

"We need to get her to shore."

We all need to get to shore.

"I saw it with the last lightning strike," Thom shouts over the storm. "It's that way." He points behind him, seeming to indicate a black abyss.

Nova nods, her breath getting too heavy to talk. She swims beside Thom, taking one of Flick's limp arms. "I'll—"

"No! I've got her. You keep an eye out for land."

Nova's mind rebels but her exhausted body agrees. She can barely keep herself afloat right now.

Lifting her arms feels like she's lifting logs, but Nova strikes in the direction Thom indicated. He paddles beside her, dragging the unconscious Flick along with him, her head lolling as he struggles to keep her face above water.

The waves lift them high then drop them low and the rain pounds from above. It's exhausting when their bodies already have so little to give.

It's terrifying when the flashes of land are few and it's impossible to tell if they're getting closer.

It's agonizing wondering if she did the right thing and whether she should've stayed in Askala.

But they keep swimming. Coughing as the waves try to climb down her throat, her chest heaving as she struggles for air, her limbs clawing more than paddling, Nova keeps swimming. As her energy progressively wanes, she tells herself at least she fought for her child's life.

When her foot hits something in the inky water Nova yanks it up, a fresh outbreak of terror screaming through her veins.

It has to be a leatherskin, coming up to feast on her drained body. And there's no more energy to fight it, no matter how much her heart is already crying for the child she never had a chance to hold.

Silently, Nova sends Kian an apology. He never knew about their child. She never said the words to him.

They should never have let Askala define their love.

As her leg falls back down through the water, Nova feels it again. Hard and unwieldy and rough.

The whoop from Thom is as startling as the realization that she just touched land. Flattening her feet, Nova lets her body absorb the solid foundation she just found, elation making her lightheaded.

She can't believe it. They're almost there!

A wave hits her, knocking her over. The warm, acidic water engulfs Nova, reminding her that her skin is starting to burn. The sensation had gotten lost in the exhaustion and fear. Scrabbling to find solid footing again, she hears Thom call out, the words barely audible over the storm.

"Nova! I need help."

He's not far behind her, struggling to gain purchase as the waves push and pull, water repeatedly flooding over Flick's face.

Nova paddles over and slips in beside Thom, taking Flick's arm and trying to lift her shoulders higher. "We're almost there, Thom. Come on."

He nods, exhaustion draining his ability to reply. Together, they fight the constantly changing current, the sensation of the water becoming shallower and shallower their driving force. Each time they stumble, they get up and keep going. Each time the waves try to reach Flick's face, they pull her higher.

The minutes it takes to half-swim, half-stagger the last yards feel too long. Like the distance is too great.

But they make it. The grit of sand is the most heavenly sensation Nova's ever experienced. They lower Flick to the ground once her feet are out of reach of the waves and collapse beside her, gulping in air.

Reaching out, Nova finds Flick's wrist, relieved to discover a faint, fluttering pulse. It's not strong, but that's not surprising considering what they just went through. Turning her head and resting it on the sand, Nova blinks in the rain, studying Flick's profile.

She's pale and motionless, her eyelashes a stark contrast against her skin. Her curls are flattened and coated in sand. Nova glances lower, focusing on Flick's chest.

The heart rate that had finally started to slow spikes again. Nova pushes up on her elbow, leaning in closer.

"What?" Thom's panicked question matches the dread blossoming like ink through Nova's veins. "What is it?"

Nova places a trembling hand on Flick's chest, confirming the awful truth.

She isn't breathing.

Nova pushes to her knees, urgency powering her shout. "Roll her onto her side!"

Together, they push Flick over and Nova presses down on her ribs. Water gushes from her mouth like vomit. Relaxing the pressure, Nova takes a breath before pushing down again. More water spews out, flowing onto the sand.

"Come on, Flick," Nova mutters. "This was your chance at freedom."

Another compression and Flick jerks forward, coughing and sputtering, and Nova falls back on her heels in relief. Coughing means air is getting into her lungs. She's no longer drowning from the inside out.

Thom darts around, falling in front of Flick and holding her shoulders as she ejects the remaining seawater. "Thank Terra," he breathes. "I thought…"

Nova crawls away, the inevitability she'd been able to stall climbing up her throat. She only makes it a few feet before her own swallowed sea water heaves onto the sand. Her body convulses as if it's trying to rid itself of every last drop, retching over and over again until her stomach feels like it's about to come up next.

Unable to hold herself up, she collapses onto her side, exhausted, relieved...aware they're far from safe.

Nova's muscles tremble with exhaustion. Even her marrow feels soaked. She tries to move but her body begs her for a break, her bones feeling too heavy.

She struggles to sit upright. They need to get up and move inland, no matter what they just went through.

"We need to find shelter," she croaks, hoping the other two can hear her.

The wail from Flick has Nova rushing back, her pulse once again a stampede through her veins.

She's heard that wail before. In the infirmary. When a life has been lost and raw grief is an involuntary flood.

She looks around frantically, trying to find Thom. He looked fine, but fluid can continue to build up in the lungs after a near-drowning. She should've kept an eye on him.

Except Thom is beside Flick, cradling her. Nova falls beside them, about to ask where Flick's hurt.

Flick lifts her fingers from her thighs, the rain instantly slashing streaks through the blood coating her trembling hand.

"Please, no," she whispers. "My baby."

KIAN

*E*very time lightning strikes, Kian's teeth clench. As the ensuing thunder rolls across the Oasis, a flash of fear contracts through him.

Nova is out in that storm.

Pregnant with their child.

And she's there because she didn't believe Kian would keep her safe.

Anguish flares so hard Kian has to close his eyes as his breath shallows. He believed he was doing everything right when he became leader of Askala. He was following the path that had been carved out for him.

And he'd done everything wrong.

Lengthening his stride, he yanks his shoulders back. It's time to make new choices.

It's time for change.

And that begins in the upper decks with the Unbound.

He's already asked Dex to find Bea so she can round up as many as possible. He wants to talk to them. Before he does what needs to be done to make this right.

Kian's just about to take the last flight of stairs when he hears someone behind him.

"Kian, stop!"

It's his father striding down the corridor, his own brand of thunder storming across his features.

Kian slows but doesn't stop. "I can't talk right now, Dad."

There's nothing else to say. His father's obvious disappointment is painful, but it's not going to stop Kian from seeing this through.

"Where are you going?"

Kian turns around. The question his father wants to ask is 'What are you doing?' Or maybe it's 'How could you do this?'

"I'm going to the upper decks to talk to the Unbound."

His father's frown only deepens. "To tell them about the rations?"

Kian clenches his hands, bracing himself. "I'm going to tell them they'll receive weekly pteropods just like the Bound do."

"You're going to do what?" His father reels back. "What are you thinking, Kian? Where will this end?"

Kian unwinds his body. His father's scared, more scared than Kian is. He's worried everything he's built is about to be undermined.

By his son.

Kian takes a step forward, reaching out. "I don't know. But there has to be a way, Dad. We can keep working toward healing our planet without the Unbound paying the price they do."

But his father retreats a step. "That's not a plan, Kian. That's little more than a dream. An idealistic one."

Kian's hand drops, disappointment dragging it down. "Isn't that what Askala was built on, all those generations ago?"

His father snaps his mouth shut, the frown doing the impossible and deepening. He gazes at Kian, everything about him trying to tell his son he's making the wrong decision.

Turning, Kian continues down the corridor. His father's support would've been nice. Heck, it would've made this much easier.

But it's not a prerequisite.

He's going to do this, with or without his blessing.

When he arrives on the upper decks, Kian has to hide his surprise as he takes in who's there.

Dex nods from the other side of the room—a spacious area where a handful of card tables and chairs have been pushed against the wall. A few Bound are with him—Aarov, Tory... Shiloh.

What has him pausing is that there are far fewer Unbound than he'd hoped.

He recognizes Bea, Vern standing beside her, and offers her a smile. She crosses her arms and settles back, her gaze challenging but also wary. She's waiting to hear what Kian has to say before she gives him an indication of how welcome he is.

Kian nods, acknowledging that's fair. He's sure whenever his father has spoken to them it hasn't been with good news.

Kian takes a step forward, hesitating when he sees one more person arrive.

His father slips in through a door on the opposite side of the room, sliding behind the small crowd. Kian looks away before his gaze can catch his, aware he's not here to encourage him, only to freeze when he catches sight of who his father brought.

His mother is standing beside him, tucking a strand of hair back from her worried face. Holding back the frown is hard. His father knows he just made this ten times harder.

Although, it's still not going to stop Kian.

Straightening his shoulders so he can carry the weight of this moment, he steps forward. "Thank you for coming on such short notice. I appreciate it."

There's shuffling as gazes slide away. They're here to support Kian about as much as his father is.

But that's okay. He doesn't expect any Unbound to trust him. Just like Nova didn't.

"As you all know, we've had successive storms batter Askala. Each one has inflicted repeated damage to the gardens. What's more, locusts decimated a significant portion before this current storm."

People glance at each other, degrees of nervousness passing between them. One or two frown as ferociously as his father.

"The loss to our food supply has necessitated rationing—"

"And we'll be the first to know when we get to eat again?" challenges Vern. "As we watch the Bound feed themselves and their children?"

The people around Vern nod, their anger holding a hint of hostility.

Kian lifts his hands in a conciliatory gesture. "We're all about to be hungry."

Bea steps forward. "Some more than others!" she spits at him.

Dean, his hair matching the florid red of his cheeks, glares angrily. "I'm tired of being hungry."

Kian sees his father lean back against the wall as he crosses his arms. He's noting that this never happened when the great Magnus spoke to the Unbound. The interruptions and thinly veiled anger weren't an issue. They always accepted his father's words, on the surface calm and compliant.

The Unbound are testing Kian.

As his father watches.

Kian looks around the room, summoning a sense of calm. Maybe it's a good thing his father and mother are here. They should hear this, too.

"No. No one will be more hungry than anyone else. I'm here to tell you that the remaining food stores will be distributed equally among the people of Askala, irrespective of Bound or Unbound status."

Stunned silence slams through the room. A gentle kind of joy fills Kian. This is the first time he's felt like he's leading with heart.

"What's more, you'll no longer earn pods."

Startled breaths break the quiet, the anger that was just banked flaring hot. Hands clench around the room as brows slam down.

"You'll be allocated weekly pods just as the Bound are." Kian consciously doesn't glance at his father. "I doubt anyone would be able to survive in the current conditions without them."

A collective breath rushes out. Looks of disbelief are passed around. Kian's father is probably the most shocked. He pushes away from the wall, his arms falling to his side.

"No," he mouths.

Bea crosses her arms. "I don't trust this. Bounds aren't this... kind."

"They're probably fattening us up for something," mutters Vern, loud enough for several people to hear.

The shuffles are back, as are the glares. Dean's lip curls, his hot gaze zeroed in on Kian. It makes Kian sad to realize how deeply the distrust runs.

"Once this storm passes, I invite you all to the pod pool. The first week's worth of pods will be handed out."

To his left, Kian sees Dex nod. "He's telling the truth. Kian proposed this at our recent High Bound meeting. The vote was in favor."

Not unanimous. Two High Bounds objected, Zali one of them, scared as to what this could mean for their children. But not enough to be able to stop this announcement.

Kian glances at Dex, grateful for his cousin's support. After what Kian did with the Remnants, it's more than he deserves.

At the front, an older woman is leaning against a young man and Kian recognizes Finn, Jay's older brother. Finn is Bound, which means he shouldn't be here. But it seems his kind heart extends beyond the lines of Bound and Unbound. Finn slips an arm around the woman as a tear trickles down her cheek. Gratitude is swimming in their eyes.

They go to speak but Kian puts up his hand to stop them. He doesn't want thanks for something that should've been done a long time ago.

Plus, there's more.

Kian glances at his father as he pulls in a breath. "There will be changes in Askala. We won't forget what destroyed Earth—human greed and selfishness. We've proven the way forward is through kindness and healing. But we'll do it with open arms, not with division and inequality. It's for that reason I believe we need to connect with the Outlands." Before anyone can recover from this next surprise, Kian gets to the punchline. "I'm going to head an expedition across the ocean. We'll take peace to them."

He scans the room. No one speaks, several eyes are wide, most of them look at him like he's lost his mind.

Dex is open-mouthed.

"Three of us have already left, running away because they thought the Outlands would be safer than Askala," Kian continues, working to keep his voice steady. Admitting this is why Nova and the others ran hurts. "I want to find them and bring them back. Whilst there, I want to forge connections with the people of the Outlands. So, we can continue to heal the Earth together."

His piece said, Kian realizes he's breathing a little heavy. No one says anything, apparently speechless.

He finally raises his eyes to the back of the room, knowing he has to face his parents' reactions. His father is shell-shocked. Kian winces. His mother looks devastated.

Dean is the first to move. He steps forward, hands clenched. "That's why you're doing this. You want to take some of us with you. You're looking for recruits. Some expendable Unbounds to go on this crazy mission."

Kian shakes his head. "I understand your mistrust, Dean. You're right, I'm looking for people to come with me. But I wanted to tell you all first because I'm offering a payment of fifty pods to anyone who does."

Dean's eyes widen as he tries to absorb the sheer wealth fifty pods is to an Unbound. It would take them more than a year to earn that many.

Kian turns to scan the crowd again. "Fifty pods. Eat them, share them, keep them for when you need them most. It's appropriate compensation for a trip that isn't without danger."

When his father finally moves, Kian looks up. Maybe he's realized this is the way forward. Maybe he's seen the distrust, the anger their system has managed to breed.

But his father doesn't look at him as he turns away and scans his hand over the sensor, his face dark with anger as he steps through the door. His mother follows, slipping a trembling hand over her mouth. Her single glance Kian's way is full of confusion.

Kian almost takes a step toward her. She looked…betrayed.

They're gone without a word, but their actions say it all.

Kian clenches his jaw. There's no time to process their rejection.

"I'll go." Several people gasp in surprise as Finn removes his arm from the old woman and steps forward. "I'll help you get to the Outlands."

Kian's shock is so strong he realizes he wasn't expecting anyone to volunteer. "Thank you, Finn."

Especially considering it was the ocean that took his brother. Kian wonders how much Finn is trying to prove that bravery runs in their family's gene pool, not the awkward nervousness Jay was known for.

"Well, for fifty pods, you can count me in."

Kian has to suppress his frown as Dean raises his hand. He's a strong, young male, just the sort of person you'd want on this expedition.

Except Kian's not sure he can trust him.

"Thank you, Dean. Your help is appreciated." He looks to the others. "There's room for one more, but I'll also ask the Bound if they would like to complete the team so there's no expectation for any of you to do this."

Bea snorts quietly. "Ain't no Bound going to risk their precious hide to open our borders, let alone to find three missing Unbound."

"I'll go." Shiloh's voice rings out high and clear as she steps forward. "I'd like to come, Kian."

It takes Kian a second to recover from the surprise. Why would Shiloh risk her life for this?

She must sense his hesitation, because Shiloh smiles. "You're right, Kian. We've closed ourselves off from valuable resources —discovering the sap proved that. We need to do this." She shrugs. "Plus, I'm a healer. My skills could be helpful."

Kian nods, noting the way her eyes shine. Is Shiloh doing this because she loves Askala, or because she loves him?

And does she know he's going after Nova?

"Thank you, Shiloh. You'll be an asset to the team."

His business finished, Kian smiles at the crowd. "Thank you for your time. I promise you'll be cared for as equals from now on." He catches Bea's eyes. "No one is unworthy."

The small crowd slowly disperses, many of them talking among themselves. Kian has no doubt the news will be quickly circulated throughout the upper decks.

The Unbound will rejoice.

It's how the Bound and High Bound react that will be interesting.

There are only a few people left when Bea approaches him. Her keen gaze assesses him. "Did you mean all"—she waves her hand in the air to encapsulate the words that were just spoken—"that?"

Kian nods. "I did."

"Not what I expected from the son of Magnus."

Kian's heart clenches. "It wasn't what he expected, either."

"So, you're heading off to the Outlands, huh?" Bea chews over her own question, looking at him like she's not quite sure what to make of him.

"The moment it's safe enough to do so."

Bea nods thoughtfully. "You bring our Nova back to us, okay?"

Our Nova.

It doesn't surprise Kian that Nova has already developed strong bonds in the upper decks. How could he have believed that Askala could decide whether she was worthy?

That she was less, somehow...

His body tightens. "I promise to find her. I promise to make right what has been wrong."

Bea steps away, an eyebrow tweaked in challenge. "I'd like to see that...Kian."

She walks back to Vern and, taking his hand, leaves the room.

Leaving only one person remaining.

Dex walks over slowly, his face unreadable. "Shiloh's gone to pack. She said she'd organize extra sap."

Kian nods. "That's good." He pauses. "Does she know it's Nova who's out there?"

"My guess is she knows exactly who left on that raft. Stuff like that doesn't stay a secret in Askala." Dex shrugs. "Well, apart from Thom. She won't see that coming."

Kian nods again, waiting to see if Dex is going to add anything.

Except he doesn't. Kian shifts his weight, trying to

remember a time when he couldn't get a read on Dex. Not one moment comes to mind.

"I know the changes are big and kinda sudden," Kian starts. "But I didn't realize—"

"That change needed to happen? And we couldn't wait for Magnus to come to the party?"

"Well, yeah..."

Dex clamps onto Kian's shoulder, squeezing it. "What you did here is a good thing, Kian."

Relief rushes through him. It's good to have his cousin back on his side. He hadn't realized how much his support meant to him.

"Going to the Outlands...it's selfish," he whispers like it's a confession. If it weren't for Nova, he never would've thought of doing this.

"Love makes pretty amazing stuff happen, Kian." Dex squeezes again before releasing Kian's shoulder. "What would Askala look like if more Bound loved Unbound, even if it was just a fraction of what you feel for Nova?"

Kian blinks. That Askala wouldn't resemble the world he grew up in.

The world he's been championing.

"So, you think I should go?"

Dex arches a wry brow. "I dare you to revoke the offer of fifty pods from Dean." But then he sobers. "I think you should go, Kian. It's the best thing you could do right now."

Unsure what that means, but not having the time to ask, Kian clamps his hand over Dex's. "I want you to be leader in my stead."

Dex jerks back. "What?"

"You heard me. It has to be you. There's no one else I trust completely."

"But—"

"And tell Wren she doesn't need to hide anymore." Kian

almost smiles as he inclines his head. "Although maybe Phoenix should keep lying low."

"There are moments I'm tempted to pummel that dude with my stump," Dex mutters.

This time, Kian grins. "There were moments I wished I had a stump so I could do the same."

Dex chuckles but the sound quickly dies. "Fine, I'll play leader while you're gone." He holds up his hand before Kian can say anything. "But don't expect those ledgers to make sense by the time you return."

Kian sobers, too. The lines are blurring on those ledgers, anyway. Where will his son or daughter be recorded? The child of a High Bound and an Unbound, he or she won't slot neatly into a column.

"Maybe the ledgers need some shaking up."

Afterall, what have those books recorded?

Two words flash bright in Kian's mind. Division and inequality.

Feeling like a traitor, Kian turns away. He knew when he started this that he had no idea where it will end up, just that change was necessary. But those ledgers are the record of Askala.

A black and white testimony of their system. One his father has maintained religiously.

Except Kian has learned about the gray between the lines. Of the pain that underlies it but has been hidden. Like dirty smudges that have been carefully erased.

And he's not willing to overlook it.

Except, how deep has his doubt penetrated? How much more will he betray his family and everything they've worked for?

Knowing those questions don't have an answer, Kian heads for the door. He needs to get the raft ready and the others briefed.

They need to realize how dangerous this will be before they totally commit.

"Kian."

Kian turns around to find Dex still standing where he left him. He goes to move only to stop. "I have a feeling Askala is going to be a pretty different place when you get back."

Kian considers this for a long moment. "I hope so," he says before resuming his path to the door.

It's time for Askala to stop being an island of privilege. It's time for Askala to become a beacon of hope.

Whatever happens, he's glad he was a catalyst for that. That his and Nova's love was a catalyst for that.

As Kian steps onto the gangplank he looks up. Rain pelts his face, but the thunder and lightning are gone. A glimmer of sun hugs the horizon.

The storm is letting up.

It's time to find Nova.

DEX

When Dex was asked to stand in as leader while Kian goes looking for Nova, he hadn't quite known what to say. Because the truth of it is that most likely by the time Kian returns, Askala will no longer exist. Well, not in the same way it does now.

Wren's father could arrive at any moment now, and the league is gaining momentum. It seems it's all going to come to a head over the next few days.

Which is why he's sheltering his eyes from the pelting rain as he makes his way to the lab. His father decided to sit out the storm out there and Dex needs to talk to him as soon as possible. He also needs to let Wren know she can come out of the secret room.

What Dex just witnessed in the upper decks has changed everything. He's no longer certain they need to take Askala by force. Kian just proved he's capable of being a fair leader. That he won't be following in Magnus's footsteps. Changes will be made. He's going to fix what's broken. But Kian can't do that with Callix and the Commander of the Outlands in charge. They need to give Kian a chance.

Dex presses his chip to the sensor and the door to the lab slides open.

They have to tell Kian what's happening before he sets off for the Outlands. He's proven he's fair. It's only right that they return the gesture and do the same for him.

Shaking off the worst of the rain as he steps through the door, Dex heads for the bunkroom. Having given his last set of clean clothes to Wren, he takes some of Jay's, rolling up the sleeves and ankles when he puts them on. He might look a little foolish, but at least he's dry.

Once he's certain Wren's not hiding under his bed, he takes in several deep breaths and heads for the computer room. It's going to feel good to be able to tell her that she can leave that hideout she hates so much.

But when the door slides open, he finds the room empty and the hatch wide open.

"Wren?" he calls. "Dad?"

Nothing but silence bounces back at him. There's not even the sound of Phoenix's smug drawl.

"They're gone."

Dex spins around to see his father at the door.

"I went to give them some fresh water, but there was nobody there."

"Again?" Dex curses. "That's the third time she's run off on me!"

He hates that he's been counting, but it's impossible not to. Each time Wren's disappeared she's left a scar on his heart. He doesn't so much have to count the occasions as he does feel them.

"Where could they be in this storm?" his father asks. "Doesn't seem like the best time to make a break for the forest."

It's then that Dex remembers Wren asking him several times over the past few days about the weather. He'd thought she was feeling cooped up in her underground prison, but is it possible

23

she was asking for another reason? She'd also mentioned some loose dirt on the ground down there and was convinced the roof was starting to cave in. Could she have decided it was no longer safe?

"What is it?" his father asks. "You've got that look on your face again."

"I'm not sure." Dex closes the hatch and rolls his chair over it. "But she's up to something. I just know it. I was hoping to talk to her just now. And to you."

"About what?" His father slides into a chair and raises his eyebrows.

"Kian." Dex swallows, trying to choose his words carefully. "He said Wren could go free."

His father's eyebrows shoot even higher. "What brought that about?"

"Nova, I'd say. He's been doing a lot of thinking. He just announced that the rations are going to be shared evenly amongst the Bound and Unbound from now on."

His father nods. "That's a start. But if he were serious, he'd offer them pods, too."

"He did. One a week. Same as the Bound."

"What?" His father's jaw falls open. "Does Magnus know?"

"Yup. He and Amity walked out when he announced it." Dex lets out a sigh. "You'd think he'd just confessed to a mass murder or something."

"In their minds that's exactly what he did. You know they see the world a little differently."

"I think we should talk to Kian," Dex ventures. "He needs to know what's going on."

His father shakes his head. "No, Dex. That's not a good idea."

Before Dex has the chance to ask why not, there's the sound of boots in the hallway. Heavy boots. Nothing like the bare feet or woven shoes worn in Askala.

"What the hell?" Dex leaps to his feet and slams his stump to the sensor with such force that he's sure he's going to get a bruise. If that's not someone from Askala, then who the hell is it?

He can feel his father's breath on the back of his neck as they wait for the door to slide open.

"Careful," his father cautions in a hushed tone.

The door slides open and Dex's heart skips a beat to see Wren's familiar form. But as the gap opens wider, he sees she's not alone. To her left, he sees Phoenix. Swinging his gaze to her right, he sees the owner of the boots.

A large red-headed guy is standing close by Wren's side, a hand placed possessively on her back. He looks enough like Phoenix that Dex is certain he must be his father.

Ronan.

The man Dex has heard so many stories about and none of them good. But what the hell is he doing here? It was Wren's father who'd been sent for. And why does he have his hand on Wren like he owns her?

The three of them are soaking wet, water pooling at their feet, but they don't seem to care. Their focus is on whatever it is they've come here to say.

"Ronan?" Dex's dad stands and stares at Phoenix's father like he's looking at some kind of ghost. Or perhaps a leatherskin. There's a mixture of confusion, fear and disgust embedded in his features.

"Callix!" Ronan steps forward making the room instantly seem smaller. Dex hadn't known that Ronan was so…large. He almost makes Phoenix look puny. "Long time, no see."

"What are you doing here?" Dex's father asks, seeming to regain a little of his composure, although failing to return Ronan's smile. "We asked to see your Commander."

"You're looking at the Commander." Ronan puffs out his broad chest and grins, having clearly waited a long time to say these words to one of his old enemies.

Dex glances at his father, checking to see if any of this makes any more sense to him. But he looks just as baffled. So, instead, Dex locks his eyes on Wren. "What's going on? You said your father was the Commander."

Wren shuffles forward and to Dex's horror Ronan wraps his arm around her shoulders.

"My father *is* the Commander," she says, looking down at the floor.

"Ronan's your father?" Dex takes a step back, his hand clamped to his chest. This can't be happening. Ronan almost single-handedly destroyed Askala. He can't be Wren's father.

"I prefer to be called Cy, now," says Ronan. "Or Commander. Ronan died in that fire on the bridge."

"Clearly not," Dex's father says.

It's only then that Dex's eyes are drawn to Phoenix, who's being unusually quiet in his father's presence.

"So, you two are…siblings?" Dex asks, hating the hope that's soaring in his chest. Wren is Ronan's daughter. There's no way they can ever be together no matter what her relationship with Phoenix is.

"We're twins actually," says Phoenix, finding his voice. "I took after Dad. Little bird here took after our mother."

Dex lets out a long sigh and sinks back into his chair, scanning back over everything Wren's ever said about Phoenix. He can't remember a single occasion she ever commented specifically on her relationship with him other than to say how much he means to her, which makes sense if he's her twin. They'd all assumed he was her boyfriend. All she'd done was not bother to correct them.

"I'm sorry, Dex." Wren goes to step toward him, but Ronan pulls her back.

"Do *not* apologize to anyone," he hisses at her. "Ever. Understand?"

Wren bites down on her bottom lip and nods.

Dex stands, every cell in his body wanting to go to Wren. To release her arm from the traitorous vice that's holding her in her place. But the look in her eyes tells him not to.

"Who's this kid, anyway?" Ronan asks Wren, tilting his head toward Dex.

"This is my son," says Dex's father, words that only seem to have Ronan's grip tightening.

"Please don't tell me Mercy's his mother." Ronan's face darkens and for a moment Dex thinks he's going to hit someone. Most likely, him.

"I'm the son of Mercy," Dex says. There's no way he could ever deny the woman who loved him like nobody else ever has.

Steam seems to pour from Ronan's ears as he lets go of Wren and slides his shirt over his head, throwing it into a dripping mess on the floor.

Now certain that Ronan is about to hit him, Dex holds up his hand, blood thrumming through his veins. "I don't want to fight you."

But Ronan makes no move toward him. Instead, he points at a series of black lines inked on the left side of his chest. They're similar to the ones on Phoenix's arms, only these lines seem to spell out a word.

"You put her name on your chest?" Dex's father is aghast.

Dex looks closer, eyes springing wide when he realizes the lines spell his mother's name.

"Mercy is *mine*," Ronan growls. "She's been right here close to my heart this whole time. Why else do you think I call myself Cy? I've honored her name every day of my life by taking on part of her name. How dare you claim her for your own!"

His anger is directed at Dex's father now, and Dex finds himself praying hard that the rumors he's this oaf's son are unfounded.

"Mercy never loved you." Dex's father pulls back his shoulders and sneers at Ronan.

"That's not true." Ronan thumps a fist on the desk, sending a wooden cup clattering to the floor. "Bring her out and let her speak for herself. I've waited a long time to see her again. You'll see. She'll tell you she was only filling in time with you until I came back for her. I'll forgive her for that."

An awkward silence permeates the air as everyone waits to see who's going to be the one to tell him that's not going to be possible. Nobody wants that task, certain that the messenger will be shot on the spot.

"Dad," says Wren, putting a hand to his elbow. Always the brave one. Nothing scares the girl they call little bird.

"My mother's dead," says Dex, doing his best to shield Wren from her father's wrath. He can handle the brunt of this man's anger. He'd like to bet that Wren's already had more than her fair share in her life.

But it's not anger that strikes Ronan. It's...grief. Raw and acute. Devastation is spilling from his eyes as he stumbles, the first sign Dex has seen of any weakness.

It's strange to see a complete stranger mourn his mother like this. Dex is so used to being the only one to struggle with her death. Even though Dex can't remember his father's initial reaction, even he seemed to take it better than Ronan is right now.

Unsure how he feels about having something in common with Ronan, Dex breathes in deeply.

"You didn't look after her!" Ronan roars, his accusation taking the place of any questions as he launches himself at Dex's father. "You should have looked after her!"

Ronan grabs his archnemesis by the shirt collar and drags him over to the nearest wall, pinning him against it as he bears down on him. Dex's father's face turns purple, his mouth flapping like he needs to say something but can't figure out what.

"Give me one reason why I shouldn't kill you right now," sneers Ronan.

"Get off him!" shouts Dex, going to Ronan and pulling on his arm only to be flicked away like a locust on a stalk of corn.

Wren leaps forward. "Dad, this isn't what we planned."

Phoenix remains rooted to the spot, not as willing as his twin to stand up to their father, despite him being twice Wren's size.

"If you kill me, I can't tell you about Mercy," Dex's father chokes out.

Ronan thinks about this for a moment then lets go of him, cursing as he watches him crumple to the floor. "Then start talking."

"Mom was attacked by an Unbound," says Dex, trying to divert Ronan's attention toward him while his father regains his composure. "It wasn't Dad's fault. He was working here at the time trying to protect her from the trouble you threw her in when you swapped over her chip."

"Trouble?" Ronan is glaring at Dex now. "You wouldn't be here if I didn't swap that chip, would you? So, I don't think you're in a position to complain."

Dex shakes his head, hating that this is true. "No, I wouldn't."

"You look like her," says Ronan, his voice softening just a notch. "Apart from that stump on the end of your arm. What happened to you?"

Dex winces. He might call it his stump, but it doesn't sound like a compliment on Ronan's lips. "The Unbound took that, too. It was retaliation for everything that happened after you left."

"And what exactly happened?" Ronan's eyes narrow.

"Near starvation," says Dex's dad, having crawled to his feet. "Without the pods, our population suffered. Greatly. So much that Magnus decided to mark the Unbound by taking the finger they'd have worn a ring on if they'd been made Bound."

"He chopped their fingers off?" Ronan's expression is one of both amusement and awe.

"We think that Mom's murder, and this"—Dex holds up his missing hand—"were revenge for that."

"Then why not kill Magnus's bitch, Amity, instead?" asks Ronan. "Why Mercy? She was so good. So pure."

"Mercy was an easier target," says Dex's father. "Simple as that."

"My poor Mercy." Ronan shakes his head, unable to free his eyes of the grief that's taken hold of them.

"Was she pure, though, Dad?" asks Phoenix. "Rumor has it that you might be this one's father."

Dex flinches as Phoenix points at him, the only thing stopping him from taking issue with Phoenix being his desperation to know the answer to that very question.

Ronan slams his index finger into Phoenix's chest. "How dare you question Mercy's integrity like that! She was pure. Innocent. Nothing like what you're insinuating. Nothing like your own mother who whored herself to me the moment I set foot in the Outlands."

Phoenix shrinks back but doesn't break eye contact with his father, no doubt having learned the hard way what happens when he disrespects him. Wren is hopping from foot to foot beside him, not daring to intervene this time.

"Mercy and I should have had ten babies together," Ronan says. "But we were robbed of the chance by that asshole called Magnus. And now some scum of the Earth Unbound has taken the chance of me ever being with my love again."

Ronan leaves Phoenix to go to Dex, who channels his inner Phoenix and tries to look at him without blinking.

"I'm not your father," Ronan says. "But I loved your mother and when I find out who killed her, I can promise you that I'm going to kill them. Slowly. And very painfully."

Dex blinks. Once. Twice. Three times. All the while doing his best not to smile. This is the first time anyone has ever sworn a vendetta against whoever destroyed his life. His father has so passively accepted what happened that Dex has never thought about channeling his anger into finding out who did this. It may not be a very Bound trait, but the taste of revenge is sitting on his tongue like a sweet cherry from the orchard. He wants it more than his pride will allow him to admit.

Wren is staring at him from the corner of the room with a strange look on her face. One that he's going to have to decipher later. She looks pleased about something, although he's got no idea what.

"We need to talk about the future," says Dex's father. "What your arrival here means. When we asked Wren to send for you, we didn't know it was…you."

"Wren told me you've assembled a league of Unbound." Ronan sits down in Dex's chair and folds his arms behind his head in the same way Phoenix is fond of doing. "Very cunning of you, Callix. I must admit I'm impressed. I didn't think you had that in you."

"We have almost a hundred Unbound on side now." Dex's father straightens out his shirt, doing his best to look powerful, yet the uncertainty in his voice is failing him miserably. It seems he's still shaken up by everything that's just happened. "We were planning to align with you to overthrow the Bound. But now that we know who you are, I have to say I'm not sure we want you working for us."

Dex bites down on his tongue, knowing now's not the right time to admit that Kian's left him in charge. Technically, his father is planning to overthrow Dex.

"That's not a problem," says Ronan, chuckling. "Not a problem at all."

"What do you mean it's not a problem?" Dex's dad's brows furrow as he tries to figure out why this wouldn't be an issue.

"I'm not exactly a team player now, am I?" says Ronan. "I'm not here to work *for* you. I'm here to take back what's mine.

Along with the two dozen trained soldiers I've brought with me. If you're lucky, I might just let *you* work for *me*."

Dex's father may have been purple only a few minutes ago, but there's no mistaking that now he's gone completely white. Dex imagines he must look the same.

The room feels like it's spinning. This can't be happening. None of this can be. When they'd invited the Commander of the Outlands to their shores, they'd had no idea who that was or what hell they were unleashing.

Dex might have been able to forgive Wren in the past for all the truths she'd held back from him. But how can he ever forgive her for something like this? She's betrayed him in the worst kind of way. This time she hasn't just left a scar on his heart, it's like she's taken his own knife from under his mattress and driven it through his chest.

He'd thought that together they could save Askala, but he knows now that's not possible.

She's going to destroy it.

And he was the one who helped her do it.

WREN

*W*ren thought she knew all about the word *hatred*. She'd been raised to hate anybody outside her inner circle.

But right now, as she marches behind Cy on their way back to the lake to collect his soldiers, the only person she hates is herself. And it's clear that Dex feels the same. She'd seen the look in his eyes. He might have been able to forgive her for all the other times she's disappointed him, but this time is different. She'd gone too far. Or rather, Cy had.

They were supposed to work together to bring justice to Askala. She'd thought she'd convinced Cy this was the right path when they'd stood under that leaky shelter by the lake.

He'd listened and nodded and made all the right noises. And then he'd said whatever the hell he liked as soon as Callix was foolish enough to trigger his ego by suggesting he didn't want Cy to work for him.

Cy doesn't work for *anybody*. Least of all the guy who ended up with the only woman he ever loved. And to top it off, Callix had failed to protect her.

Wren can see the devastation sitting on Cy's shoulders as he walks ahead of her in the easing rain with Phoenix by his side. He'd genuinely loved Mercy. And if she'd been anything like Dex, then Wren can see why. The pained look in his eyes when he'd learned of her death had been proof enough of how he'd felt.

She can't help but wonder if Cy would be this upset if something happened to Wren? Because it's clear he doesn't value anything she has to say.

"Why did you really send me here ahead of you?" she calls out as she catches up to him and falls into step.

"To find their weak spots." Cy shakes his head. "Makes it easier to know where to strike first." He gives the air in front of him a few quick jabs and Phoenix laughs.

Wren stops in her tracks, wondering how she'd never noticed just how callous this man is.

Actually, that's not true. Of course, she'd noticed. It's just that she'd never realized there was any other way to behave. Spending time with Dex and Nova has opened her eyes to so many more things than she'd counted on.

Cy and Phoenix walk on ahead, even though they must be aware she's no longer beside them. Dex would never do that. Phoenix wouldn't either if he wasn't with Cy. She'd been able to open his eyes a little over the past weeks but clearly not enough. She has more work to do. And a lot of it.

Which is the only reason she starts walking again. Returning to Dex and begging him for forgiveness may be what her heart wants to do, but she can't. That would mean turning away from the man who raised her. The man who promised her this was her destiny. There are some days she's wondered if this is exactly why she was born—to be Cy's weapon. To help right the wrong against him.

Except she never realized the destruction he planned.

Or that her understanding of right and wrong would switch sides.

Her father's soldiers are restless when they reach them. Wet, hungry and ready for the fight they were promised. She knows each and every one of their snarling faces from the Outlands. And she hasn't missed a single one of them.

"Commander," they say, nodding their heads and straightening their backs. The rain is dripping from their muscle-clad bodies. A few are wearing shirts, but most choose not to, preferring to wear the ink on their chests as their clothes. It seems the more muscles they have, the more tattoos they've adorned themselves with. Most of them have a flamethrower slung around their shoulders. All of them have Cy's wish as their command.

These are Cy's most loyal men. Any one of them would lay down their life for him.

Or Wren.

As Cy's only daughter, she has their protection. She also has their lecherous gazes. Hooking up with Cy's daughter would elevate their status beyond anything they'd ever be able to achieve as one of his minions. But she's made it clear she's not interested, which means they wouldn't dare lay a finger on her. Cy would have their head on a stick.

She hadn't thought she was interested in men at all, until she met Dex and realized she just preferred kind hearts over bulging biceps. What would Cy make of that? His own daughter in love with Callix's son. He'd have everyone's heads on sticks if he ever found out.

Still, the knowledge that Dex is not her brother has her smiling. Somehow this fact makes the impossible minutely less impossible. Just like when Phoenix had told her she had a one in a thousand chance of making it to Askala alive and she'd pulled back her shoulders and told him that at least that meant she had a chance.

Cy holds up his hand and his men fall silent. Even the rain

35

seems to ease a little further, as if it, too, wants to know what he has to say.

"The meeting went well," he announces.

Wren moves to the back of the group so that nobody can see her face. *The meeting went well?* The meeting was a disaster!

"I told them who's in charge here." Cy beats his chest and the men burst into a series of cheers.

"When do we go to the ship?" one of the men asks.

An excited murmur ripples from soldier to soldier. They've heard all about the Oasis. The stories that Cy tells about life in Askala was how he got to his position in the first place. Not that such a position had existed before he'd stood up and named himself Commander. Cy's told Wren how they saw him as some kind of all-knowing hero, the moment he set foot in the Outlands. The only person who'd experienced what it's like on the other side. He'd grasped hold of that power and taken it to the next level. Shunned by Askala for being different. Embraced by the Outlands for exactly the same reason.

"We go immediately," Cy says. "No reason to wait. They have food there. And women."

More cheering erupts and Wren feels like she's going to vomit. Women? She's seen the things that go on in the Outlands, and not all of it happens by choice. Well, not from the woman's point of view, anyway.

"Hands off the women," says Wren, stepping forward until she's standing beside Cy. She may not be able to stop them from eating the food supplies, but she can do her best to ensure the people here are protected from these thugs. "This is a peaceful world. You don't touch anyone without their consent."

The men fall quiet, seeming to wonder if she's serious. Then Cy bursts into laughter and claps her roughly on the back. His men let out whistles and howls, joining in with their leader's amusement.

"I wasn't joking," says Wren, looking to Phoenix for support.

He saw how vulnerable Nova was when he cared for her in her cabin. Surely, he understands?

He's not laughing with the other men, but he's not exactly looking like he's about to leap to her defense either.

"Consent won't be a problem, little bird," Cy says. "I remember that party deck..."

This has the men shuffling their feet, keen to fill their bellies and satisfy their salacious desires.

"Let's do this." Cy pumps his fist in the air, indicating his pep talk is over. He doesn't have Magnus's eloquence when talking to his people, but he doesn't need it. He lets his position and strength speak for him.

He marches ahead of his men, leading them down the path that will take them to the Oasis. Wren can only hope that Dex and Callix have gone ahead of them and managed to lock all the doors. Although Cy hasn't come this far to let a door get between him and the revenge he craves.

Because as Wren takes up the rear of the group and follows them down the path, she's certain that this is what it's about.

Revenge.

She'd thought Cy had wanted to invade Askala in the spirit of fairness. To give his people equal access to the resources that these people had been keeping for themselves. But she sees now that's not it at all.

Cy came here to show these people what he'd achieved after he was banished. He wanted them to see what they let go.

Which means that as much as he might claim Ronan died on that bridge, he didn't. He may have given himself a new name, but the grudge he holds is the same.

What Wren needs to decide is if she's prepared to make it her grudge, too.

The rain has cleared now but the surface of the gangplank is still damp and slippery. It groans under the weight of so many large men with heavy boots and flamethrowers full of fuel. A few people had been coming down the gangplank but had very wisely turned around at the sight of these men and scuttled back inside.

They get to the top and Wren waits for Cy to beckon her to scan her hand on the sensor.

But, instead, he scans his own.

Wren's brows shoot up as the door slides open. It seems there'd been no need to cancel the chip of a man Askala had believed dead. It's even more surprising that Cy hadn't cut the chip out of his hand. More evidence that he intended to return one day. He's been waiting for this moment for a long time.

Even from the back of the line, Wren can sense the panic taking place in the Oasis as word spreads of the new arrivals.

"I remember this stench," laughs Cy, turning to face his men. "Is it the smell of decay? Or is it the broken dreams of the Unbound? Let's go and make their day, shall we?"

Cy disappears through the door, his men following closely behind.

Wren is surprised to find Phoenix waiting for her.

"Hey, little bird," he says, wrapping an arm around her shoulders.

Wriggling away, she breaks free. "Don't you *little bird* me."

"What's the matter?" His jaw drops and he looks at her like he's genuinely surprised by her reaction to him.

"You're the matter," she huffs. "You're like a different person when Cy's around. As much as you drove me crazy when we were locked up in that room, I liked you far better than I have since we left. What is it with you men?"

"It's just talk." Phoenix falls into step beside her as they walk down the corridor. "You know that. I haven't touched a woman since I've been here"

She sighs. He's right. He had plenty of opportunity to seek out that kind of pleasure and hadn't. He'd been more focused on taking care of Nova. And making sure Wren was okay.

"You need to learn to stand up to him," she says, keeping her voice low.

He raises a brow. "Let me see you do it first."

"Maybe you will," she throws back.

He puts a solid hand on her arm, bringing her to a stop. "Don't do anything stupid, Wren. I mean it."

He does mean it. He never uses her real name unless he's serious. But is she serious? Does she really have enough courage to stand up to the man who raised her?

"The ballroom!" shouts Cy from the other end of the corridor. "Everyone to the ballroom. We're having a different kind of Announcement today and you don't want to miss it. You're all invited."

As they twist through the corridors, Cy shouts to the confused people to join him. But instead of following, the people scurry away. It will only take minutes before every person on this ship is aware of his arrival. What they choose to do with that information will be interesting. Will their curiosity outweigh their fear?

Cy leads his army into the ballroom, extending his arms and welcoming his men like he made this room himself.

"Just as I remember it," he says to his men, who all seem suitably impressed.

Two Bound women stand like statues with brooms in their hands. They slowly step away from the men until their backs are pressed against the far wall.

"Join us," says Cy. "You're just in time."

The women say nothing. It's like they're incapable of speech. Instead, they stare at these strange men as they try to figure out what's happening.

But before Cy can give them any more attention, people begin to pour through the door. Streams of them. Mostly Unbound, but Bound amongst them, too. It seems that with the peaceful, constant lives these people live, they haven't realized what danger they might be in.

Cy steps up on the stage and Wren scans the crowd, looking for Dex. But she'd need to grow three feet before she would have a hope of spotting him with this many people in the room.

"Come on," says Phoenix, tugging on her hand and leading her up to the stage.

She follows, keen to get a better vantage point.

Cy's men position themselves around the perimeter of the room, flamethrowers in hand, making no mistake about who's in charge of this gathering.

A door off to the side of the ballroom opens, and the High Bound walk in.

Dex!

Wren tries to catch his eye, succeeding for a moment. But it's a fleeting one, because as soon as Dex sees her on the stage beside the man he calls Ronan, his face falls and he turns to say something to Kian.

Kian nods and pulls back his broad shoulders, walking directly to the steps of the stage. If he's scared, he's not showing it, his face just as brave as it'd been when he'd led them through the tests of the Proving.

How could she have not seen this earlier? Kian really would make a fine leader for Askala. He's not perfect. Far from it. But he's a hell of a lot more perfect than Cy.

Kian walks up onto the stage and Wren takes a step toward him, only to feel Cy's hand on the back of her neck as he pulls her to his chest.

"Careful, little bird," he hisses, sensing her urge to run. "I don't want to have to clip your wings."

"People of Askala," says Kian, his voice loud and smooth. "I wel—"

Cy lets go of Wren to shove Kian hard in the chest, the

sudden movement sending Kian flying backward and landing on his butt.

Wren winces. That had to have hurt. She goes to him, holding out her hand to help him up, but he brushes her off, shaking his head at her, shock stinging his eyes.

"I'm sorry," she whispers.

Her words are drowned out by the hiss of Cy's flamethrower as he sends a burst of fire shooting above the heads of the people in the crowd. They cower as the flame threatens to set them alight.

Cy lowers his weapon, his message having been sent.

Kian is on his feet again, except this time he stands to the side of the stage with his arms crossed, waiting to see what Cy has to say. Kian might be brave, but he isn't foolish.

"Thank you for that warm welcome," Cy says, glaring at Kian. "From the look of you, I'd say you're the son of Magnus, am I right?"

Kian nods, the fold of his arms seeming to tighten as he grits his teeth and waits for Cy to get to the point.

"You're just like your father, the great Maggot of Askala." Cy laughs, enjoying his own joke. "He never knew when to keep quiet, either."

Kian opens his mouth to say something, but Cy waves the flamethrower in his direction and Kian seals his lips.

"We wouldn't want this whole ship to go up in flames, would we now?" Cy threatens, oblivious to the look of horror on the faces of the people he'd come here to win over.

"You're Ronan," calls out an older man from the back of the crowd. "I remember you."

There are some gasps and a rumble of voices across the room as people fear for this brave man's safety.

And they're right to be scared.

Cy turns to the crowd, his gaze locked on the man who Wren now recognizes as one of the outgoing High Bound.

41

"You're Ronan," the man says again.

"My name's Cy, I'm the Commander of the Outlands." Cy puffs out his chest as he speaks, making his shoulders even broader. "But yes, some of you know me as Ronan. Do you have a problem with that, Dorian? Yes, I remember you, too."

"You almost destroyed us!" Dorian calls out. "You were banished for a reason."

Wren's stomach drops. That was a mistake. A big one. She'd hoped this would be a peaceful takeover but there's no way that's going to happen now. Dorian really should have stayed quiet.

Cy looks toward one of his soldiers at the rear of the room and nods, a smile plastered to his face that Wren's seen many times before. He means business.

The soldier marches over and lifts his flamethrower above Dorian's head.

Dorian closes his eyes and shields his face from the fire that he's certain is about to engulf him.

But it's not fire that rains down on him. It's the barrel of the weapon as it slams into Dorian's skull with such force that he doesn't even have time to open his eyes. He slumps to the floor, blood pooling around him.

Dead on impact.

Wren doesn't need to look closer to know that's the result. It's a signature move of Cy's army. They take pride in the length of the crack in the skull they can cause. She once witnessed a man's head split right down the middle until his brains had oozed onto the dirt.

"Has anybody else got anything they'd like to talk to me about?" Cy asks, smiling across the room. "Because I'd be happy to discuss it."

Silence is reflected back at him. Wren scans the crowd for Dex, finding him standing by the wall, his eyes glued to the man once known as Dorian. He looks rightfully horrified.

"I'm your Commander now," says Cy. "You answer to me. Do you all understand?"

"I have something I'd like to say," comes a deep voice from the back of the room.

Wren tenses as she sees Dean step forward, the sick feeling worsening with each step he takes to reach the stage. Dean sure knows how to pick his times.

"Hello, brother," says Dean, as he takes to the stairs.

Cy shakes his head and smiles. "Hello, little brother."

Wren shouldn't be surprised by that response. Cy always likes to remind people that they're beneath him.

The two embrace. Dean looks like a raven who's just had a fresh bowl of crickets set down in front of him. He's just gone from an Unbound nobody to the Commander's brother, his status having elevated so quickly it's surprising he has any blood left in his head.

Cy breaks away first and steps forward to the crowd, leaving Dean standing beside Phoenix and a very reluctant Wren. She sneaks a glance at the two of them. It's strange to see them side-by-side in better lighting than they'd had in the meeting of the league. They're not quite as similar as she'd thought. It's definitely obvious they're related but they're also different. Phoenix has a longer nose and is taller, Dean has smaller eyes and is far scrawnier.

"See, my blood is from this land," Cy calls to the crowd. "This is my rightful home. All I'm doing is reclaiming what I was denied."

Kian chooses this moment to step up. "You might want to know what this brother of yours tried to claim just the other day."

"Ah, the son of Maggot speaks," says Cy, fingering his flamethrower. "I thought I told you to be quiet."

"Let him speak," says Wren. "I want to hear what he has to say. What did Dean try to claim from you?"

"Five pods." Kian looks at Phoenix. "In exchange for bringing me Phoenix. Not that he was able to find him for me."

Cy's hand slips from his weapon, only for a few seconds but it's enough to show Wren that he's rattled.

"That's right, Ronan," says Kian. "Your brother—your blood —was prepared to serve your son up to me for the prize of five pods. How do you feel about that?"

Wren's got to hand it to Kian. She's impressed with him standing up to Cy like that. Especially after what they just witnessed with Dorian.

"Is this true?" Cy asks.

Dean shakes his head, but the fear in his eyes betrays him. He's even worse at lying than he is at finding lost nephews.

But it's Phoenix who finds his backbone and grabs Dean by the throat. "You were going to sell me out? I didn't think you were serious when you mentioned it at the meeting."

Dean is still shaking his head, eyes bulging. "No!" he croaks.

"Let go of him," says Cy. "I want to hear the weasel speak."

Phoenix releases his grip and Dean bends over and clutches at his throat, drawing in desperate breaths.

Cy stands over him, his anger palpable. "Did you, or did you not, agree to turn my son in for a prize of five measly pods?"

"I was only pretending!" he says. "Playing both sides so I could keep Phoenix safe. We're family, Ro. Family!"

"Do. Not. Call. Me. That." Cy's teeth are gritted, his eyes flaring with a rage he's never found a way to control.

"It's true," says Dean. "Ask Wren. She'll tell you how happy I was to meet Phoenix. She'll vouch for me."

All eyes in the room turn to Wren and she freezes. Does she stand up for Dean and reunite this family? A choice that feels very much like she's also choosing this family for herself.

Or does she tell the truth? That she was excited to meet Dean but very quickly realized he isn't a person who can be trusted? A choice that somehow feels like she's siding with Kian.

44

"Well?" prompts Cy. "Tell us. What do you make of this little brother of mine? Would he sell his nephew for some pods?"

Wren looks for Dex. He's moved from where she last saw him. She's going to have to make this decision on her own.

Imagining Dex with his eyes on her, she draws in a breath.

"He *would* sell Phoenix for some pods," she says. "I believe it."

"Get out of my sight," Cy spits out at Dean. "Go, before I have one of my men knock some sense into you, just like they did to that old man. You should be ashamed of yourself."

"I'm sorry, Ro! I mean, Cy!" Dean drops to his knees. "I'm sorry. Please, forgive me."

"I said"—Cy grits his teeth—"get out of here."

Cy's men step forward, banging the end of their flamethrowers with the palms of their hands.

"Get out of here," Wren hisses, not wanting responsibility for what might happen next. "Quickly!"

Dean glances up at her and seeing the desperation on her face, he rises.

And takes off, down the steps and through the parting crowd. Cy's men hold still when Cy fails to give the signal to intercept Dean on the way out.

It's then that Wren sees Dex. He's crouched over Dorian's body. Shiloh is by his side. They're trying to do what can't be done. Save a man who it's far too late to save.

"So, that's two people we've heard from now," says Cy. "Does anybody else have anything they'd like to add?"

Nobody says a word. People are barely breathing, let alone willing to speak up.

"Great!" Cy claps his hands together. "The message is clear. You either join me or you come up against me. It's your choice. But I promise you that if you choose to fight me, then you're not going to win. If you don't like the sound of that, then you're very welcome to follow my beloved brother out that door."

Nobody moves.

"So, now that the formalities are out of the way, I promised my men here a good feed when they arrived. One like they've never had before."

"We don't have any food," says Kian. "We're all on rations."

"The kind of food we want, you have plenty of, don't worry about that, son of Maggot." Cy is grinning hard now, his yellowing teeth flashing in the light.

The ballroom fills with the sniggering of Cy's men scattered around the room as they pat their bellies.

"To the pod pool," Cy declares, smacking his lips together. "Anybody who chooses to stand with me, may join us. I don't care how many fingers you have. Askala...it's time to eat."

Wren stands, helpless, as she watches people file out of the room. Cy knows exactly how important those pods are for human survival. And how difficult it is to collect more. How is she supposed to talk sense into someone who's prepared to ignore all of that?

"That went well," says Cy, looping an arm around each of his children. "Pity about Dean turning out to be so pathetic, but you can't win them all."

Wren swallows as she allows herself to be led from the stage.

Cy's right. He *can't* win them all.

And it's hard to deny that she doesn't want him to win this one by settling his grudge with Askala. Not in the way he's made it clear he wants to.

But she can't turn her back on her own flesh and blood.

Can she?

NOVA

*a*s the sun rises the following morning, Nova gets to see exactly where they'd arrived…and it's nothing like she imagined.

The rocky outcropping that they'd curled up against in the rain felt instinctively protective. It had sheltered them from the bulk of the wind and rain enough to fitfully doze through the night.

Flick needed to rest after losing the baby.

She'd cried more water than what the skies poured down on them, Thom holding and rocking her. Nova had sat close by, wet and curled, wishing she could tell Flick she understood, but knowing she couldn't.

The thought of losing her own child paralyses Nova. The grief would be unimaginable. But she can't tell Flick she's pregnant. Not now.

So, she'd kept a surreptitious eye on the bleeding, relieved to see it steadily slow, falling into a fitful sleep only after Flick and Thom did the same. As the crashing of the storm eased, she'd held the hope close to her heart that they've done the right thing by coming here

The first peek of sun is almost timid, as if even it's embarrassed at what it's about to illuminate. Nova stretches tired, wet limbs as she looks around. At first, she's disorientated, wondering if she's in a nightmare. There's too much black, too much...nothingness.

The landscape around her is everything the High Bound used to describe when talking about the desecration humans had wreaked. Burnt. Empty. A world of charcoal.

Nova wipes her hand over her face. A quick glance at Thom and Flick reveals they're still asleep, holding each other with curled, desperate fingers. She's glad. As she pushes to her feet, she knows they're going to need all the rest they can get.

The sound of the ocean isn't far away as she uses the solidness of a boulder to pull herself upright. A few steps and she stops, slowly turning around, deciding the High Bound were wrong. They'd failed to capture the abject desolation of the Outlands. They'd said it was a burnt desert, the odd black skeleton of a tree clinging to the depleted soil. But they hadn't described how the place feels exhausted and hollow.

That it's a void hope could never survive in.

Swallowing down the panic, Nova takes a few more steps, gazing as far as she can one way then the other. No sign of life. There are no birds or bugs let alone humans.

Sweet Terra, what have they done?

There's the sound of movement behind her and Nova rushes back. Flick is struggling to sit up, pushing away Thom's arm like she's just found herself tangled in vines. "I need to get up! I need air."

Thom shuffles back, looking hurt. "I was just trying to—"

"Yeah, well, don't." Flick frowns. "I need to breathe, okay?"

Nova kneels beside Flick, keeping several inches between them. She hopes Thom understands Flick's hurting and that's why she's pushing him away. "How you doing, Flick?"

Flick turns to Nova, her curls limp and wet around her face.

Her eyes fill with tears as her lip trembles. "It wasn't a dream, was it?"

Nova stays where she is, trying to block the truth that the nightmare of the Outlands only continues to stretch out behind her. "No. We got caught in a storm." Nova grips her hand. "I'm so sorry about the baby, Flick."

Flick nods, the movement short and fragile. "I'm Unbound, the baby probably wasn't meant to be," she whispers.

Nova's hold on Flick's hand tightens. "That's not true. It will never be true. The stress of all this was just too much."

"She's right," adds Thom. "Next time will be different."

Flick stiffens and Nova works not to wince. She's heard men say that before in the infirmary. They think they're helping by painting a future that will be different. But Flick's present is painted in pain, thinking of another child doesn't acknowledge that.

Flick angles her back more fully toward Thom, looking at nowhere but Nova. "So, my baby didn't die because it was... wrong?"

Heart constricting painfully, Nova holds Flick's gaze. "No. Your baby was proof that life can be conceived irrespective of some cruel law, and that's beautiful."

Flick throws herself forward, wrapping Nova in a fierce hug. "Thank you," she whispers through her tears.

Nova's own tears threaten to spill. Her baby's heart is fluttering deep inside her, also conceived despite the harsh laws of Askala. How can she feel so lucky and so guilty at the same time?

Thom clears his throat behind them and Nova knows what he's trying to communicate. They can't stay here, with no food or water.

Nova pulls back, pushing Flick's slack curls from her face. "Now, we need to get up and get moving. But you need to know, what's out there isn't..." *What we'd hoped.* "Pretty."

Flick frowns. "It can't be worse than what they told us."

Exactly what Nova assumed.

Nova stands and steps back, watching Flick's face as she tries to absorb the abused land around them. Her eyes widen. Her jaw slackens. The tears pool in her eyes again.

Nova holds out her hand. "You're stronger than this, Flick. Come on, the sooner we find food and shelter, the better."

Flick takes Nova's hand, hauling herself to a stand. Nova watches carefully but doesn't see any signs she's about to faint. It's hard to tell how much blood Flick lost with the miscarriage.

Thom comes to stand beside Flick, looking at her apprehensively. "You could lean on me if you like."

Flick clenches her jaw. "Like Nova said, I've got this."

Nova passes Thom a sympathetic look. Hopefully he won't give up too easily. Once the freshness of this pain passes, Flick is going to need him just as much as he needs her.

Nova looks left then right. "I suppose we just follow the coastline. We've got to find water, maybe even something we can eat, eventually."

Surely all of the Outlands can't look like this.

Thom joins her. "I reckon you're right. We need to find one of those villages Wren spoke about."

Flick takes a few cautious steps, her face tight as she stoops slightly. Nova wants to go to her, but she doesn't. As hard as it is to watch, they all need to be strong right now.

Their survival depends on it.

They strike out, the deadly ocean to their right, devastation everywhere else. Agitation hums through Nova's veins, wanting her to lengthen her stride. But she knows she can't. Not only is Flick not capable of that, but they have no food or water.

They need to conserve what little energy they have.

The horizon changes—at times hills and mountains rise to their left, other times what would've been grasslands stretch out like desert—but one thing stays the same. The desecration. The damage that feels like it can never be reversed.

Is this what Askala once looked like? Before such an extreme regime was implemented, one that dictates the child she's carrying isn't supposed to exist? Nova glances down at her left hand, the garish gap evidence of what was done in the name of that regime.

Where does the truth lie? And what will it mean for Nova and her child?

Flick stumbles and Thom is by her side before she can crumple to the ground. She stiffens, the frown that hasn't left her face deepening.

"Let me help you," pleads Thom. "Who knows how much further we're going to have to walk."

Flick begrudgingly slips an arm around his shoulder and Nova lets out a breath. She didn't want to have to be Flick's crutch. Her feet are already dragging over the seared soil. Her mouth is parched, her stomach aching for food. She tucks her head into her shoulders, missing the shawl that was lost in the storm.

Thom's right. Who knows how much further they're going to have to walk. With no shade. No food. No freshwater.

They trek for hours, the sun climbing high into the sky. The warmer it gets, the more the wind batters them. Without trees, there's nothing to stop it, and it blasts through them, savage and unrestrained. Nova feels her energy drain as her body temperature slowly climbs in this hot, desiccated landscape.

It's slow going, with Flick needing frequent rests. Several times Thom rushes to the ocean, bringing back a strip of his shirt soaked in water so he can wash away the blood trickling down Flick's legs. Each time she holds still, staring at the horizon like she's been carved in stone.

Eventually the burnt trees give way to stumps, the world no

longer painted in fire, now shaped by greed. They've barely said a word as they've walked, but now their silence is absolute.

The dead slabs of hewn trees, any sign of sap long gone, are undeniable proof of human habitation. They've got to be getting close.

It will either mean their salvation.

Or it will be the end of this foolish, naïve grasp at freedom.

Nova hears it first and she freezes, holding her hand up for the other two to stop.

"What?" Flick croaks. "What is it?"

Nova shakes her head, miming to keep her mouth closed. Flick looks around in panic, probably suddenly aware of how out in the open they are. Nova thought that long ago, but nothing could survive out in this wasteland. Especially a top predator like a polar grizzly.

Thom half-walks, half-drags Flick closer and they stand together, barely breathing. The undeniable sound of voices trickles over, peaks and troughs of noise that are impossible to tell whether it's shouts or laughter.

They stare at each other, all conscious there's no way of knowing whether they're friend or foe. Above, a raven circles, feeling as if it's watching them like a vulture. Nova shrugs. "We have no choice. We lost what little food we had, we have no water, and Flick can't continue for much longer."

"I'm...fine," Flick croaks just as her knees give out. Thom clamps her to his side as her head lolls, her cracked lips parting as she loses consciousness.

"Surely they'll take pity on us. She needs help."

Nova nods. They're certainly not a threat. "Let me help you."

Tucking around the other side of Flick, Nova and Thom follow the trail of sound. The closer they get, the harder Nova's heart thumps against her ribs. Wren wouldn't have turned them away, would she? She was tough and defensive, but not heartless.

The first shelter appears ahead, a trail of smoke creeping up into the air beside it. Nova glances at Thom only to find him looking even more frightened than she's feeling. She straightens her shoulders, pushing in closer to Flick. She needs to be strong, for Thom, Flick, and her baby.

No matter what happens next.

They shuffle forward, the weight of Flick seeming to grow with each step as their tired bodies begin to falter. She slips in and out of consciousness as they approach the village, moaning occasionally. Her obvious state of vulnerability has to be in their favor. Nova grits her teeth as she realizes she really is starting to think like Wren, seeing Flick's weakness as an advantage if they have to beg for food.

They approach the first few huts, all scattered around a dusty road. Nova feels her eyes widen as she tries to absorb what she's seeing. The small shelters are built of rough hewn timber, but they've been supplemented with scraps of rusted metal and cracked plastic. Everything looks sturdy, but somehow decaying.

It's a village made of timber and rubbish.

A small child darts out of the first hut only to freeze at the sight of them. Nova smiles, taking in the grimy skin and matted hair. He or she is skinny in a way they've never seen in Askala.

"Hello, could we speak to your parents?" she asks gently.

The child startles then streaks away, but not back into the hut like Nova expected, instead running up the ashen road into the village.

Thom grunts. "Well, I reckon our arrival just got announced."

It turns out he's right. As they stumble further into the village, people come out of their ramshackle homes, staring with a mix of suspicion and curiosity.

Curiosity is good, Nova tells herself. They want to know more about these strangers who just arrived in their midst.

Nova draws to a stop, Flick hanging between her and Thom. No one moves and she can feel the weight of their gazes. How many people are here? And why won't anyone say anything?

She catches one woman, her hair color indistinguishable beneath the soot that seems to cover everything, studying Nova's waistline. Nova startles. Surely the woman can't tell Nova's pregnant?

But then she realizes the woman is studying her clothes. Nova glances down, realizing how different their hemp cloth is compared to what's around them. Some people wear leather, some a strange patchwork of scraps. One or two have fragments of plastic tied to them like armor. Many of the men and children are shirtless, the grime being their protective layer.

People start shuffling as tension climbs in the air. Nova relaxes her wound-up body, pulling up a small smile. "We come in peace. We seek food and shelter for ourselves and our sick friend."

Disgust creeps up several of the faces, one or two turning away. One man, lean yet with enough muscle to be intimidating, steps forward. "What do you have to trade?"

Nova's gut clenches. "We have nothing. We seek your kindness and generosity."

The man laughs, the sound harsh and without humor. He turns away, several others doing the same. Nova sees the woman at the edge of the dispersing crowd, tucked behind the corner of a hut. Her face is full of sympathy. No, pity.

She knows no one here will help them.

"She just lost her baby, for Terra's sake!" Thom spits out desperately.

Several of the men grunt in disgust as the women look away. Someone mutters, "Who the hell is Terra?" They don't care. Nova realizes they can't. These people are barely feeding themselves, let alone three people who look healthier than themselves.

She never realized how much Askala was a land of privilege, even as an Unbound. No wonder the Remnants came at them with violence and hatred. They would've thought the people of Askala were just as selfish as Nova had been raised to believe the Remnants were.

And yet they were desperate. Wanting to save their own lives and those of their children. Just like Nova is now. Their world is one of survival.

Still, surely the Outlands haven't killed all shreds of compassion and kindness...

Nova looks at a woman nearby who's grimacing at them with yellowed teeth. She has to try one more time. "Please, maybe we could just rest beside your hut."

Untangling from Flick and having a break from the sun and wind would be enough to have them recharging. They could show they're not a threat. Maybe find out something that could show them how to find food and water.

The woman recoils. "What do you think I am? Stupid?"

The man beside her snarls, exposing black gaps where several teeth used to be. "Get the hell outta here, we don't need more dead bodies stinking the place up."

Nova flinches. He's already decided their fate. But the thought of dragging Flick between them as they try to find another village sends panic through her. Who knows how far away that is? And what are the chances they'll receive the same welcome?

Flick's head lolls. "Tell them we know Wren," she whispers hoarsely.

"What?" Thom asks before Nova can object. They don't know if aligning themselves with Wren could be dangerous.

"Wren." Flick croaks louder. "We're friends of Wren."

The muscled man steps forward, eyes narrowed. "You know Wren? The daughter of the Commander?"

Nova swallows. "Yes. She's a friend of mine."

A second man, shorter but stockier, steps up next to the first. "They ain't friends with no one." He gazes at her assessingly. "Unless they have something of use."

Which means Wren may have only befriended Nova so she could infiltrate Askala.

But Nova doesn't have time to think of that right now. Something about the way the second man is looking at her makes her uncomfortable. She straightens her shoulders, looking at the first. "Wren believed you would help us."

It's not exactly what Wren said when telling Nova about the Outlands, but Nova has to believe that's what she'd meant. Wren had told her that she could build a life here, Nova just has to find a way to get food, first.

The first man goes still, his dark eyes seeming to glint. "Luckily, my hut is just here." He jerks a thumb toward the wooden structure behind him. "I have some broth."

Nova sags with relief. "Thank you."

Dragging the semi-conscious Flick, she and Thom follow the two men into the shadowy interior. Inside the room is largely empty. A mat that's more holes than string is in the corner, some wooden cups and utensils litter the ground. In the middle stands a dented pot.

The muscled man jerks his chin to indicate they sit in the corner and Nova and Thom gently lower Flick to the ground. She groans as her eyes flutter, but doesn't wake.

The second man collects two cups from the dirt floor, tapping out the dust. He passes it to the first, who ladles a small spoonful into each one.

Nova takes a cup while Thom reaches for the second. "There are three of us," he points out.

The man barely glances at Flick. "You feed the strong first."

The man retreats, sitting beside his friend, one on either side of the pot, guarding it. Nova glances in the cup. Small, indefinable lumps—gray like everything else in this world—float in the water they call broth. And yet their stares tell her they're guarding the pot with their life.

Smiling, she takes a sip. It's cold and tastes like ash. But it's liquid and her body welcomes it. She works hard not to drain it all in one gulp. Unlike what the man just said, she's not going to let Flick get any weaker.

Thom already has her head in his lap, looking a little lost about how to feed her without spilling a precious drop. Nova places a hand on his arm. "Drink some of yours, then it'll be easier to pour. Then give her the rest of mine when you're done."

Thom nods, relief filling his face as he takes a drink.

Behind her, one of the men snorts, the sound full of derision. They think Nova and Thom are fools for caring for Flick. How Nova wishes they could see the way things are done in Askala. There, kindness isn't a weakness. There, these men could learn to live differently.

Gently, Thom lifts Flick's head and tips the cup to her lips. At first Flick grimaces, but then she opens her mouth. It feels like color flows into her face along with the broth. The men watch them like they're some freak show, glancing at each other in some silent communication.

"Your hut looks sturdy," Nova comments, trying to make conversation as she distracts herself from the remaining liquid sitting in the bottom of her cup. Sturdy would be important in this windblown, parched land.

"Phoenix built it. Do you know him, too? He's never far from Wren's side."

Phoenix. It doesn't surprise her that he's good with his hands. They were always sure and firm as he nursed her through her fever.

She nods. "Yes, I know him."

"He built it in exchange for my son," the man adds, his face impassive.

Nova has to work not to blanche. "Your son?"

"They needed recruits for their army." The man flexes his bicep. "Said he came from good stock."

"Did he want to go?"

The man's eyes fill with disdain. "You ask like there was a choice."

Nova can't keep his gaze. Thom passes her his cup and she swaps it for hers. She glances down realizing it's empty. And yet she can't ask for more.

She passes it back. "Thank you. You've been very generous."

The muscled man takes it from her. "I wasn't being generous," he growls like she just insulted him. "Nothing is free here, girl."

"I'm sorry..." Nova stammers. "I thought—"

"You thought you'd get something for nothing?" The man stands, shrinking the small hut as the doorway becomes obscured.

The second man stands too, and the room darkens further. "The Commander and his family always paid."

Like a hut for a son. Which means dropping Wren's name didn't ensure them food and shelter. It meant these men fed them in good faith believing they would be compensated.

Nova glances at Flick, who's fallen into a fitful doze. Panic climbs up her throat. All they've done is put themselves in more danger.

Thom's hands are fisted. "We don't have anything. We told you that."

The shorter man grins. "There's always a way to pay."

"We could take your clothes," the muscled man suggests, the glint in his eye feeling like the only light in the room.

Nova shrinks around herself. "What?" she whispers.

The man's gaze scans her from head to toe. "We ain't seen that sort of material around here. I reckon it would fetch quite the price."

The shorter man nudges him. "Might even get ourselves some rabbit or somethin'."

The first man nods, Nova suddenly conscious of the corded muscles that shift with the movement. "We wouldn't have to spend hours in Fairbanks risking our lives trying to trap them."

Nova shakes her head. "But...we need our clothes."

The man's grin is slow and deliberate. "Nah, they're only going to get in the way when you pay for the first cup."

KIAN

*T*he ballroom is almost clear. Except for Ronan—Kian refuses to call him Cy—standing on the stage like an inflated carcass as he watches. He grins as Dex and Shiloh drag Dorian's dead body away, making Kian grimace.

Helplessness courses through Kian. They have to stop this. He takes a step and Ronan spins around. His violent glare unmistakable in its message. *Move and you're dead.*

Only a few of Ronan's goons are left, waiting to follow the crowd to the pod pool, some practically salivating, when Kian's father storms into the ballroom.

"What is the meaning of this, Ronan?" he bellows, still so sure of his position of power in Askala.

Ronan's lip curls. His fists clench. "Magnus," he growls. "You'll rot in the brig like the maggot you are. When I'm ready, I'll banish you just like you did me. Except you won't survive the Outlands like I did. Your foolish principles won't protect you there."

"Stop this, Ronan." His father widens his stance, telling Ronan he isn't going anywhere. "You're going to finish what you failed last time—you'll kill us all."

"My name is Cy!" Ronan shouts. "And I am the savior for all, not just those you've deemed worthy." He slams his fist into his hand. "People like Mercy."

As Ronan roars so hard his mouth foams, Kian creeps around the stage. He needs to get to his father. He doesn't realize how vulnerable he is.

How unhinged Ronan is.

Ronan flicks his fingers and two men move in, their flamethrowers clutched high against their chest. "Take him away. I have places to be."

"No!" Kian shouts. He runs at the first man, the image of what happened to Dorian still too fresh. His father will fight these men, having no idea of their capacity for violence.

The man spins around, lifts his weapon and slams it into the side of Kian's head without hesitating.

Agony explodes, bringing him to his knees and robbing him of breath. He falls forward, slumping onto the ground. His cheek pressed against the floor, blood turning his vision a hazy red, Kian watches helplessly as his father is dragged to the brig. The triumph on Ronan's face is sickening.

Ronan steps over Kian's prone body. "Leave him to die," he orders. "I'll never be able to have a firstborn son with the woman I loved. It's only fair that Magnus doesn't either."

Then, there's nothing but blackness...

As Kian wakes, he can sense time has passed, but he has no idea how long he's been here. He lies on the floor, the blood feeling dry and caked on his cheek. He listens, hearing only his shallow breaths.

The Oasis has been transformed in the time he was out. He knows it with the same certainty as he knows this is only the beginning. The ballroom is empty, which he expected. But the hallways are quiet, the world has fallen silent. It's as if the whole ship is holding its breath.

An entire ecosystem has been invaded and it's now waiting to see who will be predator and who will be prey.

He pushes himself up from the floor onto all fours, his mouth dry yet tasting of copper. His head swims and the room spins, black spots of pain throbbing everywhere he looks.

Nova's soft voice caresses through his mind. *You should rest. You might have a concussion.*

If she were here, that's exactly what she'd say. She'd take his head in her lap, stroke his brow, ask someone to bring her a damp cloth. She'd lean down, say the words…

But Nova isn't here.

Nova chose the Outlands because she believed it would be safer for their baby than Askala.

"Nova…" he moans. "I was coming to get you."

The room remains silent. Collapsing back on his haunches, Kian feels the dried blood crusted at his temple. He glances at his fingers, surprised to find sticky sap matted in his hair. Before he can wonder how it got there, another wave of nausea swells up his throat. Clenching his jaw, he waits for it to pass. He doesn't have time for this.

The people of Askala are about to become the prey.

The nausea passes but the throbbing pain doesn't. Kian gingerly feels the lump in his hair, wincing, but glad it's no longer bleeding.

He groans as he pushes himself upright. Staggering, his hands fly out as he tries to find something to hold, only to grasp air. The room spins again and he slams his eyes shut, keeping away the blackness by force of will.

He can't afford to lose consciousness again.

The night that was trying to swallow him retreats. Drawing in slow, measured breaths, Kian walks to the door. Before he scans his hand over the sensor and leaves, he realizes he needs a plan.

Ronan has declared himself leader of Askala.

Kian's father is in the brig.

And Ronan assumes Kian is dead.

Right now, his best bet is to find somewhere to lie low and heal. Then he has to stop Ronan before he destroys Askala and everyone who depends on it.

But before he does that, he needs to check his mother is okay. Kian frowns, pressing his fingers to his forehead when the movement hurts. His mother would've demanded she joined Magnus in the brig the moment Ronan put him there. But the brig will be heavily guarded. It would be foolish to go there.

Then Kian remembers Ronan announcing he was taking everyone to the pod pool for a feast. Those pods have been his mother's way of growing and nourishing Askala. They thrived under her dedicated care. She would've done whatever she could to stop Ronan plundering the pods. That's where she'll be.

Keeping his hand on the walls for support, Kian makes his way there. He notes the corridors are empty. People are either asleep or too scared to come out.

Or they've aligned themselves with Ronan.

Clenching his hand so it's a fist skimming over the peeling paint of the walls, Kian realizes he can't blame them. How many Unbound would've jumped at the chance for freedom? With a gutful of pods to sweeten the deal, no less.

How ironic. Askala planted the seeds of its own downfall.

As Kian reaches the steps that will take him to the pod deck, he pauses, listening. When he hears the same eerie silence that's invaded the Oasis he makes his way up. The door slides open with a whoosh and Kian is instantly on high alert. If Ronan and his goons find him, they won't be as gentle with the butts of their flamethrowers.

But there's no one on the other side. The familiar scent of saltwater fills the air, the gentle sound of water lapping at the edges of the pool reaching him. Maybe Ronan decided to leave the pods alone.

Maybe his mother convinced him to follow the rations they've implemented for all.

Except as Kian steps through the door, he realizes there isn't silence on the pod deck. There are snores and grunts as satisfied bodies loll beside the pool like slumbering seals.

He looks around, shock icing his veins.

People, a dozen or so, are littered around. Most are the shirtless guards with their flamethrowers still strapped to them, but some are Unbound. The odd pod, dead and gray, lies in their open palms. All of them look like they've gorged themselves into unconsciousness.

Kian creeps around them, drawn to the pool. The surface is like he's never seen before. All his life it's been covered with islands of phytoplankton, floating buffets for the pods below. It always reminded him of the pictures of the globe he'd been shown—pockets of green dotted on beautiful blue—back before the fires and the droughts and the destruction.

But now, they've been fractured and shattered. Pockets of sparse green are being pushed around by the wind, spinning listlessly. The water's been tainted green with thousands of the orphaned organisms, probably contaminating the water for the remaining pods.

Kian kneels down, scanning the murky water. A few glowing bodies flit past but there are only a fraction of the number there were yesterday. There could be more, swimming in the safety of the deep. *Please let there be more down below.*

"I tried to stop them. I tried to tell Ronan."

Kian spins around to find his mother walking from the corner of the deck, her arms wrapped tightly around her middle. Her voice cracks. "He wouldn't listen."

Kian strides over, taking her in his arms. She buries her head in his shoulder, silent sobs wracking the shoulders that suddenly feel fragile. His mother feels everything so deeply. The devastation of the pods would be cutting her to the marrow.

When the shuddering subsides, Kian pulls back, looking down into watery eyes. "Dad's in the brig."

"I know," she breathes on a trembling sigh. "Ronan told me if I visit him, he'll kill him."

Anger seethes like lava in Kian's gut. "He can't get away with this."

His mother blinks, frowning as if she's seeing him beyond the tears. She reaches up to touch the sap covered wound tucked in his hairline. "What happened?"

Kian winces as she probes the swollen flesh. "I tried to stop them taking Dad."

"My strong, brave son." She shakes her head. "They could've killed you."

Like they did Dorian. And probably anyone else who objected to this invasion.

"It's just a bump. Ronan left me for dead, the fool. We need to figure out a way to stop him."

His mother steps away, her arms wrapped around her middle again. "He said if I look after the pods and don't make a fuss, the kids will be fine."

Kian's siblings. Willow, Holly, and sweet little Jasper. Their future has just been stolen from them. Possibly their lives.

His hands clench, heat building deep in his palms. "We can't let this happen." Kian's heart aches for him to stop as he says the next words. "I can't leave for the Outlands. This is too important."

Every cell in his body wails one word. *Nova.* It's like his body is composed of a million screams, all rejecting that he has to choose Askala over her. Again.

But Kian was too late. Too late to save Askala. Too late to tell her. And this is his punishment.

He fortifies himself. At least this decision Nova would understand. "We have to fight this."

"We can't, Kian." His mother's face fills with helplessness.

"Our society is a peaceful one, we don't have the skills or the means to fight them."

Because they have flamethrowers. And training. And muscles. His shoulders sag. "And they have the advantage. Ronan knows our ways. Our vulnerabilities."

Taking hold of Askala had to be the easiest hijacking of an entire society in the history of man. The blood that was shed was purely Ronan's need to exert power. It was totally unnecessary.

His mother's face lights up as something strikes her. "Then we do the same."

"What?" Kian frowns, trying to figure out what his mother is suggesting. How do they get the advantage?

She grips his arms. "You have to go to the Outlands. You need to. Learn about the Remnants and their world, how Ronan came to power. The key to solving this is *there*."

"But I can't leave Askala. Not now."

"Ronan probably believes you're dead, Kian. What do you think will happen when he discovers you're not?"

Kian doesn't answer, but images of Dorian's face lying in his own puddle of blood plunge through his mind.

"This is the best thing you can do for Askala." Her voice drops with urgency. "Find out how we win this."

One of the men groans and rolls over. Kian and his mother freeze but the man's face goes slack again. Although they relax, it's a reminder Kian can't stay. He can't be seen.

Kian nods. His mother's right. This is what he needs to do. He grasps his mother and presses his lips to her forehead. "Do what you need to do to keep Ronan happy." It's the only way she and his siblings will stay safe. "I'll be back as soon as I can."

His mother's smile is small and sad as she steps back, but it's a smile nonetheless. "You were right. Askala needed to change. I'm sure your father realizes it, too. Just not like this."

For some reason, Kian doesn't feel the same certainty that's shining from his mother's eyes, but another groan has him striding for the door. It's time to do the only thing he can to save Askala. A notion that was as alien to him as losing Nova.

Leave.

"Kian!"

Kian turns back at his mother's urgent whisper.

"Find Nova. You can't fight this war when you're only half alive."

He nods. There's no way he's coming back without her. She's just as much the key to save Askala as any of them.

The walls of the corridors start to echo with the sound of movement. People are waking and getting hungry. They'll want to see what their future is going to look like.

Kian half-runs through the hallways. He doubts even the Unbound will like what they see. Freedom should never have come at this price.

Kian stumbles as he leaves the Oasis, the sun painfully bright as he covers his eyes, trying to shield himself from its harshness. The shards of light feel like skewers in his brain. He slows but doesn't stop, ignoring the wave of nausea that climbs up his throat.

He has to talk to Dex before he goes into hiding. Tonight, he'll take the raft the Remnants arrived on and sail for the Outlands. Please let Dex be in the lab. Kian can't afford to wander around the Oasis looking for him.

He doesn't glance at the gardens as he lurches past. If the storm didn't finish them off, then Ronan and his army will. He just has to hope Ronan knows enough from his time in Askala to realize that a portion of their reserves will be needed to reseed it.

Arriving at the lab is a relief. His head throbs and his body's demanding a rest. Kian finds Dex asleep at the desk, the computer screens blank around him. Sighing with relief, Kian grasps his shoulder, shaking him gently. "Dex. We need to talk."

Dex jerks awake, pushing Kian's hands away in alarm. Jumping to his feet, he blinks hard trying to bring the room into focus. He pauses, then frowns. "Kian?"

"Only me. Sorry, I didn't mean to take ten years off your life."

Dex wipes his hand down his face, then peers at Kian a little closer. "What happened to you? You look like a polar grizzly played tag with you." He arches a brow. "Then threw you to a leatherskin when he was done."

Kian rubs the lump on his head. "One of Ronan's goons happened to me. It was a blessing in the end, Ronan thinks I'm dead." He glances around. "You're alone?"

Dex nods. "Dad went out a little while ago to get a sense of where things are at. I'd say he'll be back shortly, reporting things have gone to hell." Dex rubs the back of his head. "I must've fallen asleep."

Probably after spending part of the night sending Dorian's body out to sea and the rest of it encrypting Askala's data.

Knowing he doesn't have much time, Kian gets to the point. "I'm leaving for the Outlands tonight. We need to learn what we can about Ronan and the Remnants.

Dex frowns, opens his mouth, then shuts it again. He nods slowly. "I think that's the best thing you can do."

"I want you to come with me." Dex's eyes widen with shock. Kian rushes in to fill the surprised silence. "We can find Nova, learn how to defeat Ronan. Who knows what we could find out there. You said yourself we should never have closed ourselves off from them."

Dex gives the idea some thought. He steps back, rubbing his chin as he stares at the floor. Kian relaxes a little, glad his cousin can see the merit of his proposal. The key to undermining Ronan is in the Outlands.

Slowly but undeniably, Dex shakes his head. "I'm going to stay."

"What?" If Dex's gaze wasn't so serious Kian would assume this was another of his jokes. "As a High Bound, it's just as dangerous for you to stay as it is to go to the Outlands."

"It's not that. I…can't leave."

Frustration cramps between Kian's shoulders. "This is about Wren, isn't it?" Dex's jaw tightens giving Kian the answer he needs. His arms explode outwards. "She's a traitor! She betrayed every one of us, especially you, so she could hold the door open for Ronan to invade!"

Dex looks away. "Believe me, I know. But I can't go. I'm the only one who can reach her."

"You think you can get through to her?" Kian asks incredulously.

"I have no idea, but I have to try." Dex winces. "I can't shake the feeling that Wren is going to play an important role in all this."

Of course she is. She's going to fight for Askala's downfall just like her father raised her to.

"So, you're not coming?" Kian still can't believe he's hearing this.

Dex shakes his head emphatically. "No, I'm not."

Kian collapses into a chair, jamming his hands into his hair only to stop when he winces with pain. "Who will I take then?" He blinks, already restructuring his plans. "I'm going to need to find somewhere to hide out for the day."

"Take Shiloh and Finn if they still want to go. It's not safe for them here." Dex sighs. "If we knew where Dean was, I'd say his brawn would be useful to have on your little excursion."

"And turn his back on his own brother?" Even as he asks the question, Kian knows the answer.

"The higher the prize, the quicker he'd do it." Dex frowns. "Although it would mean you'd have to watch your back."

Kian nods. He's not the only one talking about aligning

himself with someone who's proven they can't be trusted. "And you watch yours."

They hug, briefly but fiercely, and Dex pulls back. "Don't make me wait too long till the next brug, okay?"

Kian swallows the jagged lump crawling up his throat. "I'd say wish me luck, but it's possible you're going to need it more than I will."

Dex grins, making Kian shake his head. Only his cousin could do that at a time like this. He slaps Kian's shoulder. "Let's hope you haven't used all yours up already, then."

Kian watches in amazement as Dex steps back and leans down, pulling up a hatch in the floor. "I'll tell Ronan that you died and I disposed of your body in the ocean just like Dorian." He pouts. "I'll be suitably devastated. In the meantime, I know exactly where you can lie low for the day."

Kian stares down the hole into the black room below them, realizing this is where Dex must've hidden Wren and Phoenix. But who built it and why?

As he climbs down the ladder, he acknowledges something else. This is where he'll spend his last hours in Askala. The room that's proof that secrets and lies have been undermining the land he loves for far longer than he realized.

DEX

*D*ex leans back in his chair and rubs his face. *He did it!* It's hard to believe he'd been able to encrypt every last one of those files before Ronan came looking for him.

It seemed like an impossible task, but the fact he'd managed to achieve it is further proof of how disorganized Ronan is. Dex doubts he thought much past his arrival here. He's so focused on revenge that he forgot to consider what life might look like after he'd wreaked his havoc. Ronan must be as big a fool as everyone has always said he is.

But he's Wren's father...how is that even possible? And it's not her looks that are confusing. It's the two qualities the Proving tested her for that she managed to pass with flying colors. Her intelligence. And her heart. How exactly had Ronan sired a daughter like that? She must take after her mother in more than just her appearance.

There's a loud banging on the door to the lab. For one crazy moment, Dex wonders if it's Nova. Then he remembers she's gone. Plus, she'd never knock with such force. Whoever this is wants his immediate attention.

He flicks on the screen that has a feed from the cameras

normally used for surveillance in the Provings. If that's Ronan out there, then there's no way he's letting him in.

Because before Dex encrypted all the files, he did one other thing.

He canceled two chips.

Ronan's.

And Wren's.

Let them try to get around the Oasis now.

Squinting at the screen, he sees Wren pacing as she pulls at the tufts of her hair that have begun to grow back. She looks adorable…in a grumpy, traitorous kind of way.

She also looks frustrated. And that makes Dex smile. Hopefully it's more than just the locked door that's annoying her. He'd like to think she's not having an easy time with her recent actions. Which would mean that maybe—just maybe—he hadn't been wrong about her.

He watches her for a while longer, wanting to be certain she's alone before he lets her in. She alternates between pacing, tapping the sensor, cursing and knocking. Each time she knocks it gets louder than the time before.

He gets up and walks with slow and measured steps to the door. Pressing his chip to the sensor, it slides open to reveal Wren staring at him with crossed arms and a tapping foot.

"Oh, look," he says, blocking the doorway, even though she's more than capable of crash-tackling him out of the way. "There's an angry little bird on my doorstep."

"You canceled my chip." She steps up to him, expecting him to move, but he holds his ground.

They're nose to nose now. Well, nose to neck, really, given their height difference. The air around them feels charged with some kind of energy he hasn't felt between them before. Is that what pure frustration feels like? Because they both have enough of that to fill Askala's solar power banks ten times over.

"Of course, I canceled your chip," he says. "What else did you expect, daughter of Ronan?"

She blinks at him and he tries to figure out exactly how he's feeling now that he's looking at her. He's angry. Of course, he's angry. But the white heat he'd felt seeing her next to Ronan in the ballroom has simmered. It's almost like the intensity of all the emotions he's felt for this girl have scorched his ability to feel anything except an almost wry amusement.

"Let me in," she says. "I need to talk to you. Quick, before someone sees me here."

He steps aside and she passes.

A quick glance around before the door closes tells him she really has come alone.

She heads for the computer room and he follows her, drawing in a series of deep breaths as he tries to still his heart. He has to tread very carefully here. It doesn't matter what they shared in the Proving. Her recent actions have *proven* far more.

He can't trust her.

Wren perches on the edge of his desk, drumming her fingers on the timber surface.

"You're still wearing your ring," he points out, watching her fingers come to a sudden pause.

"And you're still wearing my pendant," she retorts.

He swallows, wishing he'd done a better job at tucking it into his shirt. He's not even sure why he's still wearing it. It's not like he's going to be sending another raven any time soon.

"Do you want it back?" He slips it over his head and holds it out to her, immediately noticing how bare his neck feels without it. "Go on. Have it back."

She hesitates, then takes it from him, and it's like she's thrown a spear through his chest, unwanted proof that he hasn't lost the ability to feel. He hadn't expected her to take the pendant. But then again, why should he think he'd be able to predict anything she does? He really doesn't know her at all.

Not the real her.

Wren runs her fingers over the leather cord and loops it around her neck. Then, taking off her Bound ring, she extends her palm.

He rakes his fingers through his hair. Surely she can't be serious?

The small piece of curved silver sits in her hand and it's obvious that she means it. This is her symbol of her connection to Askala. Proof that she was deemed worthy. And the steadiness of her outstretched hand shows that she no longer wants to be a part of it.

She's no longer Bound.

He's shaking now, both with rage and grief. He'd had such hope when he'd witnessed her accept that ring from his father. Hope for her future. Hope for his own. A future woven around each other just like the roots of the mangrove pine before it had been dipped in zinc to form the ring that he doesn't want to take back.

"You're angry," she says.

"Of course, I am! You think you can continue to dish this out and I'm just going to take it like some kind of doormat? Even I have my limits." He snatches the ring from her hand and jams it into his pocket. Why does it feel like they just broke up? Like they've stepped over a line that he never wanted to cross.

"Dex…" She bites her lower lip as she looks up at him.

He crosses his arms, unwilling to help her out with whatever it is she seems to want to say. She's the one who's always run from him, not the other way around. It's Wren who needs to explain herself. He has nothing to apologize for.

"Dex…" Her words fail her again. He's never seen her so unsure of herself. Where is that cocky Remnant who marched into their Proving and showed them all how foolish they really are?

"What are you doing here?" he asks on a sigh, wishing she'd

just get on with it. He really can't stand this much longer. "Haven't you hurt me enough already?"

"I wanted to... I wanted to see you."

He does a mock tap dance, aware his moves are more aggressive than they are comedic. "Now, you've seen me. Anything else? Any other possessions you want to exchange?"

"That was you!" Her eyes pop open. "You told me to take the pendant. I thought you wanted the ring. Why mention it otherwise?"

He stares at her, wondering if that's how it really happened. It hadn't felt like that to him.

"It doesn't matter." She casts her eyes down. "I just wanted to talk to you."

"Then talk to me." He's determined not to make this easy for her. She's never in their short history made anything easy for him.

She swallows, still studying the floor. "I wanted to say sorry. I hate the way you looked at me in the ballroom. How you're looking at me now. I can't stand the thought that this is what you think of me."

"It's a little late for an apology." He crosses his arms and shakes his head, not wanting to get reeled in by her again, but aware his anger is starting to ebb.

She doesn't move. Doesn't meet his eye.

He waits for her to argue with him.

But she remains silent and it's only then that he notices tears trailing down her cheeks.

Is this the real Wren? He didn't even think she knew how to cry.

Slowly, she lifts her face and his feet move, almost against his will, as he takes a step toward her.

They lock eyes.

"I never meant to hurt you." Her voice breaks with emotion

as a new set of tears spill from her eyes. "You're the best person I ever met."

Dex draws in a breath, trying to decide how he feels about this. Hearing these words is all he's ever wanted from her. He's reached out to her so many times only to have her run the other way. But was it really him she was running from? Or was it Askala and everything it represented to her? He wants to forgive her. He *really* wants to forgive her. But no matter how rapidly his heart is beating, he knows it's too late.

"Wren..." Now it's his turn for the words to get lost on his tongue. He might not be able to forgive her, yet he's also not sure if he can ever change the way he feels for her.

"You don't have to say anything," she says. "I've been awful to you. I know I have, b—"

Dex holds up his hand. "Stop it, Wren. It's not just me you've hurt. Your father almost killed Kian, did you know that? And left him for dead."

"I know." Her voice is a moan laced with anguish. "I was there. I'm the most horrible person who ever lived."

"You were there?" He takes a step back and throws out his arms.

"I felt sick when I heard it." Wren launches off the edge of the desk but seeing the thunder on his face she's wise enough to keep her distance. "I was just outside the ballroom. As soon as we all got to the pod pool, I turned around and went back. I rubbed in some sap to stop the bleeding. I stayed with him as long as I dared, but I was afraid Cy would notice me missing. Are you saying he survived?"

Dex nods, taking in what she just told him. She saved Kian's life? Just like the Wren he thought he knew would do.

Wren swipes at her tears and gives him a small smile. "I'm so glad to hear that."

"Did you know that Nova's gone?" he asks, realizing that with everything happening it's likely she has no idea.

"Gone where?" she asks. "To nurse Kian?"

Dex shakes his head. "To the Outlands. She's pregnant."

"What the hell? No, Dex! No!" Wren looks stricken as she clutches onto his arm. "She won't survive there."

"What do you mean?" he asks, a sickness spreading to his gut. "You said it was safe there!"

"No woman is safe there alone." Wren lets go of his arm to press her fingers to her temples. "You asked me about Felicia and Thom. Not Nova. She's different. She's too kind. Too innocent. A girl like her will never blend in."

"She's with Felicia and Thom," he says, hoping that makes a difference. "They'll look after each other."

"You're sure she's pregnant?" asks Wren. "I thought you said the Unbound—"

"That's a long story." He doesn't want her thinking about this too much. "But yes, I'm sure she's pregnant. Kian's going to go and look for her."

Wren lets out a breath, almost like she actually cares about what happens to any of them. "That's good. He should go. He needs to go."

"And you should go back to your father." Dex is unable to decide if he wants to shake this impossible girl or kiss her until the last star in the sky burns into oblivion. "He might notice you missing again."

"Don't be like this, Dex." She takes a small step toward him and he crosses his arms. "Please, Dex. I really am sorry. For everything. Please don't look at me like you hate me."

He sighs, determined not to let her get even further under his skin when she starts fiddling with the hemp shirt she's wearing. Before he has a chance to wonder what in sweet Terra she's up to, her shirt falls open at the front.

"I'll do anything to make it up to you," she says, making no move to cover herself.

"Wren!" Dex steps forward and pulls her shirt together, but

not before catching a glimpse of that pendant hanging innocently between her breasts. "What are you doing?"

A pink color rushes to her face and she turns away from him, fixing her shirt. "I thought...It's just that...That's how it's done back home."

"Well, that's not how I do it." Dex shakes his head, unable to believe she was prepared to throw herself at him like that. "Is that what you think of me?"

"Of course not." Her voice is a whisper, her face filled with shame.

"Wren, you can't just come in here and apologize and throw yourself at me and expect things are going to go back to the way they were. This isn't the Outlands. Too much has happened for that."

"I don't blame you," she says, her face still aflame. "I'm a bad person. You're nothing but good. I should never have expected you'd want someone like me."

Now she doesn't look like an angry little bird. She looks like a baby bird who's fallen out of her nest.

"It's not that." His own sense of shame washes over him for making her feel like this. She hadn't read the situation all that wrong. He wants her. He's always wanted her. She knows that. Practically everyone in Askala knows that. But he'd never take advantage of her. If she's going to come to him, he has to be certain it's because she wants him, too.

"It's okay." She holds her shirt closed even further, showing him the most vulnerable side of her that he's seen yet. "I get it. I wouldn't want me, either. The things I've done are awful. I really am the worst."

"What are you doing here, Wren?" His voice softens. "What are you *really* doing here?"

She shakes her head, looking just as confused as he is. "Honestly, I'm not sure. I just couldn't keep away. I didn't want to keep away. I missed you. I miss the Dex who used to look at me like I wasn't a bad person."

"Come here." Unable to help himself a moment longer, he reaches for her and pulls her into his chest. "You're not a bad person."

She buries her face in his shirt and wraps her arms around his waist. The contact both soothes and burns at his soul. He wants her and wants to push her away.

But it seems she's not going anywhere.

He releases his grip enough so he can reach for her chin and tilt her face upwards. Her big brown eyes blink up at him, no longer filled with tears, but with something he's never seen before.

Longing. And not the sort like she'd been implying a few moments ago. This is a longing to be loved. To be held. For him to make her feel worthy.

It's not her fault she was raised the way she was. He knows she's a good person.

She opens her mouth to speak. Apologize perhaps. But he moves his hand from under her chin and presses his index finger to her lips, his Bound ring reflecting the light.

"You're not a bad person," he repeats.

"I am." She tries to pull away, but he holds her firmly in his arms needing her to believe him.

"You've made some *interesting* choices," he says. "But the Proving tests didn't lie. You have a good heart. I see that. The soft girl who hides underneath that feisty exterior. I see *you*, Wren. And you're a good person."

She relaxes into his arms once more. He can feel her heart beating against him in an elevated, rapid rhythm. She's as frightened as he is about whatever's passing between them.

"I don't deserve you, Dex." She shakes her head before burying her face in his chest. "I don't."

"Why does love have to be about deserving?" he asks,

thinking about his mother. "Sometimes we don't get what we deserve. Good or bad. Sometimes we just have to be grateful for what's in front of us right now."

Wren nods. Pulls back her shoulders. And lifts her face to him.

The girl he dragged from the water on the shores of Askala has returned once more. The girl he fell in love with. The girl he's never known if he can trust.

"I apologize for throwing myself at you earlier," she says, blinking at him. "It wasn't the right way to fix what's broken between us."

He nods. This is an apology he's prepared to accept. She'd been raised in a world that treats everything like a commodity. Including all the parts of yourself that should be most sacred. He can't blame her for that. If only he could show her what true love is…

"How do we fix what's broken?" he murmurs.

"Dex." Her voice is breathy. A different voice to any he's heard from her before. "I swear if you don't kiss me right now I'm going to have to kill you."

This time, Dex can't catch the smile that ambushes his face.

He's dreamed of this moment so many times he's lost count. He's imagined what those stubborn lips taste like. What it would be like to feel the warmth of her mouth pressed against his. And as much as he knows he shouldn't, he also knows he's about to find out.

Leaning down, he closes his eyes wanting to feel this moment with all his other senses. His mouth finds hers and he hesitates, drawing in a sharp breath at the heat of the contact.

She slips her hands behind his head and brings him down to her.

Hard and desperate.

Their lips open and mesh, and Dex's heart contracts then

expands as if needing to take in every part of this moment. Every part of Wren.

The energy that's been swirling around them ever since he saw her on the doorstep—scrap that, ever since he saw her in the ocean—rises and spins through his core and he dares to deepen the kiss.

Her lips are soft and sweet, her tongue cautious yet welcoming. Their connection soars as she presses her body against him. Unsure if he feels like he's just been born or he's about to die he spears his fingers into the spikes of her hair and cradles the back of her head. He needs her close. Every whisper of air between them is too much.

He's never kissed anyone like this before. He's not sure he'll ever kiss anyone like this again. Which means he needs to savor this moment. Remember it. Worship it. Because he also knows that even if he lives to regret trusting Wren, he'll never regret this kiss.

Wren lowers her hands from his head.

Slowly.

Achingly slowly.

Trailing her fingertips down his back until he shivers with the intensity of what he's feeling for this girl.

Her hands find their way to the hem of his shirt and she slips them underneath. When her palms touch the bare skin of his lower back he gasps, certain he's going to melt under the fire that's flooding him in all the right, and wrong, places.

Still kissing him, she gently bites down on his lower lip, letting him know she's not finished with him yet. Her movements are playful yet demanding. She's telling him this isn't one-sided. Everything he's been feeling, she feels it, too.

But it's too much. The feeling of skin on skin, her breath mingling with his, her soul laid bare before him…

If he doesn't break away now, he's never going to be able to. And that could be even more dangerous than any test he's ever faced before. Because if he lets this go where he wants it to then his life is forever entangled with hers.

And she's the daughter of the man who threw Magnus in the brig and tried to kill Kian.

He can't love Wren. He can't!

But as he breaks away, he knows without doubt that he does.

Wren whimpers and he takes two steps back, dragging in air like he's just run all the way to the beach and back.

"We can't do this," he says, bringing his fingers to his lips.

"I think we just did." She grins at him. "Dex, that kiss was incredible."

You're incredible! he wants to scream. But he doesn't.

"We need to talk," he tries instead.

Wren tilts her head. "If you don't mind, I'd rather kiss."

Dex lets out a gentle laugh as he shakes his head. "Stop it. We can't. Not until I know where you stand."

"I'm standing right here." She extends her arms then takes a few small steps until she's right in front of him again. "But I'd rather be standing here."

The sound of an alarm echoes through the lab. It's the alarm from the Oasis. The one used to call for help when there's danger. The same one used when Nova was found in the brig in the place of Wren.

"Something's happening," he says.

Wren's eyes widen. "I have to go." She takes a step toward the door. "It could be Cy."

"Are you kidding me?" All the warmth he'd just been feeling for her whooshes straight out of his body as it's replaced with the familiar feeling of betrayal. "After everything that's just happened, you're choosing him over me. *Again.*"

"Look, I know Cy's not perfect." She turns from the door, clearly torn. "But there's goodness inside him. I've seen it. Your tests even proved it. How else did he become Bound?"

"He wasn't Bound!" The words are out before he can stop

them. But why should he have to? There's no Bound or Unbound anymore. They're all just people from Askala fighting to keep hold of their homeland. "He's not the man you think he is."

"He has a chip in his hand," she says. "And it opens all the doors."

"So did my mom. And she was no more Bound than Nova." There! He's said it now. His greatest secret is out. And instead of regretting it, he feels a weight lift. "Ronan stole chips from two deceased Bound and swapped them over. Both my mother and your father failed their Proving. I've seen the results myself."

"But..."

"But nothing, Wren. You and I are both the children of Unbounds. Yet somehow we passed our Proving."

"Which shows just how screwed up your system is."

"*Is?*" he asks, wondering if they even have a system anymore. "Or do you mean *was?*"

"I have to go." She has her brave face back on. If what he'd just said to her meant anything, she isn't showing it. Her walls are back up. And they're higher than ever. "I told you that I'm a bad person."

"I thought you came here to make things right between us?"

She looks genuinely confused now. "I thought we did. You didn't think that meant I'd turn my back on my family, did you?"

Disappointment punches him in the gut. "Just hurry up and go, Wren. After all, you're good at that."

"I'll come back as soon as I can." She lifts her hand to the sensor, then remembers her chip no longer works.

"Please, don't," he says.

"But I have to go."

"No, I meant don't come back." He slams his stump to the sensor and the door slides open.

Wren stares at him open-mouthed. "I just need to see they're okay. That's all. Surely, you understand that?"

He pushes past her and heads for the exit, keen for her to leave so he can work out what the hell just happened.

Opening the door, he steps back. "Just go, Wren."

"No matter what you think of me, Dex"—she loops the pendant from around her neck and puts it back over his head—"I'll always love you."

Before he can process what just happened, she disappears into the fading light.

She loves him? Did he just hear that right? His hand flies to his neck and he feels the warmth of the pendant, proof that he didn't dream that last bit.

Spinning around slowly, he returns to his computer lab, only to see the hatch open and Kian's head poke out. With everything that just happened, Dex had totally forgotten he was down there.

"Well, that was intense." Kian grins at him.

"You were listening?" Dex feels heat rush to his cheeks. "I didn't even tell you there was a radio down there!"

"Needed something to do while I waited." Kian climbs up and closes the hatch. He looks so much better for the rest he just had. "It seems we're even now."

"How so?"

"That time on the beach with Nova." Kian arches a brow. "You know?"

"Oh." Dex tries to blink away the memory of those bare bodies on the sand. "That."

"Yeah, that."

"How's your head?" Dex asks, changing the subject.

"Feels like a polar grizzly sat on it but I'll be okay."

"You ready to set out?"

Kian nods. "You sure you don't want to come with me? It might be safer for you. You know, if Ronan finds out about that little bit of tongue wrestling that you two just participated in he'll come after you."

"You could not possibly know if there were tongues." Dex crosses his arms. "But you have a point."

"So, you'll come?" Kian's face lights up.

But there's no way Dex is going to the Outlands. Not before. Not now. Probably not ever. "Someone has to stay here and try to protect what we have, you know that."

"Then you be careful, okay?" Kian puts a hand on his shoulder, all the joviality of only moments ago having vanished. "Be very careful with Wren. I know how you feel about her, but you need to be cautious. She's still loyal to Ronan."

Dex nods, then remembers something else. "You heard what I said to Wren, didn't you? About my mom."

Kian visibly swallows as he nods. "Why didn't you tell me?"

"I haven't known for long. I wasn't sure how you'd take the news. If it would change the way you see me." Dex holds his breath as he waits for his cousin's response.

"You forget that my son or daughter is going to be the child of an Unbound." Kian's words are laced with worry. "If anything, this news gives me hope."

Dex frowns. "You still think there will be such a thing as Bound or Unbound in your child's future?"

Kian shakes his head. "I meant it gives me hope that my child might turn out to be like you."

"What? Funny? Smart? Devastatingly handsome?" He grins and bats his eyelashes. "World's best kisser?"

"Now that's one thing I don't want my child to be." Kian laughs. "And hopefully their jokes are better than yours."

"Don't worry. I'm running out of material trying to keep the mood up around here lately."

"Which is why I need to get across to the Outlands." Kian wrings his hands as his expression turns grave. "We need to know what we're dealing with here."

"It's not easy for you to leave, though, is it?"

"It's really not. Do you think it's the right thing?"

Dex thinks about this, wanting to give the question the consideration it deserves. "I do think it's the right thing. For Askala. For Nova. And for your baby. Bring them home, Kian."

But before Kian can respond, the constant ringing of the alarm from the Oasis falls silent. Both Dex and Kian pause as if turned into statues as they listen.

"What do you think's happened?" Dex asks.

"I don't know." Kian takes a step toward the door and presses his hand to the sensor. "But it can't be good."

"Don't go to the Oasis!" Dex grips Kian on the arm, bringing him to a halt. "They'll throw you in the brig with your father."

Or worse. Ronan's men might finish what they started.

"I'm not going there." Kian puts his hand on Dex's. "You were right with what you just said. I need to bring my family home. And I need to leave before whatever's just happened hits the fan."

"You're leaving right now?" Dex isn't at all sure he's ready to say goodbye. He thought they'd have more time. A few hours at least.

"I'm ready." Kian nods. "It's time to go."

WREN

*W*ren's heart is pounding as she races up the gangplank to the Oasis, and she's pretty sure it's not from the run.

It's Dex.

Who knew he could kiss like that! Holy hell. It was like he was making out with her entire soul. She'd never felt so damn worthy in her life.

And now she's gone and screwed it up.

Again.

Because when she heard that siren, it didn't matter that she'd just experienced the kiss of a lifetime, she knew her family was in trouble.

Except now the siren's stopped and she's not sure what that means.

Reaching the door to the ship, she realizes she's not going to be able get in until someone comes out. She should've had Dex reactivate her chip before she left him. But she'd been in too much of a hurry, and he hadn't seemed in the mood to help her once he realized she wasn't going to hang around.

Wren bangs on the door but nothing happens. There are

always people coming in and out of the Oasis. Surely, she won't have to wait long? But seconds turn to minutes and still, she's waiting.

What's going on in there?

Maybe she should head back to the lab?

No! She can't do that. Because Dex and those lips are there. And the fact she's already thinking about the next time she might get to kiss them tells her that her heart is choosing a side in this war that she's not ready to follow.

Not yet.

Truthfully, maybe not ever.

She needs to think with a clear head. And kissing Dex hasn't helped with that.

At all.

Walking back down the gangplank she lets out a sigh. Nope, her head is upside-down like it's been turned around a thousand times. Perhaps she'd be better off to do less thinking and concentrate more on actions.

Or maybe not. It was her actions that got her head in such a state in the first place.

She'd gone to the lab to beg for forgiveness, unable to stand the thought of Dex looking at her with anything but love in his eyes. But she hadn't counted on transforming that look of disappointment into one of...pure lust. And then back to disappointment again.

As if she didn't already have enough to make up to him, now she has to add that to the list. There's going to come a day when he's unwilling to forgive her. He's almost reached that point already. She could see it in his eyes before he'd let his guard down and given in to whatever this is between them.

Wren jogs around the ship, heading for the ladder on the other side that leads to the small beach, hoping this will be a faster way to get onboard. Nobody's coming anywhere near that front door.

Her dread grows with each rung of the ladder that she climbs. It's quiet. It doesn't sound like anyone is about. But then again, not many people spend a lot of time up there. If she's lucky, there might be someone who can let her in.

She reaches the top quickly, her lungs barely complaining at the exertion. In fact, it feels good to burn off some energy like this.

But she quickly discovers the energy was wasted when the upper deck is also deserted with the door to inside left firmly closed.

"Phoenix!" she shouts, more out of sheer frustration than any belief he can hear her.

Knowing there's only one other way into this rusted hulk of metal, she scrambles back down the ladder.

She has to get inside. Something isn't right. What if something bad has happened to Phoenix or Cy? They might not be perfect, but they're the only family she has.

Although…are they? Because there's no question that Dex and Nova have started to feel like family. And Kian. She'd had to try to help him in the ballroom. There was no way she could have left him lying there like that. She only wishes she could have done more. But at least he'd survived and that's something.

Wren continues to jog around the Oasis until she reaches the door used for the Proving. It looks like it was cut into the side of the ship when that temporary tunnel was built to lead the participants directly to the ballroom. There's a spider's web on it now, evidence of its lack of recent use.

Before she knocks, she presses her ear to the paneling and listens. There are voices on the other side. Shouting. Screaming. Crying.

Wren knocks, her knuckles pinking up at the force.

"Cy!" she calls. "Phoenix! It's me! Let me in!"

But it's clear they can't hear her amidst the chaos going on inside. Then she remembers they can't let her in even if they wanted to. This door is one-way, only opening from the outside, symbolic of the commitment they make after the Proving. Except she no longer has a chip that works. This door is as useless to her as that pledge she made to Askala.

"You don't want to go in there," says a voice behind her.

Wren spins around to see Nova's mother. Her face is covered with lines that Wren can't remember having seen before. Her hair has streaks of gray and her shoulders are hunched forward. It seems everything that's happened lately has taken its toll on this poor woman.

"Thea," says Wren. "Can you open this door for me? I have to get inside."

Thea rubs her hands down her dress. "You don't want to go in there."

"So, you keep telling me," Wren says. "But you haven't told me why."

"Your father woke up at the pod pool and realized his chip didn't work." Thea flinches as if the memory is painful. "It put him in a bad mood."

"Oh." Wren's very aware of what one of Cy's bad moods look like. It's no wonder Thea is reacting this way.

"He's called everyone into the ballroom. Attendance is compulsory." Thea uses her fingers to make quote marks in the air at these last few words.

"Then why aren't you there?"

"I was in the forest at the time, collecting more sap. Shiloh came out and warned me not to go back inside. It's not safe."

Wren takes a closer look at the bushes surrounding them and startles to see several sets of eyes watching her from between the branches. How many people are hiding out here?

A young child darts out into the open air and her mother emerges and hauls her back in, her eyes spilling over with fear as she sees Wren. *Is she scared of her?*

"I won't hurt you," Wren calls out, unsettled by the behavior, although after what happened to Dorian, she supposes it isn't entirely uncalled for.

"Nobody's allowed to leave," says Thea. "Not until…"

"Not until what?" Wren takes a step closer to this frail-looking woman who'd seemed so strong and capable when she'd worked on Wren's injuries when she'd arrived.

Thea steps back, keeping her distance. Is she frightened of her, too?

"Ronan says he's going to run his own Proving." Thea wrings her hands. "He's going to decide who's Bound and Unbound."

"He's what?" Wren is aghast.

Thea nods. "Says he can do a better job of it than Callix."

Wren would like to think Thea's making this up, but these words ring true. That's something Cy would say.

"Why are you telling me this?" Wren asks. "How do you know I'm not going to turn you in?"

"Because you're my daughter's friend. And you're Bound." Thea glances down at Wren's left hand and her eyes widen to see it's bare.

"I'm no longer Bound." Wren remembers the hurt look on Dex's face when she returned the ring. She'd honestly thought that's what he wanted when he mentioned it. Especially, given he'd just returned her pendant. "But I'll always be Nova's friend."

Thea lets out a breath and nods. "You need to stop Ronan. Please? Someone needs to stop him."

"Will you open the door for me?" asks Wren, not making any promises. Thea is placing far too much confidence in who she is and what she's capable of doing. "I can't do anything from out here."

Thea grips her firmly by the hand and eyeballs her. "You can't fix something by smashing it to pieces. Remember that."

Wren nods, not needing to ask Thea what she means. Askala may not have been perfect, but it could have been repaired.

Can it still?

"I heard about Nova," Wren says. "I'm so sorry."

"Will she be okay?" Thea lowers her voice, still making no move to open the door. "Will your people look after her?"

Wren hesitates, wanting to be as honest as she can. It all depends on who Nova encounters. "There are good people in the Outlands, just like here. Nova's stronger than I think any of us ever realized."

"She *is* strong." Thea's face lights up with pride. "And so are you. You're better than your father."

"You don't know anything about me." Wren steps back, not used to so many people putting her father down after spending her life hearing people sing his praises. Even though she knows where it's coming from, it makes her uncomfortable.

"You're right. I don't know you," Thea agrees. "But Nova does."

Thea presses her hand to the sensor on the door and dashes away to join the people peeking out from the bushes.

The door opens and Wren blinks at the scene inside, trying to take it in. It's almost silent. The screams of only minutes ago have been swallowed by the unmistakable terror that's permeating the room.

Cy is standing on the stage wearing his tight leather trousers and no shirt, his Mercy tattoo shouting at Wren from his muscled chest in a way it hasn't before. It's strange to think the name she's grown up knowing belongs to Dex's mother.

There's a group of people behind Cy. Their eyes are downcast, their expressions brimming with the same defeat evident in Thea when she'd approached her.

There are more people milling in the ballroom, their faces a rainbow of indecision and fear. Cy's men are roaming amongst them, waving their flamethrowers and herding them toward the stage.

"Wren!" says Cy. "So glad you could join us. Which reminds me…where have you been?"

"Didn't realize you were calling a meeting." She shoots Cy a nervous smile as she avoids his question.

"It's my fault," says Phoenix, crossing the stage to get to her. "I asked her to see if she could find me a deer like that one we told you about. Fancied myself a feed."

Cy tips back his head and laughs. "Don't we all, son. Don't we all."

Wren slips her hand into Phoenix's, needing the comfort of her twin's touch. He's always made up excuses for her to keep her out of trouble.

He squeezes her hand. It's nice to know that with everything that's changed recently, the bond she has with Phoenix will always remain true.

"Well, you're just in time for the Proving, Wren," says Cy. "Come and stand with me. These people are lining up for their first test."

Wren takes cautious steps toward him, still gripping Phoenix's hand. "What are you testing for?"

"Well, it's not intelligence, as you can tell by looking at our new Bound behind me." Cy laughs again, the bad mood that Thea had described seeming to have vanished in a cloud of newfound power.

Wren studies the solemn faces behind her father, recognizing some as previous Bound and others as Unbound. What exactly have they done to all be considered Bound now?

"He's testing for loyalty," Phoenix explains.

"The only quality worth testing for." Cy nods for one of his men to bring the next person forward. "Anyone can be taught to be a soldier if they're loyal enough."

A woman is dragged onto the stage and deposited at Cy's feet. Wren recognizes her as Zali, the woman who prepares their meagre meals each day.

"Excellent," Cy says to her. "You're practically kneeling already. Now it's time for your Proving."

Cy winks at Wren and she scratches her nose to hide her cringe.

"Who's the Commander of Askala?" Cy asks.

Zali pulls herself to a stand and clears her throat, only for Cy's man to knock her back to the timber floor. Phoenix tightens his grip on Wren's hand, warning her not to react. It takes all of her strength to obey.

"Kneel before your leader!" the guard sneers.

Zali kneels, unable to stop the tears streaking down her cheeks.

"Who's the Commander of Askala?" Cy asks again, cracking his knuckles.

"You are," Zali says, keeping her eyes down.

Cy nods. "First test passed! Well done. Next…do you have anything you'd like to give me?"

Zali removes her Bound ring with a little difficulty and passes it to him. Her hands are shaking. It's obvious she doesn't want to part with it. Those rings aren't supposed to be removed. Not ever. But Zali's not being given much choice.

"A High Bound ring." Cy raises his eyebrows as he takes it from her. "Want to be a High Bound, Phoenix?"

"Sure." Phoenix lets go of Wren's hand to take the ring from their father.

He returns to Wren's side but this time she rebuffs his hand, not wanting to feel that traitorous sliver of metal against her skin.

"Cover for me," he whispers. "I need to do something."

She watches, open-mouthed as he leaves the stage.

"Now, tell me what use you are to the new Askala?" Cy asks Zali, drawing her attention back to him. "What skills will you serve me with?"

"I'm responsible for the gardens and the kitchen," says Zali. "You need me here."

"I can see how that will be useful," says Cy, nodding. "Excellent. So, that's the first three tests of the Proving. Now, you saw what the others did for their final test. It's time to *show* me your loyalty."

Zali turns a paler shade of white and Wren can barely stand it. What the hell is he making these people do?

Cy folds his arms across his broad chest and smirks down at Zali who leans forward, bringing her face closer and closer to the floor.

She kisses one of Cy's dusty feet.

This can't be happening. Surely, not!

Wren goes to say something to Phoenix, before remembering he's no longer there. She looks to the back of the room and sees him slip out the door.

"Please join your fellow Bound," says Cy. "Congratulations."

Zali gets slowly to her feet, her disgust written all over her beaten face, as she wipes her mouth and joins the others standing behind Cy on the stage.

"What's he doing to those who don't pass?" Wren whispers to the man standing next to her.

He points to a dimly lit back corner of the ballroom where there's a small group of people being stood over by two of Cy's men. It's hard to see, but Wren's certain some of them have bruises and others are awkwardly cradling various body parts. She sees Amity sitting amongst them with a swollen black eye. Clearly, she'd been one of the first to have to prove herself to Cy. And it's no surprise she failed miserably.

"Next!" Cy announces and an Unbound is brought before him and asked the same series of questions. He doesn't have a ring to hand over and is a lot less anxious about his answers, promising his new Commander that he's a good hunter and prepared to bring back as many polar grizzlies as he desires.

Something that Wren seriously doubts, but it seems people will promise anything if their life is on the line.

The man kisses Cy's feet and moves to the back of the stage without fuss, leaving Wren wondering if this is how it will be for all the Unbound—keen to start a new life judged as being more worthy than their counterparts. It must make for a tempting change, no matter what they've had to agree to.

The next person to approach is Bea. An Unbound. And one who has good reason to be upset with Askala. Her brother would be alive right now if he'd been given the medical care he needed.

But when she's asked to identify the Commander of the Outlands, her response has everyone in the room holding their breath.

"Kian."

"Don't do it, Bea!" calls a man from the corner of the room, who Wren thinks she recognizes as her partner.

Wren winces as the man is savagely kicked in the thigh by one of Cy's men. He grimaces but doesn't let a sound escape his lips, even though he must be in agony right now.

Wren fights the urge to run to him. To tell her father's men to leave them all alone. Then she reminds herself that at least nobody here is losing a digit.

"The son of a maggot is your leader?" asks Cy, his attention focused only on Bea. "Are you sure about that? Or would you like to change your answer?"

"You will never be my leader." Bea spits at Cy's feet and Wren watches as the saliva flies through the air, spelling out her fate.

The man who'd dragged her to the stage raises his flamethrower in the air, but just before he brings it down, Cy holds up his hand.

"Be sure not to kill her." He smirks. "There are some fates

worse than death. Add her to the other filthy Unbound at the back of the room."

Cy's man grabs Bea roughly by the wrists, hauling her across the stage in such a way that it's surprising her arms aren't ripped out of their sockets. Cy may not want her dead, but it's clear she's not exactly going to make it to the back of the room unharmed.

As Wren watches the people of Askala face Cy's Proving one-by-petrified-one, she knows she should have listened to Thea and stayed away.

Because there's nothing she can do to stop this nightmare.

And each and every time someone passes or fails Cy's Proving, her heart aches for them in different ways. Being Cy's enemy is undoubtedly dangerous. But as she's fast learning, being his ally can be even worse.

It feels like it takes an eternity for everyone to be sorted into their new groups and Wren lets out a breath as Phoenix sneaks back into the room just as the last person is made Bound.

The group on the stage is far larger than those remaining shoved in the back corner. The new Bound are spilling off the raised platform and down the stairs. It seems Cy was right. When it comes to being a soldier, anyone can be taught. Or perhaps bought—with fear as the currency.

There are about twenty of the new Unbound, including Bea and her partner, and Amity. Wren studies their stoic faces, thinking about the irony. These people are the true soldiers in the room, the only ones willing to stand up for what they believe in, no matter what the cost. Cy would be better off to dump his new Bounds in favor of this group, but she knows he'll never do that. He has hundreds of loyal subjects now.

At least this whole debacle is over now.

But just as she's about to let out a long breath, the doors at the back of the ballroom open once more, revealing the last person she wants to see in here right now.

Dex.

He walks across the room, taking in the dejected faces of the injured people in the corner. It's obvious that whatever it is that Cy's up to, it isn't good. And there's Wren, standing right beside him.

"You're just in time," says Cy, grinning at Dex. "Welcome to your Proving."

Dex gasps and Wren prays he won't look at her. She wills his gaze away, unable to bear the disappointment she knows she'll see.

But, slowly, he turns his head and his eyes find hers.

And the look he gives her crushes her soul.

Her greatest fear has come true.

This time, she's gone too far. He'll never forgive her for this.

NOVA

*I*n the gloomy hut, the two men look like grimy monsters. They loom, large and menacing over Nova as she subtly moves between them and her friends. Fear quickly swells to become the third beast in the room, bringing certain details into sharp relief.

The men's faces, their intent clear in their half-grins.

The door—the only point of light—that now feels like a mile away.

The sound of Flick behind her, awake and whimpering. The silence from Thom, probably frozen with the same dread that has Nova's muscles rigid.

How foolish they were. How naïve.

The men glance at each other, their smirks growing. The smaller man wipes a hand across his mouth as if he's salivating. Nova's stomach recoils at their excitement.

Then she cringes at herself, sitting there, waiting for them to take what they want.

She pushes to her feet. "Don't do this, please." Seeing them pause, Nova struggles to find the words to stop this. "It's…it's wrong."

The taller man's leer only cements deeper. "Wrong is taking something from someone and not paying. We're making it right."

"By taking us by force?" Nova shoots back, courage she didn't know she had clenching her fists tight.

The shorter man's eyes rake her body. "Most of the women just take off their clothes like the good girls they are."

There's a shuffling sound and Thom comes to stand beside Nova. "I'll work off what we owe you. I'm probably stronger than most men here."

Which is true. Thom's stocky body has had a lifetime of pods and food. Unlike these people's lifetime of poverty and desperation.

The men glance at each other and Nova senses Thom lean forward ever so slightly. She holds her breath. Maybe she could help Thom with whatever task he's given. It shouldn't take them long to work off two cups of watery broth.

The men burst into raucous, forced laughter. They slap each other on the back. "They think we need muscles." The taller man turns back to them. "Look around. There's nothing left to build with. The Commander made sure of that." He impales them with a glare. "We need food and water, just like he promised us." The smallest of steps has Nova shrinking back. "Until then, we need something to brighten our day." His gaze slides over Nova's fair hair. "And we don't get to see your sort of sunshine very often."

The shorter man pulls in a long breath as if he's trying to smell her from where they stand. "I reckon she's gonna taste like sunbeams."

Nova's gut plummets as her breath splinters. The intent in their eyes tells her they planned this all along, whether they could've paid or not.

So foolish. So stupidly naïve.

She tries to prepare herself for what's coming next. She

stares back, unblinking. "Leave Flick alone. She recently lost her baby."

The shorter man shrugs. "Happens all the time." He takes another step, telling her it doesn't matter.

The fear is back, bigger and far more suffocating than before. Nova raises her hand as if she has the power to stop them. "Please no." She desperately throws out the last plea she can think of. "I'm pregnant."

There's a gasp behind her, then another. Flick and Thom.

The two people who only just lost their own baby.

Nova flinches at her selfishness, but she's not just trying to save herself. She's futilely trying to find hope in a hopeless situation.

The taller man gapes at her left hand, the missing ring finger unmistakable. "What the hell happened to your finger?" he asks, horror stamped across his face.

The second man is peering at Flick's hand. "Hers is missing, too!"

Instinctively, Nova knows not to tell them they're from Askala. This is their opportunity to escape. "It was taken. Cut off. Because...because we're defective."

The shorter man pulls back. "Defective how?"

"They're both diseased," Thom jumps in. "It shows they're highly contagious."

The short man glances at Thom's left hand. "And yet you've got two of these defective women. It doesn't seem to have stopped you."

The other hasn't taken his gaze off Nova. "You sure as hell don't look diseased to me, girl." His face fills with excitement. "And there's only one way to find out."

He lurches forward and grabs her arm, his fingers digging into her flesh. Nova struggles, yanking back as she jams her heels into the dusty ground. "Run—"

Her plea to Flick and Thom is cut short by the slap across

her face. Her head snaps to the side as her cheek flashes with pain. Eyes stinging, Nova bites her lip.

Who was she kidding? She doesn't stand a chance in this fight.

The man raises his hand to strike her again and Nova slams her eyes shut, the sound of roaring echoing in her ears.

When the man's grip is torn from her arm, her eyes fly open again. The roaring wasn't in her head.

It was Thom.

He's launched himself at the man, his hands grappling to reach his throat. "Stay away from them, you bastards!"

The first man stumbles, trying to keep Thom's solid body at bay. Thom pushes them backward, the man's foot kicking the pot of broth over.

"No!" the other man screams. He reaches to his side, the glint of silver the only sign he has a knife as he lunges at Thom.

Nova's mouth forms around her own denial, but it's too late.

The blade pierces Thom's side and he collapses with a groan.

The man he attacked steps back, looking at him in disgust. The other man is kneeling over the wet ground where the broth has seeped into the dust, mingling with Thom's blood.

Nova rushes to Thom, Flick behind her. A quick assessment tells her what she wishes wasn't true.

The cut in the side of Thom's abdomen is deep, with crimson blood flowing freely. Nova quickly pulls his shirt back down, covering the flash of white intestine that was peeking through the wound. She presses her hands to it, knowing it's useless.

Flick falls to her knees, not needing Nova to tell her what's painfully obvious.

Thom's dying.

"No, no, no." Flick moans the word over and over again. First, their child. Now Thom.

Thom lifts his hand only for it to drop to his chest with a

wince. "I…" He swallows the blood pooling in his mouth. "Wasn't…running…again."

"You didn't run." Flick whispers as she takes his hand. "Just like you didn't leave us in the storm."

Nova's chest feels like it's been excavated. Although Thom left her to deal with the polar grizzly, he put his life at risk to save Flick and their unborn child when she lost consciousness in the ocean. And now he's here, like this, because he tried to protect them.

There's a gurgle of blood and Thom's chest deflates. An eerie silence blooms as it doesn't move again.

The tall man straightens, righting his clothes. "We'll dispose of him shortly." He turns back to Nova, the glint in his eye laced with steel. "Now you owe us for a full pot of broth."

His friend chuckles, the sound low and threatening. Flick scuttles back beside Nova and they huddle together.

There'll be no more talking. No more fighting back.

There's no one left to save them.

As Flick and Nova contract together, the men each step to the side, widening the gap between them. They move in from each flank, their leering faces dominating the room.

"Askala! Askala!"

At first the words are faint, the voice high-pitched as if from a child, and Nova almost thinks she imagined it. How else would she be hearing it? Who would be calling the name of the island they should never have left?

But Flick stiffens and the men straighten.

"Askala has fallen!" the child's voice carries through the open doorway, this time clear and excited.

The men snap to attention as they look at each other in surprise. Without glancing at the girls, they rush outside, jostling their way through the door.

Nova pushes to her feet, hauling Flick up with her. They hold each other, listening to the commotion outside.

"It's finally happened," says a woman in a reverent tone.

"Just like the Commander promised!" a man shouts with jubilation.

There's the sound of feet shuffling in the dirt as if people are dancing. "When are we joining them? When?"

No one seems to have the answer to the last question, but the child continues to run up and down the village, repeating the broadcast. "Askala! Askala has fallen!"

What? How is that even possible? Kian would never let that happen!

Nova snaps out of her state of shock, realizing this is their opportunity to escape. She rushes for the door, peeking out into the bright sunshine only to find the backs of the two men only a few feet away. They want to hear the news, but they're not leaving their prisoners unattended.

"We have to find a way out," she hisses, scanning the hut frantically..

Flick glances around, her eyes wide and glassy. Blood loss. Shock. The promise stamped on the men's features. Thom's dead body, still warm and only a few feet away. It's all taken its toll on her.

Nova squeezes Flick's hand. "Wait here. I'll find us a way out."

Flick nods obediently, letting her curls fall around her face.

Heading to the wall behind her, Nova's fingers work over the slats of timber, looking for any weakness she can find. But it's been built to withstand the harshness of the Outlands. The wood is thick and rough, each length jammed close to the next.

Her breath harsh in her ears, Nova moves to the back wall. They don't have much time. Halfway along she finds a patch of corrugated iron. Heart beating so hard it's making her dizzy, Nova follows the edge with her fingers. Maybe they missed a screw. Maybe it's loose somewhere.

Hope soars for a split second when the metal bends outward,

only to be shattered when a sliver of light streaks through and nothing else. The gap, maybe an inch, isn't wide enough for them to fit through. Nova pushes and pushes, but it's secured firmly. Feeling more and more frantic, she looks for where it's attached. Maybe they can try and undo it enough to slip out. Her fingers find nothing.

The screws are on the outside.

"I think they're coming back," Flick says in a small voice.

The sound of voices outside is quieting, as if people are moving away.

"I've almost got it," Nova lies. The metal isn't moving.

Feeling the surface, Nova registers the roughness of rust. Her head falls forward, resting on the rough wood in front of her. Their only chance is to kick it in, hoping it's weak enough.

Which will make a racket and have the men rushing in before they can get out.

They're trapped.

"We need to be prepared." It's the man. The tall one. Not far away. "Good thing we'll have that cloth to trade for food. We're gonna be the first ones on those rafts for the land of food and water."

"After we..." The other man chuckles and Nova imagines him indicating his head toward the door.

She crumples to the floor, her hand resting on the warm metal. Defeat feels like black tar in her chest. She indicates to Flick. "Come here. We should stick together."

If she can protect Flick from what's coming, then that will be her victory in these moments of despair.

Flick tucks herself in beside Nova, her gaze even more blank than before. Nova realizes it's probably a good thing. No one wants to be conscious during what's about to happen.

There's a quiet scraping behind her, the twisting of metal into metal. Nova spins around, jerking Flick back with her.

They watch, silent and panting, as the noise stops and the

metal moves. Nova gasps as it swings open an inch like the cover over a peephole. There's a softly muttered curse and it opens further, the shaft of light suddenly feeling too bright.

Nova glances over her shoulder but the men aren't there yet. When she looks back, she recoils in shock at the face staring at them through the hole.

It's a woman, but a deeply scarred woman. Her face is angled so only the right side shows, the skin melted and twisting her features. She's wearing some sort of hood and cape made of brown material, obscuring her hair and the rest of her face.

Flick lets out a squeal, but Nova quickly claps her hand over her mouth.

The woman pulls the metal further to the side, creating a gap large enough for them to slip though. "Quick," she hisses. "You're running out of time."

Nova has pushed Flick through the hole and followed her without giving herself time to think or glance back. She has no idea who this woman is, but whatever she wants with them can't be worse than what was about to happen.

The moment they're through, the woman pushes the metal back and jams a rock in the base. With the briefest of glances at them she turns and runs.

Nova grabs Flick's hand, following her as she winds around the back of the huts. Within moments, they leave the village, the expanse of the Outlands opening up. Nova has no idea where they're going, but she can sense they're moving away from the ocean.

They're running inland.

The strange cloth the woman has wrapped around her billows like a parachute as she runs. Occasionally she glances back to make sure they're keeping up, but apart from that, she doesn't speak or acknowledge them.

Their choice is to follow her to who knows where, or stay in the village. Tugging on Flick's hand, Nova breaks into a trot, doing her best to keep up.

The first time Flick stumbles, Nova wraps her arm around her waist.

"I can't." Flick goes to stop but Nova doesn't let her maintain momentum.

"You can," she tells her through gritted teeth as she matches her gait to Flick's.

They keep moving, the exchange counting out their steps. "I can't," pants Flick.

"You can," retorts Nova.

"I can't."

"You can."

When something appears on the horizon, Nova squints, knowing this is where the woman is taking them. It grows steadily like an island in the vast charcoal wasteland they're traversing, gaining height and hugging more of the skyline. After only a few minutes of their shuffling run, Nova recognizes it.

She's only read about places like this. She'd thought they were all nothing but rubble.

It's a city.

She realizes they're on a road, the dirt more compacted than the rest. Ahead, the skyline rises and spreads, broken and crumbling, looking like it's held together by nothing but shadows.

The woman only stops when she reaches the edge of it, breathing evenly compared to Nova and Flick's puffing.

She turns to them, and Nova sees she's largely scarred on her right side only. The left is smooth, far cleaner than she's seen in the Outlands, quite beautiful and almost...familiar. The woman sweeps her arm toward the decay behind her. "This is Fairbanks. They won't look for you here."

Nova's heard of Fairbanks. As the continent had slowly changed, shrinking and submerging, capital city after capital city being lost to the ocean, Fairbanks had been the last fort of human habitation in this area. Some of Askala's ancestors had hailed from there.

Now, it's hard to imagine it being habitable. Shells of rusted motor vehicles litter the ground, the glass long gone, panels missing and exposing their corroded intestines. Every building that rises up is either crumbling straight back down or leaning like a giant, drunk monolith. Many are both, several collapsed onto each other like dominoes. In the background, a towering mangrove pine grows through one building, the winding trunks and branches punching through in multiple places, yet the thick, serpentine roots that spear into the ground look like they're the only thing holding it together.

Before them, a massive beam of steel has fallen over the road, a diagonal shaft of metal reaching to the sky. There's no way around it, looking like some strange bridge that's the only way in. Except there's nowhere to step off on the other side. It looks exactly like Nova's life feels right now—unknown and dangerous.

The woman faces Fairbanks, cupping her hands around her mouth as she mimics the call of a raven. Nova waits, wondering if this is where more people dressed like her will come swarming out. It's time to find out if they've run from one trap straight into another.

But no one comes out. The woman turns back. "It's safe to enter now."

The woman indicates they should continue up the beam with a wave of her arm before tucking it into the folds of the material swathed around her. Nova realizes it's a fine netting of some sort, like closely woven webbing, and a lot of it.

Flick frowns. "You're not going first?"

The woman shakes her head. "I'll be right behind you."

Crossing her arms, a flash of the old Flick starting to show, she shakes her head. "I'm not walking over that," she states flatly. "I'm not even sure we should go in there."

"Inside the city is the safest place for you right now."

Nova hesitates, realizing exactly how fragile their situation is if they're considering entering this abandoned metropolis. Everything looks as if it could collapse any moment and who knows how stable that beam to nowhere is.

Flick moves a little closer to Nova, not bothering to hide her frown. "Who are you?"

"My name is Avis." She regards them steadily. "I live in there."

She lives in Fairbanks? Nova glances at the ruins behind her, wondering how that's even possible. A mosquito buzzes past her ear, reminding her of the stories of disease that broke out in these impoverished, decomposing cities. All the moisture of the newly temperate areas were a breeding ground for malaria, cholera, and dengue.

"I'm Nova and this is Felicia." Nova smiles a little, not wanting her to be offended. "We're grateful for your help."

Flick keeps her arms firmly crossed. "Why exactly did you help us?"

Nova watches Avis, wondering the same thing. The Outlands doesn't look like a place that engenders generosity and kindness.

Not without a price.

Avis's lips tighten. "The Commander took my children from me when they were barely two years old. For his army."

In the same way the man in the hut said he lost his own son.

"Then he did this to me when I tried to stop him." She points to her face, anger vibrating through her. Now that they're no longer running, the bright sun hiding nothing, the scars are even worse. Half of Avis's face has melted, the skin red and shiny. Part of her nose is missing, her eye and mouth drawn down in a permanent expression of sadness.

Nova refuses to look away, compassion filling her. The burns this woman endured would've meant months of pain. Nova's not even sure how she survived.

Avis looks Nova in the eye. "If you didn't escape, your child could've suffered the same fate."

Nova's hands fly to her stomach. Her child. Used for labor or war. With her unable to stop it in a world that values strength over kindness.

"Thank you," she whispers. She eyes the world of atrophied gray and overgrown green. "Is there a way in?"

Avis half-smiles, her scarred side barely moving. "There's always a way in." She steps back, waving her arm for them to pass.

Nova doesn't move. "And somewhere safe to stay?"

This time, Avis's smile grows until her sad-angry side compresses up, too. "Safe is a relative term in the Outlands." She shrugs her shoulders under her layers of netting. "Unless you have somewhere else to go…"

Flick grips Nova's hand, leaning in to whisper. "I don't like this. She isn't telling us everything. We don't know what we're getting into."

Nova's jaw tightens. Neither did they when they chose to come to the Outlands. Right now, they have two choices.

Enter Fairbanks, with a scarred woman who claims she's doing this to help them. If she were in Askala, Nova wouldn't hesitate. But a snippet of conversation with Phoenix flashes through her mind.

"Look after yourself, Phoenix."

"Will do, Blondie…It's the first rule of the Outlands."

Why exactly is Avis helping them? And will she want something in return for the kindness she's shown them?

Nova glances over her shoulder. Their alternative is to try and find another village. One of them recovering from a miscarriage, the other pregnant, with nothing to trade...but their bodies.

She looks to Flick. "From what I've seen, I'd rather face this unknown than the known we've already encountered."

Flick bites her lip. "You'll stay with me?"

Nova's hand tightens around hers. "We'll stick together, Flick. I promise."

Turning back to Avis, Nova finds her watching them, her gaze sharp and assessing. Why does this woman feel so familiar? Taking a step toward the beam, Flick close by her side, Nova levels her gaze at Avis. "Thank you for saving us." She straightens her shoulders. "We'll try to repay you any way we can."

Avis chuckles. "You don't need to worry." She arches a brow as she turns away. "I won't be asking for much."

KIAN

"*I* think that's everything." Finn dusts his hands on his pants as he steps back from the raft, eyeing it like it's going to fall apart any second.

Shiloh nods, pulling in a shaky breath. "Just the food and water to strap down."

Kian stops himself from pointing out one last time it's not too late to back out. Each opportunity he's tried they've both been adamant. Shiloh is convinced this is the way to save Askala. Finn said he can't stay and watch Ronan destroy it all.

Not after his brother died protecting everything they're trying to save.

Kian just hopes this mission won't have casualties like the Proving did.

When Dean materializes from the trees, Kian straightens. He was hoping he wouldn't have to have this conversation.

Dean narrows his eyes at them. "Figured you wouldn't be sending me the memo. Good thing I decided to hang around and wait."

Kian angles a brow. "There was no memo." He sincerely

doubts bringing Dean will be a good idea, despite Dex trying to convince him that his brawn would be useful.

Dean is certainly strong and healthy. With only Shiloh and Finn to row with him, the trip to the Outlands wouldn't be quick. But Dean's double-crossed his own family. Kian doesn't trust him any more than he'd trust a leatherskin.

Dean angles his head. "Running away, huh?"

Not bothering to point out that those words just cemented his decision, Kian turns away, strapping down the small bag of food they're bringing. Inside, Dex has slipped a few jars of pods, pointing out that the concept of rations doesn't seem to exist in Askala anymore.

"I could raise the alarm. Get the guards here," Dean growls behind him.

Kian doesn't even glance at him. "No one will believe you," he states flatly. "Not to mention the moment you show your face, your own brother will consider roasting you with his flamethrower."

Thanking Shiloh for the bottles of water she passes him, he straps those down, too. Nodding at Finn, the three of them shove the raft across the sand to the edge of the water. As Kian rights himself, he isn't surprised to find Dean not far behind them.

He shakes his head. "I can't pay you, Dean. You've got a better chance of weaseling your way back in with Ronan than getting fifty pods out of me."

Who knows if there are even fifty pods left in the pool.

"I was originally part of this team. I said I'd go, so here I am."

"You want me to believe you're here because you're keeping your word?" Kian asks, incredulity hiking up his voice. He turns back to the others. "Climb on and I'll push it the rest of the way out."

Shiloh and Finn jump onto the raft, Finn taking an oar and

digging it into the sand as Kian pushes. Water laps at his ankles and his heart rate picks up.

I'm coming, Nova. I can't fix this on my own.

There's splashing beside him as Dean takes hold of the raft, too. "Take me with you."

Kian doesn't miss the note of pleading in Dean's tone. "I can't afford to be watching my back in the Outlands, Dean." This is dangerous enough as it is.

Shiloh looks away as Finn starts to paddle. Neither acknowledges Dean's presence.

"I'll work hard." The water wraps around their calves as Dean's grip tightens on the raft. "I'll row stronger than either of those two."

Kian pauses, and it's all Dean needs. He pushes in close, his eyes bright in the fading light. "I'm a dead man if I stay. It's Ronan or the forest, and neither of those are going to welcome me."

Kian hauls himself up to the raft, frustrated that he can't turn his back on Dean like Ronan did. He picks up an oar and holds it out to Dean. "We row through the night."

With a grin, Dean pushes up beside him and grabs it. "Looking forward to it."

The sun sets behind them as they draw their oars through the water. As darkness sets, they establish a steady rhythm, the water calm and black. Shiloh dozes in the middle of the raft, her head lolling on Finn's shoulder. Several times they both offer to row. Both times Kian refuses, surprised when Dean does, too. It seems they both have something to prove.

They slip through the silent night, Askala dissolving behind them like it never existed, no way of telling how far away the Outlands are. It turns out luck is on their side—the cloudless sky allows for easy navigation as the stars guide them, the gentle tailwind encouraging them over the water.

It's like fate wants him to find Nova.

Weariness tugs at Kian's muscles as the night draws on, but he doesn't stop. Each pull of the oar is bringing him closer. As much as he wasn't sure taking Dean was a good idea, when their raft hits the shores of the Outlands the following morning, he admits his strong rowing arms didn't go astray. They wouldn't have made it in the time they did without him.

As dawn caresses the horizon, they drag the raft to hide it among the rocks. Kian straightens, about to congratulate the others on their effort, when he notices their frozen expressions.

His eyes widen as he sees what they're looking at.

It's a world drawn in coal, smudged and gray like a battle-field. Kian's chest aches at the nonexistence of life. Nothing breathes, nothing grows. No healing has happened here.

It's like Mother Nature has been made barren—the seeds of life she carried shriveled up and died in this wasteland.

Slowly turning on the spot, Kian wonders if the only thing they're going to learn here is what acres of death looks like. How could the Remnants have anything of value to share?

Maybe this is a warning of what will happen if they don't stop Ronan.

Pulling in a steadying breath, Kian looks further than the annihilation in their immediate vicinity. In the distance, a curl of smoke rises to the sky. They've obviously landed close to habitation.

Kian points it out to the others. "There. That's where we'll go first."

Finn swallows. "You reckon they're friendly?"

"If not, stick close to me." Dean slaps him on the back. "They'll regret anything they try."

Kian frowns. "We come in peace. We're here to learn what we can and find the others. Not to make trouble."

Dean clenches his jaw as he looks away. "Sure. I was just showing I had his back."

Grabbing their food and water, Kian looks to Shiloh. "You okay?"

"I didn't expect it to be so...empty." She bites her lip. "I suppose it just shows how important it is that we succeed."

"I was just thinking the same thing," replies Kian.

"Yes!" Shiloh's face lights up. "This is why we needed to have the Bound and Unbound. What we did ensured nothing like this could happen. I knew you'd see it, too."

What? She thinks this is evidence for the segregation that fostered the collapse of Askala? Kian's about to point that out, thinking she sounds like his father, when Dean steps past him.

"What's that?"

He's squinting at some rocks further down the beach. Kian peers closer, realizing there's something sprawled over the ash-colored boulders. A quick scan shows there's nothing else around.

"Do we really want to know?" asks Finn.

An ocean breeze tugs at Kian's clothes, as if it's trying to draw him toward whatever it is. "The more we can learn about the Outlands, the better. It's why we're here."

Shiloh slips in close to Kian as they make their way over. Every muscle on high alert, Kian positions himself slightly in front of her. Who knows what they're approaching.

The smell hits them first, the undeniable stench of decay making Kian's stomach recoil.

Followed by the realization they're looking at Thom's dead corpse.

Shiloh gasps as Finn retches. Dean walks over, staring down at the bloated, pale body. "Now that can't be a good thing..."

Kian is frozen, staring at Thom's glassy eyes and gaping mouth. He looks like he died screaming.

"Does this mean—" Shiloh stops herself before she finishes the question, her hand clamping over her mouth.

It doesn't matter. Kian's already thought it. Does this mean Nova and Felicia have met the same fate?

Every shred of Kian's body screams a denial. The wail that surges deep from within his soul robs him of breath, collapsing his chest, and he discovers he's lost the ability to find it again. A part of him doesn't want to. Nova can't be dead.

She just can't be.

It never occurred to him that he would be too late.

Kian spins around, frantically looking for other bodies. It's only when he doesn't see anything else that he allows his lungs to inhale the oxygen they're shrieking for.

Nova isn't dead. He would feel it. They're too closely connected, no matter how far apart they are.

Or what tries to come between them.

His heart still pumping hard, Kian turns back to the others. "This means they could be close."

Finn looks away, avoiding his gaze, while Shiloh's eyes fill with compassion. Kian doesn't bother to explain. He would know if Nova was dead. He refuses to believe anything else. Holding his breath, he walks around Thom, avoiding looking at him. "Give me a hand, Dean."

Dean curls his lip in disgust. "I'll catch something."

Kian glares at him. "He deserves to be sent to sea." He stares at Dean until he moves to stand beside Thom's feet. If he wants to be trusted, then he needs to work hard no matter the circumstance.

Trying not to breathe, Kian lifts Thom's upper body while Dean grabs his legs. Together, they heave Thom into the ocean. He lands with a splash in the rusty water, his body bobbing back up before rolling onto its stomach.

Kian turns away as it starts to sink. Thom died running away from the life Kian was raised to believe was right. His father would think it's what Thom deserved because he defected. That as his body slowly dissolves, it's returning to the cycle of life that Thom wasn't contributing to.

Kian, on the other hand, can't help but feel responsible.

When did they stop caring about anyone but the Bound? When did they decide anyone below their cut off is undeserving and nothing more than a burden?

Picking up the food bag Kian finds Dean's already carrying the water. "Let's keep moving. Maybe someone in the village can help us."

They trudge over the scorched, ashen soil in silence. Thom's dead body was a stark welcome to the Outlands. It's shown Kian they need to find Nova and Felicia, and fast.

The village materializes ahead and although Kian doesn't slow, he indicates for Shiloh to stay close to him. They don't know how Thom died. He could've drowned just trying to reach the Outlands, but he also could've—

"Thom was stabbed." Kian glances down as Shiloh's whispered words whoosh out.

"Stabbed? How do you know?"

"When you threw him into the sea. I saw the wound in his side. He was murdered, Kian."

Looking up, Kian sees Finn is glancing around like a polar grizzly's about to jump out any second. Dean's staring ahead at the approaching village, but the angle of his chin shows he's trying to hear what they're saying.

Kian leans closer to Shiloh. "Don't tell the other two." Finn will just freak out more, and who knows what Dean will do with the information. "Let's know for sure what we're up against."

Shiloh nods, her hands tucked tightly around herself. "This place is worse than we thought, Kian."

Straightening, Kian does another sweep of their surroundings. Maybe there's something else here, something below the surface they're not seeing.

Surely, it can't be as desolate and barbaric as they've been led to believe...

"Just stay close," Kian mutters. "We're stronger and safer if we stay together."

Finn must hear those last words, because he contracts into Kian's other side. Dean does the same, coming up the rear and Kian's not sure how he feels about the fact he can't see him easily.

The first hut comes into view, quickly multiplying to reveal a mottled bunch of them built of timber and trash. A small child sees them, freezes, but scuttles into the village before Kian can say anything.

"They know we're here," growls Dean from behind.

Kian raises a hand as if he can stop the hostility he can hear in Dean's voice. "Remember, we come in peace."

There's no answer, but Kian doesn't feel like he can turn around to see what Dean's response is. People are coming out of the huts. Dirty, barely dressed, and thin, they stare at the four strangers as they enter the village.

Several whisper, but Kian can't grasp much of what they're saying. "Their clothes...something to trade...just like the others."

Just like the others.

Kian's pulse picks up another notch. Nova must've come through here!

He stops in what looks like the center of the village, his heart demanding answers. People crowd around, staring, their faces cautious but curious.

"We come in peace."

"Good for you," one old man sneers. "Do you have anything to trade?"

Kian resists clenching his hand around the bag he's holding. He shakes his head. "We're looking for some friends of ours."

Several people turn away, their lips curling in disdain. A

woman wails in the background somewhere. The old man spits into the dusty ground before disappearing into one of the huts.

Kian takes a step forward, conscious the others come with him. "There were three of them. They would've been looking for shelter."

More people leave, either looking disgusted or disappointed. Kian frantically tries to catch someone's eye. All he needs are some answers. He isn't asking for any more than that.

But no one looks.

"Please, we just need to know if they passed through here." He pauses. "There may have been two. One of them is my—"

A man steps forward, a dark frown pulling down his brows. "If you don't have anything to trade, then get lost."

"We just want some information—"

The man shoves in closer. "Nobody can afford to give anything away for free out here." He glances down at the bag clutched in Kian's hand. "You want something, it comes at a price."

A hand grips Kian's arm from behind. "They want our food," Dean growls in his ear. "And they'll tell you anything to get it."

The man's eyes flare, his dirty face contracting in a scowl. "You don't look too peaceful to me," he grinds through gritted teeth.

More people leave, the space around them suddenly empty. No one wants the trouble they can see brewing.

Kian steps to the side, breaking their staring match. "If someone knows anything about our friends, then I'd be willing to negotiate."

"Well, now we're starting to talk the same language." The man leans back, crossing his arms. He glances behind Kian where Shiloh is tucked in, taking a long look. "Bringing a woman was a good start."

Tension feels like a hot current tangling his muscles. Another step to the side and Kian obstructs Shiloh from their line of sight. "First, we need to know that you have any information."

The man chuckles, a sound that grates down Kian's nerves. "I bet you're kicking yourself for letting that one with the pretty yellow hair get away. Much nicer than the one you've got left."

Shiloh tucks into Kian's back like she's trying to crawl in there.

Another man steps up next to the first. "Yep. Even with the missing finger."

Finn gasps, echoing the sound that Kian just swallowed. Nova. She was here.

The first man, taller than his friend, elbows him. "This one's just as clean, though."

"Where did they go?" Kian demands.

The first man inflates as he fills his chest. "Sounds like we're getting to the negotiating stage." His gaze flickers as he tries to glance around Kian.

Kian straightens, broadening his shoulders. "The girl is off bounds. We have pteropods. They should be more than enough."

"What the—" Dean jumps out and Kian grits his teeth. It would've been better if he'd stayed in the back and helped protect Shiloh. "You can't give them the pods!"

The smaller man frowns. "Whatever they are, we don't want them. It's the girl or—"

Kian jerks the bag up, scrabbling to pull out a jar. "They're our food source. What we eat to stay healthy." Kian indicates to Dean, Finn, and himself. "Where we come from, they're extremely valuable."

The men glance at each other, their suspicion obvious.

Finn nods rapidly. "They taste horrible, but they pack one heck of a nutritional punch."

Kian lifts a jar, three pods packed inside. He'd changed their water several times throughout the night as they made their way to the Outlands, meaning the little animals are still alive.

Their opaque wings slap against the clear walls containing them, their orange centers looking like tiny, throbbing suns.

The men quickly wipe the fascinated looks from their faces. The shorter one has already started shaking his head as the taller one opens his mouth.

Dean grabs the jar. "The fools don't even know what they are. You're not giving them our pods." He shoves it angrily back in the bag.

The men straighten, something in their eyes changing. It seems Dean not wanting them to have the pods just increased their value.

The taller man crosses his arms. "We'll do a trade. But if those things turn out to be nothin' but goop, you'll regret it."

Kian grabs the bag off Dean, frustrated that he has to yank it out of his clenched hands. "Deal."

He takes one of the jars out and passes it to the men. The taller one grabs it and shoves it up his shirt, tucking it beneath his arm.

"They came here, looking for food. They didn't have anything to trade so we took them in."

Dean snorts and the man glares at him. "We shared our broth."

The shorter man nods. "Even with the sick girl. The one with the curls."

Felicia was sick...

The men fall silent and Kian waits, wondering why they're not continuing. The first man holds out his hand. "My memory is getting hazy. Must be the lack of food."

Dean jumps forward, shoving his arm away. "No. You're not getting any more, you greedy bastards. Tell us the rest."

The man drops his arm as he steps back. "As far as I remember, that's all there is to tell."

Kian grits his teeth as he pulls out another jar. He thrusts it at them. "Here. There will be no more after that."

The smaller man snatches it and it quickly disappears like the first. He glares at Dean in triumph. "They'd just finished eating when a kid came through with the news."

"The news?" Finn asks.

The taller man snorts. "Fat lot of good it did us. Anyways, when we came back, the girls were gone. There was a sign of a fight and the guy was dead—stabbed in the side."

Just like Shiloh noticed.

"They knocked over our broth, the bastards," adds the second man, anger vibrating through him.

Kian frowns. "What do you mean, gone?"

The men glance at each other. "There are tribes who live out in the city. They come to the villages sometimes."

The other man spits on the ground. "Wild as polar grizzlies, they are, and meaner. We've lost a good few from our village to them."

Finn's eyes widen. "They take people?"

"Mostly women and children. Slavery or death is all they have to look forward to."

"If the city itself doesn't kill them," adds the shorter man. "That place is more dangerous than living out in the open."

Bile stings the back of Kian's throat. Everyone knows the cities became uninhabitable decades ago. "Are you saying..."

No. Not Nova. Not Flick.

The man shrugs. "We tried to take care of them, but they were taken."

Dean shoves his way to stand beside Kian. "They're lying."

Something about Dean's tone tells Kian he's sure. Plus, he grew up with Ronan so he should know how to spot a liar...

"We ain't lying," the taller man growls.

He strides around the back of a nearby hut and they follow. There, he pulls back a sheet of metal, exposing a hole in the wall. "The moment we turned our backs they were taken. Which means you won't be seeing them again."

123

Kian reels back, noticing the way Dean clenches his jaw as he looks away.

Because the man isn't lying. Conviction is shining from his dark eyes as he glares at them unflinchingly.

Kian staggers, gripping onto the rough timber of the hut to steady himself. Nova's been taken. Pain has his knees wanting to buckle. His lungs fill with the need to scream a denial.

Righting himself, he lurches at the taller man. "Where? Where is the city?"

The man sneers, his sour breath prickling Kian's nostrils. "That'll cost ya."

Dean leaps between the two of them. "No! No more pods!" He shoves Kian back, pushing up into his face. "We'll find the city on our own."

Breathing like he just ran to Askala and back, Kian jerks his shirt straight as he steps back. As much as he hates to admit it, Dean's right. He can't give away the last of their pods. It wouldn't be fair to the other three, no matter how much he would give away every shred he owns to find Nova.

Each man grips their jar. "Pleasure doing business with ya," taunts the taller man.

Kian turns away, disgust making him feel like he needs a wash. Maybe another village will be able to give them the information they need. Otherwise, they head inland to see if they can track the scum who took Nova and Felicia.

The others follow him, everyone silent as they make their way through the village. The wails of the woman they heard earlier steadily grow louder, the screams seeming to roll over the other in a steady rhythm. Kian grits his teeth.

"She's in labor," mutters Shiloh.

Finn swallows, his Adam's apple bobbing. "It doesn't sound like it's going too well."

Shiloh shakes her head. "It's been going on since we arrived.

I would've expected the baby to be born by now with contractions that close together."

Kian frowns. "You're saying she's in trouble?"

The next scream hits fever pitch, climbing higher and higher until it feels like it's trying to reach for the heavens.

Dean cringes, turning his face away. "Well, she isn't having fun, that's for sure."

Shiloh hesitates and Kian realizes what she's thinking. He grasps her shoulder. "Yes, you should go to her."

"Are you serious?" Dean demands. "These people just took half our food in exchange for two sentences."

They were here. Thom was killed and Nova and Felicia were taken. Make that three sentences. *We doubt you'll ever see them again.*

"We don't owe these thieves anything," snarls Dean.

Except that's not who they were bred and raised to be. Not to mention they need time to plan where they're going next. Another village in the hope they can find out where the city is, without losing more of their supplies? Or head blindly further into the Outlands, hoping to Terra they stumble across it before they run out of food and water?

Kian squeezes Shiloh's shoulder. "You should go to her. See what you can do."

Shiloh swallows as she nods. "We lowered the mortality rate for childbirth in Askala. We should at least try."

The hut with the screaming woman is easy to find. Hugging the edge of the village, stumps of hacked trees pepper the expanse behind it.

An old woman, hair almost as gray as her skin, is squatting out the front, her hands over her ears. "Not long now, not long now, not long now," she repeats in a monotone.

She looks up as they approach, her eyes wide and wounded. "It'll be over soon. It'll be a blessing."

Kian realizes she's not talking about the birth of the baby.

She was praying for it to end. For the mother or baby's death. Maybe both.

He indicates to Shiloh. "She can help."

The elderly woman shrinks back. "We don't have nothing to trade."

Kian shakes his head. "No payment. Shiloh has helped with births before."

"Liar," the woman hisses. "Of all the times you want to steal from us, you choose now?"

Hiding his shock at the woman's accusation, Kian indicates behind his back. As the old crone glares at him Shiloh ducks past them and into the hut. The woman spins around, her mouth open to shout.

Kian reaches out to assure her they only want to help but the woman flinches. He withdraws his hand as she curls back into her squat. "It doesn't matter anyway. There's nothing to take no more."

Kian retreats and Dean and Finn join him. There's another hut not far away, this one looking abandoned. Dean and Finn sit against the wall, tiredness evident in their stooped shoulders and splayed legs.

Kian knows how they feel. Exhaustion is dragging down on every one of his muscles, pleading with him to rest. But something else is pulling at him.

The desire to find Nova. To beg forgiveness. To do whatever he can to make all this right.

Dean rests his head back against the rough wall, his eyes closed. "You know the longer we stay, the more chance there is they'll rob us."

Kian ignores him. He refuses to be someone who would walk past a person in need when they could be helped, no matter where we are.

Dean snorts, the sound barely discernible above the screams

coming from the hut. "Not that it matters too much. You gave away half our food within an hour of arriving here."

"You know where the raft is," Kian states flatly. "No one is forcing you to stay."

Dean doesn't respond, making a show of drawing in a deep breath and turning his head away.

"What's next?" asks Finn wearily.

"We find the city. We find Nova and Felicia. We take back what we've learned."

"Is everything that simple in that righteous brain of yours?" growls Dean. He bangs his head back against the wall. "All we've learned so far is you're a crap negotiator."

Kian doesn't point out exactly how much they have learned as another scream pierces the air, this one the longest so far. They've learned the Remnants are starving. They're desperate. And Ronan would've leveraged that to gain power.

And they've learned where Nova and Felicia are.

Kian sighs as he rubs his temples, trying not to regret that he'd agreed to bring Dean. "So, do we walk to the next village, or do we try and find this city?"

Dean's eyes open as he regards Kian incredulously. "You're asking us, esteemed leader?"

"I never said I had all the answers, Dean."

Dean opens his mouth with a retort Kian doubts he wants to hear when a cry fills the air.

The cry of a baby.

They shoot to their feet as the old woman staggers out of the hut, cradling a bundle wrapped in rags. "It's a son," she croaks.

Shiloh steps out behind her, smiling wearily. "The baby was breech. But he and the mother should be fine."

Kian's breath whooshes out. At least something good came from all this. He smiles at Shiloh. "Well done." She probably saved both their lives.

The old woman clutches the baby to her chest. "You can't take him, please. We'll pay you any other way we can."

Kian doesn't glance at the poverty surrounding the dirty woman. They have no way to pay...apart from with a newborn baby. "I told you we don't want anything."

Shiloh comes to stand beside him. "You should go help your daughter. Let her hold her son."

The woman doesn't move, as if she's frightened they'll attack her the moment she does.

Kian wraps an arm around Shiloh. The only way the woman will feel safe is if they're gone. It hurts to know the woman couldn't trust them even after this. "Let's find another village. Maybe they can tell us where the city is."

Even as he says the words, Kian knows how naïve it sounds and he glares at Dean before he can point it out. He'd assumed that the people of the Outlands would have some capacity to help.

To care.

But they're unable to care for themselves, let alone anyone else.

Which leaves Kian and the others fighting for survival just like they are.

Figuring they need to continue following the coastline, Kian shoulders the bag with the last of their food. "We'll walk till nightfall then get some sleep," he tells the others.

Finn groans aloud. "The walking sounds like hell, but I like the sound of the sleep part."

Dean strides up beside him, his gaze on the horizon. "Staying here will be a worse hell."

They fall into step and Kian knows this is going to be a long, silent walk. Hopelessness tugs at his consciousness, and he realizes he's going to have to battle it every step of the way.

When he's exhausted already.

"Boy!" Kian turns around to find the old woman eyeing them

warily from the doorway of the hut, the baby nowhere to be seen. "The city of Fairbanks. It's due west. You can't miss that rotting graveyard."

Kian's brows shoot up. "Thank you."

She turns away, shaking her head. "You're a fool if you're thanking me. You saved my daughter's life and that of my grandchild, only to wish death upon yourself."

Hope and fear war for dominance inside Kian as he changes direction, the others doing the same.

He glances at Shiloh, Finn, then Dean, to find their faces streaked with ash and worry. Fear won their battle and he can't blame them.

Hope can survive as well as everything else in this barren wasteland.

Straightening, the sun becoming his compass, Kian strides out. Mother Nature remained resilient. She was able to recover. Askala proved that.

Now he has to do the same.

I'm coming, Nova.

Please don't let it be too late.

DEX

*W*alking Kian down to the beach had been difficult. But returning to the Oasis and finding Wren on the stage next to Ronan is worse.

Far worse.

It's obvious by the faces that fill this room that something terrible is going on. There's a hopelessness pervading the air. It's so intense that Dex can actually smell it. These people are broken. He needs to stay strong. He can't let Ronan destroy his spirit, too.

Wren is mouthing a word at him, but it's hard to make out what it is. Lip-reading has never been Dex's specialty. Is it *run?* Perhaps. That would make sense. But whatever she's saying, he's not going anywhere.

Dex's father had found him walking back to the lab and warned him not to go to the Oasis. But when he'd heard exactly why he was being asked to keep away, he knew he couldn't. Kian left him in charge. He can't just hide under a blanket while Askala is being put through something like this. It wouldn't be right.

So, he'd watched as his father had gathered as many people

as he was able and took them to the lab to hide them there. Dex promised to join them when he's able.

But now he's wondering if it's more a case of *if* rather than *when*.

Dorian's demise was proof of exactly what Ronan's capable of. And with Magnus in the brig and Kian having been left for dead, there's no reason for Dex to think he'll be spared.

Which makes him wonder how Wren can continue to stand by this monster. Dex could never support someone guilty of such heinous crimes, no matter the motive behind them.

Dex makes his way through the ballroom and steps up onto the stage, ready to face Ronan. Well, as ready as he can ever be.

"Let's begin." A bead of sweat runs from Ronan's forehead down the side of his face. The light of the chandelier above him is bouncing off his cropped hair, making it look even more orange than the last time Dex had seen him.

"First, let these people go," says Dex, aware of the sea of wide eyes and shaking limbs around him.

Ronan laughs. "Oh, sorry. I wasn't asking a question just now. I was telling you. It's time to begin."

Dex isn't sure what to say to this. Then the realization dawns on him that it doesn't matter what he says. Ronan has his own agenda. He's already decided the outcome of whatever's about to happen here.

"Let these people go, Ronan," Dex repeats, aware of the goons standing close behind him.

"Or what?" jeers Ronan. "You'll hit me with your stump? And I don't know how many times I have to tell you...my name's Cy."

"A new name doesn't make you a new person," says Dex. There's no way he's ever calling this creep anything except the name he was born with.

Ronan sneers at him and another bead of sweat runs down

his cheek, landing on his bare chest and trailing across the tattoo of Dex's mother's name.

Dex understands why she chose his father over Ronan. For all his father's faults, he'd never treat anyone like this. When she'd told Dex that he should trust the man who raised him, she'd had good reason.

"I'm glad you're not my father." Dex pulls back his shoulders, subtly checking Wren's pendant is tucked beneath his shirt. "Even if you hadn't been banished, there's no way my mother would've had a baby with an evil scumbag like y—"

A sharp blow lands on his right shoulder. The pain is blinding, flashing behind his eyes and sending him falling to the floor.

"No!" Wren screams, crouching beside him.

"Careful, little bird," says Ronan. Then he whispers something else that Dex can't hear and Wren's dragged away to the other side of the stage.

Clutching at his shoulder, Dex rises to his feet and stares Ronan in his watery blue irises.

"Test number one," says Ronan, shooting an empty smile to the crowd. "Who is the Commander of Askala?"

"Commander?" Dex asks, his body still throbbing with the pain that's radiating from his shoulder. Askala has never had anyone call themselves a Commander.

"You heard me right." Ronan crosses his arms, blocking Dex's view of his mother's name.

"Who is the Commander of Askala?"

"I am," says Dex, plainly. "Kian left me in charge in his absence."

"Kian's dead."

Two simple words that provoke a collective gasp in the crowd, almost as if Ronan had slapped each and every person here.

Dex is about to take great pleasure in reassuring his people and correcting Ronan but he bites down on his tongue to stop himself. It's better if Ronan thinks Kian's dead. It means he won't send out a raven to make sure the job he failed at is finished off in the Outlands.

"That's right," says Dex. "Kian's dead. But before he died, he left me in charge."

Ronan turns to Wren, who's squirming beside a goon on the other side of the stage. "You didn't tell me this guy's so funny."

"I'm not joking." Dex juts out his chin. "You're not in charge here. A true leader doesn't hold his people hostage. He earns their respect and they follow him by choice."

He really should have expected the second blow that lands on his left shoulder. But he hadn't. And the intensity of it not only sends him to the floor once more, but this time an involuntary scream escapes his lips.

Clutching his shoulder, he pulls up his legs, wincing as he waits for the next blow that's certain to come.

But it doesn't.

This time, Ronan crouches beside him instead of Wren.

"I'm not going to kill you," he hisses in a hushed tone. "But only out of respect for your mother. Declare your allegiance to me in front of these people and I'll let you go."

Dex sits up and glares at him, weighing up his choices. He can say the words Ronan wants to hear and go free. After all, they're just words. They don't have to mean anything.

Or he can speak his truth.

He looks at the defeated people standing behind Ronan on the stage, the light of the ancient chandeliers sending their shame and hopelessness bouncing around the room. Then he looks at the huddle of brave souls in the back of the ballroom. Those who found enough courage to stand up for what they believe in, no matter how much the consequences might knock them off their feet. He blinks as he sees Amity amongst them, one of her eyes black and swollen.

There's no question in Dex's mind which group he'd rather stand with.

"I am the leader of Askala." Dex pulls himself to his feet and projects his voice for all to hear. "And these here are my people, no matter what words you've forced from their lips."

Ronan rises and glares at him. This guy is twice his size and it's obvious by the look in his eyes that he wants to kill him. Right now, the only thing keeping Dex alive is his mother who's somehow managing to protect him even so many years after her death.

"You're nothing like your mother." Ronan's fury is burning so bright it's surprising it doesn't set his flamethrower alight. "Mercy was smart enough to know who to follow."

"She followed you." Dex nods. "But she loved my father."

Ronan grabs Dex by the arm and flings him from the stage, so fast and hard that Dex doesn't have time to do anything to prevent it.

He sails through the air, a memory of Fern doing the same thing when she slipped from the cliff coming back to him with force.

But thankfully, he doesn't have quite the distance to fall as she did.

He lands with a hideous thud, every cell in his body on fire and screaming in shock as the air is sucked out of his lungs. The momentum of his fall sends him skidding across the well-worn floor of the ballroom until he comes to a stop a couple of yards from the group of people in the back corner.

Ronan's aim was annoyingly accurate.

Lying completely still, he assesses his injuries, deciding he'll need to add a few cracked ribs to his list of complaints. The pain is throbbing, making the bruising to his shoulders feel like nothing more than a couple of mosquito bites. But he's alive.

Amity scuttles up beside him and drags him back to the

group, although the smooth floor now feels like a prickly cactus as it claws at the pain in his sides.

"You're amazing," Amity whispers as she smooths back his hair from his forehead. Her black eye looks even worse at this close proximity. How dare Ronan do this to her! She's one of the kindest people Dex has ever met. This isn't right.

"I'm fine," she reassures him, noticing the way his gaze is fixed on her eye. "Your mother would be so proud of what you just did. And your father."

It's then that Dex takes a closer look at the faces around him and realizes that many of them are familiar from his father's meeting of the league. The very people who were meant to align themselves with Ronan are the ones who've turned against him.

"You guys are the amazing ones," breathes Dex, wincing as even these words are a struggle to get out.

But he means it. These are the true heroes in the room. The ones willing to stand up for what they believe in. The ones who are demanding change no matter what it might mean to them as an individual.

"Now I believe that's everyone sorted." Ronan's voice echoes across the ballroom. "Congratulations to our new Bound and Unbound!"

There's the muted sound of clapping, and with Amity's help, Dex manages to pull himself into a seated position to see people with nervous smiles applauding their self-appointed leader.

"I can't give all of you a ring," says Ronan. "But I can give you food and as many pods as you desire. You're now free to roam the Oasis and Askala as you please."

"And what happens to us?" calls out Vern.

Bea slaps a hand to Vern's arm to silence him, but it's too late. The question has been asked.

Dex feels the bodies around him tense as they wait for Ronan's answer.

"Are you worried?" asks Ronan with false sweetness.

"Because you shouldn't worry. I won't do anything to you that wasn't done to me when Magnus decided I wasn't worthy of living here."

Amity lets out a quiet gasp at the mention of Magnus's name.

"Mag—"

This time it's Dex who grips Amity on the arm and she falls silent.

"Don't draw attention to yourself," he whispers. Her eye is swelling even more now. The last thing she needs is a matching one.

Ronan jumps down from the stage, not even bothering with the stairs. He strides across the room and Dex does his best to move forward to shield the others, noticing that Bea and Vern do the same.

"Refresh my memory, Amity," says Ronan. "What did your beloved Magnus do to me?"

Amity shakes her head, refusing to answer.

"Come now. I remember you were there with that pretty braid hanging down your back, standing right by Magnus's side. What did he do to me?"

"He banished you." Amity's voice is low. She's more than aware this is a trap.

"Correct!" Ronan sweeps his hand out toward the crowd. "He banished me. Sent me out across a bridge, then burned it down to make sure I could never come back. He separated me from my family, from the woman I loved."

He bangs at the tattoo on his chest and Dex flinches, tempted to point out that Ronan hadn't seemed especially fussed to find his family again when he'd returned.

"You're going to send us to the Outlands," says Bea, seeming almost resigned to the fact.

But Dex isn't resigned. Every cell in his body is fighting against that. If he'd wanted to go to the Outlands, he could have gone with Kian. His place is here. It's his job to make things right in Askala again so that Kian can bring Nova home and they can safely raise their baby. Perhaps he'd have been better off to have said the words he hadn't wanted to say.

Ronan laughs at Bea, his jaw opening so wide that Dex can see he has several teeth missing from the back of his mouth. "I'm not sending you there. The Outlands are far too good for the likes of you."

Dex's shoulders relax at this news until he realizes it's anything but positive. Where could possibly be worse than the Outlands?

"I'm banishing you to the forest," says Ronan, smiling. "I've only spotted one polar grizzly since I arrived here and I've never seen anything so sorry and skinny in my life. Wasn't even worth the kill. Nothing like a good human or two to fatten them up."

"You're using us as polar grizzly food?" asks Vern. "But that's brutal!"

"And sending me across a burning bridge wasn't?" Ronan is sneering now, the memory of his banishment wiping the smile from his face.

But Dex isn't as horrified by this news. The forest is better than the Outlands. It's familiar. And at least it's only predators of the non-human variety they'll have to worry about. And with any luck, they won't have to go to the forest at all...

"What about my child?" asks a woman, forcing herself to her feet. "My son is in my cabin. I can't leave him."

"You can take your filthy offspring with you. One less mouth for us to feed. And one more meal for the grizzly." He laughs and Dex shakes his head. What kind of deranged person laughs at the idea of a bear eating a child?

"I won't leave Magnus." Amity also rises to her feet. "Let him out of the brig. I'm not going without him."

"Oh, sweetheart." Ronan reaches out a hand and drags his

thumb down Amity's cheek. She blinks back at him with one eye, the other swollen completely shut now. "I never said anything about you leaving. You're staying right here with those pods you love so much. We need someone to keep their population up and I've seen how much you care. Were those real tears you cried when we had our little snack on our arrival? They were, weren't they?"

"Of course, they were real tears!" Amity steps back, leaving Ronan's hand hanging in mid-air. "Those pods are the lifeblood of Askala. Survival without them is almost impossible. As we already discovered thanks to you."

Ronan swings back his hand and brings it down fast. Dex doesn't have time to think before he acts. He jumps in front of his aunt and takes the force of Ronan's blow across his cheek. His head snaps to the side, jerking more pain from his broken ribs.

Clenching his teeth and squeezing his eyes shut, he tries to brush off the agony that's slicing through him. Bringing his hand to his face, he feels the warm stickiness of blood spilling from a gash just under his eye. He's grateful he could do this one thing for the woman who helped raise him. If she'd taken another blow like this to her already injured face, she may not have been able to recover.

"You're just as stupid as your father, aren't you?" says Ronan. Then seeming to realize something, he looks around the room. "I thought someone was missing! Callix has run off. Always the coward, that man. But he'll keep..."

There's movement on the stage and Phoenix steps down and walks across the ballroom.

"We've got things to do, Cy," he says. "Why don't you send this lot off so we can get started? You've wasted enough time on them already."

"Good point, son." Cy slaps Phoenix on the back. "Always the thinker, you are."

Dex rubs at his cheek wondering what Phoenix is up to. Because if Wren is difficult to trust, then Phoenix is impossible.

"I'll take them out," says Phoenix. "I'll make sure they go nice and far, so they don't come back."

Ronan narrows his eyes at Phoenix and studies him, also clearly suspicious of his motives.

"I need to get my son first!" cries the woman who'd spoken up earlier.

"Go on then," says Phoenix, glancing at his father as he injects more venom into his voice. "Get the little turd and be back here in one minute or you're both history. Understand? Same with anyone else. And don't try anything stupid or you'll live to regret it."

Three people rise and take a step toward the door, but before they get there, Phoenix scoops Amity from the ground and holds her to his chest, producing a large knife from the back of his pants that he holds to her throat.

It's Dex's knife from the Proving! He never should have let Phoenix hold onto it. He was supposed to protect them with it. Not use it as a threat.

"One minute!" shouts Phoenix. "If you're not back in one minute, this bitch dies!"

There's a gasp from somewhere on the stage, but Dex doesn't have time to figure out if it was Wren. Or someone who actually has a heart.

A different kind of smile creeps over Ronan's face now. One filled with pride. A direct contrast to the anger Dex is feeling. If that blade pierces even the tiniest bit of Amity's skin then he's going to kill that guy. Even if it means he has to die himself.

The three people scurry out of the room, jostling to get through the doors to their cabins to fetch their children.

Phoenix stands with Amity's back pressed to his chest. She's clearly terrified, but holding still, waiting for this nightmare to be over.

139

Ronan circles them like some kind of leatherskin herding his prey.

"I reckon I'd eat you first," he says, poking one of the larger men in the back with his foot. "You won't last long out there."

The man looks to the ground, refusing to meet Ronan's eye, just as he'd refused to declare his allegiance to this bully.

"I reckon that's been a minute, Phee," Ronan says, returning to stand beside his son. "Although it does leave us with the problem of who's going to look after those pods."

"Not rocket science," says Phoenix, licking his lips and tightening his grip on Amity. She swallows, only to stop when the motion presses her skin closer against the knife. "I reckon we could figure it out."

"Few more seconds," says Ronan, nodding.

Dex tenses, resisting the urge to leap up and tear the knife away from her throat. He holds steady onto the hope that if Phoenix wanted to kill her, he could have done it by now.

Another noise comes from the stage. Like there's a struggle going on. But there are too many people up there for Dex to be able to tell who it might be.

Then there's a clatter at the door, and the three people reappear with five children between them clutching at their legs.

Their eyes go straight to Amity, relief visibly sliding over them when they see they've made it back in time.

Phoenix pulls the knife away in one quick movement and she collapses, holding her neck with both hands.

For one horrifying moment, Dex fears Phoenix has done the unforgivable.

But her throat is clean.

"Go and breed me some pods," says Ronan, forcing Amity from the floor and shoving her in the direction of the door. "I'm hungry."

Amity looks back at Dex, clearly torn.

"Go," says Dex. "Your children need you. I'm fine."

And he is fine. With thanks to so many people, including Amity who raised him like one of her own. But there's no time to tell her that now.

Amity reaches for Dex's hand and squeezes it briefly. Her skin is warm and soft and the familiarity of it threatens to send tears to the corners of Dex's eyes. This could likely be the last time he'll ever see her.

Amity heads for the door, not looking back once she's made the decision to leave. It was the right choice. Her place is here on the Oasis. With her pods. And her children. And the only man she's ever loved. If he ever manages to get himself out of the brig.

"Come on, then." Phoenix strides to the door and motions for the rest of them to follow. "We're going on a little hike. But don't worry. You'll only need to walk one way."

Dex heads to the door first, even though his feet don't want to move. Each step is agony. His face, his ribs, his shoulders. It's the worst physical pain he's ever felt. But it's nothing compared to the ache that's wrapped its way around his heart. Everything and everyone he's ever loved are falling apart. How can they come back from this?

Ronan chews on his bottom lip as he watches them, the only sign that he's questioning if this is a good idea.

"Don't you trust me, Dad?" asks Phoenix, noticing the same thing and winking at Ronan.

"Course I do," says Ronan. "How many of my men do you want to take with you?"

"Two should be enough for this bunch of weaklings." Phoenix pushes the closest person to him, laughing when she stumbles.

This seems enough to satisfy Ronan who turns back to his new followers and spreads his arms out wide as if he's about to impart some kind of wisdom that he couldn't possibly possess.

Dex doesn't stick around to find out what it is. He's out the door and heading down the corridor. He'd much rather be in the forest with the people who'd proven themselves to be the bravest that Askala has to offer than be stuck on that ship breathing the same stale air as Ronan.

Phoenix steps onto the gangplank first, with Dex right behind him. Ronan's men herd the rest of them down and take up the rear.

"Phoenix," hisses Dex. "We need your help."

"Quiet." Phoenix spins around briefly to glare at Dex.

"This isn't you," Dex persists. "I know this is an act. You were never going to kill Amity. You wanted to take us out here so you could help us."

But Phoenix doesn't answer. He steps onto solid ground at the bottom of the gangplank, then spins around and punches Dex hard in the stomach. Intense pain sears through him as the force of the impact takes not just the wind from his lungs but any hope he had that Phoenix might be on their side.

"I thought you were different to your father," says Dex, struggling to regain his breath as the rest of the group file off the gangplank. He's not sure how many more injuries he can take. His lean frame wasn't built to withstand this kind of brutality.

"This way," says Phoenix, leading them toward the lab.

Dex winces as he clutches at his ribs, battling to catch up to Phoenix.

"Lead us past the back of the lab," says Dex, hoping to convince him to take pity on them. "If the gate to the courtyard is unlocked, I can get most of these people inside before your men realize what's happening. It's our only chance."

Phoenix walks on in silence.

"Please," says Dex. "For Wren. You know she cares about me."

"Does she?" Phoenix asks, the impact of his words hurting even more than the punch he just gave him.

"She does." Dex is nowhere near certain of the truth behind these words. Sure, she'd gone to him when he'd first hit the floor, but she hadn't exactly tried very hard to stand by him after that. She could have gotten away from that goon who'd held her if she'd really wanted to. She'd fought and won against a leatherskin for crying out loud!

To Dex's disappointment, Phoenix doesn't take the path that leads around to the back of the lab. Instead, he leads them right up to the front door and knocks loudly.

What the hell?

The two goons shuffle nervously at the back of the group. "The Commander said to go to the forest."

"Just making a little stop first," says Phoenix. "To pick up another passenger."

The goons jostle each other and laugh at the prospect of more people to bully.

"Don't open the door," shouts Dex. "Dad! Don't open the door!"

Phoenix grabs him roughly by the arm, sending fresh pain shooting through his body. "Do I need to cut off the rest of your arm to use your chip, or are you going to open it for me?"

Dex shakes his head, refusing to cooperate. His father is sheltering countless people in there. It's not just him he's protecting.

"Can you take care of this for me?" Phoenix asks the two goons, rolling his eyes as he pushes Dex toward them.

The men step forward, grabbing Dex roughly by the arms, sending agony sliding through his core. The one on his left forces his stump to the sensor and the door slides open.

"Run!" Dex shouts. "Get out of there!"

But the sight he's greeted by is not what he was expecting. There's a crowd of people in the doorway who rush at them the first chance they get.

There's so much color and movement that it takes Dex a

moment to realize what's happening. Two men leap forward with long knives in their hands.

They slash at the goons holding Dex, and he closes his eyes, unable to witness the amateur job these peace-loving people are doing with this gruesome task. But whatever they do, it's enough. The guards fall to the ground, releasing their grip on Dex as the blood gurgles in their throats.

Dex winces as he's pulled forward into the lab. His companions follow behind him, trampling the bodies of the men in their desperation to get inside.

"Where's Phoenix?" Dex shouts. "You have to get him."

Dex's father appears from the doorway. "He's gone."

"Why the hell did you let him get away?" Dex cries. "He was our best bargaining chip."

"He still is," his father says.

"What do you mean?"

His father puts a hand on each of his bruised shoulders.

"Phoenix is on our side," he says. "I asked him to bring you to me."

"He wasn't bringing us to you," Dex argues. "He was coming here to get you so he could dump us all in the forest."

Shaking his head, his father wraps an arm around Dex.

"Phoenix is one of the good guys."

"Are you sure about that?" Dex asks.

"They're coming!" someone shouts.

"Activate the lockdown!" Dex's father is running away from him now. He heads for the wall beside the door and pulls out a secret panel to reveal a series of buttons.

"What the Terra?" Dex's eyes spring wide open. First a hidden room and now this. Just how many other secrets does this lab hide?

His father types furiously on a keyboard and there's a clunking noise at the door.

Aarov comes running down the hallway toward them. "The courtyard is secure."

"Get comfortable, everyone," his father says in a loud voice. "Because we're going to be here a while. You're safe now."

Safe?

Dex leans against the wall behind him and slides painfully and slowly to the floor, unsure which part of his body hurts the most. They're not safe here. Not even close.

But at least just for one sweet moment, he can breathe.

There's an explosion at the front door that shakes the lab and the hallway fills with terrified screams.

Dex realizes his sweet moment is over.

This is war.

WREN

*P*hoenix bursts back into the ballroom far too soon. Walking the people deep into the forest should have taken longer than that. His face and chest are covered in black soot and his eyebrows are distinctly missing. He has two flamethrowers, one in each hand. What the hell happened out there?

The last of Cy's Bound have left the room, ready to start their new lives in the Oasis. Some joyful. Some tearful. Most apprehensive.

Wren steps down from the stage, no longer being held back by her father's soldier with his vice-like grip on her wrists that had prevented her from running after Dex.

But Phoenix's eyes are fixed firmly on their father.

"We were ambushed," he says, panting heavily.

"Is that what that noise was?" Wren asks. "We thought it was a clap of thunder."

Phoenix shakes his head.

"But I sent two more men to go with you!" Cy shakes his head, steam practically pouring from his ears as he leaves the stage to stand beside Wren. "Five of you should have been more than enough to control that bunch of losers."

Phoenix closes the gap between them, setting the flamethrowers down at his feet and wringing his hands. "They're all dead. All four of them. There was an explosion. It's a miracle I got out of there alive."

"Dead?" Cy roars. "That's not possible!"

Wren's heart almost stops at the thought of anything happening to Dex.

"Who's dead?" she asks. "The guards or the people you were transporting?"

"The guards." Phoenix shoots her a desperate look as he rakes his hands over his cropped hair, some of it falling away in his fingertips. "I made a terrible mistake."

"Get in here and tell me exactly what happened." Cy grabs Phoenix roughly by the arm and drags him to the small room where the High Bound used to meet.

Not willing to let them get away from her, Wren follows. She has to know what happened.

"We don't need you in here, Wren," says Cy, manhandling Phoenix into the room.

"Too bad," she says, right behind them. "Because I'm here. With no plans to be anywhere else."

She slumps into a chair and crosses her arms.

Cy rolls his eyes but makes no move to eject her from the room.

Phoenix goes to sit down, too, but Cy kicks the chair out from underneath him and he crashes to the floor.

"Was that necessary?" Phoenix grumbles, picking himself up.

"Actually, it *was* necessary." Cy kicks at Phoenix's shins now, sending him to the floor again.

Phoenix doesn't try to get up this time.

Cy is purple in the face now, red veins appearing in his eyes as he shakes with anger. "If you weren't my son, I'd have killed you already. Now, stop lying about on the floor. Get up and tell me what the hell happened out there!"

Wren remains quiet, aware that one wrong word could have her thrown out. Cy's always treated them like this. She just wishes Phoenix would give up wishing that's ever going to change. Impossible dreams are dangerous for the heart.

"I made a mistake." Phoenix hauls himself to his feet and slumps into a chair across the table from Wren.

"Four of my men are dead." Cy sits on the table in front of Phoenix, sliding his powerful thighs back and ignoring the groan of the old timber under his weight. "I'd say that's more than a mistake."

"We were on our way to the forest," says Phoenix. "I decided to make a stop to check the lab for Callix. I didn't think it was right to let him hide out there like that. He needed to be banished, too."

"I was going to handle him." Cy wipes his hands on the table, leaving black streaks of soot he'd collected from Phoenix. "There was no need for you to get involved."

"I know." Phoenix bites down on his bottom lip as he looks up at Cy looming over him. "But I wanted to make you proud."

Wren hasn't been sure that anything Phoenix has said up until this point has been true, but she doesn't doubt this last statement for a moment. He's always wanted to make Cy proud. It's one of the reasons he calls him Dad, despite his request for them to call him Cy. It's like Phoenix wants to remind him every chance he gets that he's Cy's son.

Cy waves his hand at Phoenix, urging him to continue.

"We went to the lab but as soon as we got the door opened, we were ambushed. They had knives. Big ones. Like machetes. I never should have gone there."

"Knives?" Cy launches himself off the table and paces the room. "I've never seen any of those around here."

"We used them in our Proving," says Wren, forgetting that she was supposed to remain silent. "They're huge."

Cy's brows shoot up. "Sounds like the Proving has changed a bit since I did it. Pity. I'd have been awesome at a test with knives."

Wren's been trying to tell Cy about her Proving ever since he arrived, but he hasn't been interested. Perhaps now he'll want to listen.

"They attacked Karlos and T-Bone," says Phoenix. Wren's not surprised he knows their names. To her they're all the same. She couldn't pick any of them from a line if her life depended on it.

"But they were trained fighters," says Cy. "Those losers shouldn't have been any match for them."

"Trained fighters who were taken by surprise." Phoenix shakes his head. "There was very little they could do to stop it. They dropped to the ground and the people—your Unbound—rushed through the door inside."

Wren breathes a sigh to know that Dex made it safely into the lab. Surely, from there he'll be able to figure out his next best step.

"And why didn't they kill you?" asks Cy. "With these knives you say they have."

"I was at the back of the group, making sure nobody ran away." Phoenix leans forward on the table, his pupils wide. "I saw Taco and Thrash come running over as back up, so I went to them, but by the time we got back, the lab had gone into some kind of lockdown. These shutter things rolled down over the doors, sealing everyone inside. Thrash and Taco got their flamethrowers onto them and for a moment we thought it was going to work. But then the fuel barrels exploded. I've never seen that happen before. I was thrown back by the force. I'm afraid they didn't make it either."

Cy goes to Phoenix and leans down over him until they're

face to face. The resemblance between them is strong from this angle, except Cy is a larger, meaner version of his son.

"We. Do. Not. Have. Men. To. Spare," hisses Cy. "I came here with twenty men, which means now we're down to sixteen. Do you know what that means?"

Phoenix shakes his head.

"It means we've lost strength," says Cy, his teeth bared as he looms over his son. "Each man we lose puts us in danger."

"You're blaming the wrong person." Wren leaps from her chair and attempts to separate them. She's seen Cy this angry before and the result hasn't been pretty.

"Keep out of this, Wren," snarls Cy, turning his face to look at her.

"He was trying to do the right thing," she says. "It's not his fault it was an ambush. Or that Burger and Bob were stupid enough to fry themselves."

Cy's full body turns to her now, veins throbbing in his temples.

She bites down on her tongue, realizing her joke has fallen flat. It seems Dex is far better at deflecting anger with humor than she is.

"It's Thrash and Taco," says Cy stepping away from Phoenix to direct the full force of his anger at her. "Have some respect and use their names."

"No offense," says Wren, pleased to have been able to deflect Cy away from Phoenix before he beat him to a pulp. "But I doubt those are the names their parents gave them."

Cy shakes his head in disgust. "You know, I honestly thought that after your bitch of a mother died that I could raise you two to be just like me. But I see that her genes were stronger than I realized. You're both just as pathetic as she was. Get out of my sight."

Wren takes a step to the door, but it's clearly not fast enough for Cy's liking.

"Get out of my sight!" Cy repeats, the sudden volume of his voice causing Wren to jump. "Before I remove you permanently!"

Cy picks up a chair and throws it against the wall, the timber splintering and scattering across the floor. He reaches for another one and Phoenix stands, grabbing Wren by the hand and leading her out of the room.

They run through the ballroom to the sound of Cy trashing the room. To think that furniture had withstood so many generations, only to be destroyed by one man in a fit of rage.

"Where are we going?" Wren asks as they head down the hallway. Surely, he's not thinking of taking her to the lab?

"I just need to get out of this stale air for a moment," says Phoenix. "There are a few things I need to tell you. In private."

"Slow down." Wren drags Phoenix to a halt, still clutching at his hand. "There's no need to run. Cy isn't coming after us."

"Why do you call him that?" asks Phoenix. "He's our dad."

"A name is just a name." She throws him a grin. "Just ask Burger or Bob."

"I can't believe you actually said that." Phoenix suppresses a smile.

"Couldn't help myself." She grins.

Phoenix shakes his head, refusing to laugh.

One of Cy's guards is near the door leaning against the wall. For a moment Wren thinks he's injured, until she notices an Unbound—no, newly Bound—woman tucked between the guard and the wall.

Wren's about to tell him to get his filthy hands off her until the salacious smile on the woman's face makes it obvious she isn't there against her will.

"You okay?" Phoenix asks her, not seeming as convinced as Wren that this isn't a damsel in distress.

"Never better," the woman says, slurring her words. "Got meself everythin' I ever wanted. A belly full o' pods, access to any part of this stinking ship, and now a big, bad man to keep me warm at night."

The guard laughs as he thrusts himself at the woman. "Long live the Commander!"

The woman giggles. "Long live the Commander, all right! And long live you."

Wren and Phoenix glance at each other with rolling eyes and head for the gangplank. Phoenix is right. It's time to get out of this stale air for a bit so they can think properly.

"The garden?" asks Phoenix.

Wren nods. Maybe they'll be able to find something to eat while they talk. With all the fuss of Cy's Proving, she can't remember the last time she filled her stomach. It's like being in the Outlands.

But when they near the bottom of the gangplank, it becomes obvious the garden is no more. The carefully curated vegetable beds have been trampled. The citrus trees have been stripped bare—of both leaves and fruit. The herb garden looks more like a mud pit, and the rows of corn and sugarcane are lying flat and broken.

Wren walks with wide eyes, feeling as damaged as the plants around her as she tries to take in the scale of the destruction. This isn't something that can be salvaged like she's seen after a storm. This is catastrophic. How could anyone be so short-sighted as to do something like this?

"Fools," says Phoenix, coming up beside her. "What do they think they're going to eat the next time they're hungry?"

"The non-existent pods, I guess." Wren scowls at a man who's fallen asleep with some kind of purple stains around his mouth.

"We were wrong to come here," says Phoenix, steering her away from the man.

"What the hell's going on with you?" Wren kicks at a pile of leaves. "I didn't buy that story you told Cy. Not one word of it."

"Then you don't know me very well." He lifts his chin and stares her down. "Because almost all of it was true."

"Start with the bits that weren't true, then." She sighs, fast losing her patience. "It'll save time."

"Remember when I left the ballroom during the Proving earlier on?" he asks.

"How could I forget?" She shakes her head. "Where did you go? You were gone for ages! I was sure Cy was going to notice."

"I went to talk to Callix in the lab," he says. "I wanted to know if our alliance still stood."

"Why would you do that?" She reels back. Of all the places she'd imagined he might have gone, the lab wasn't one of them.

"You saw what was going on in there! Someone had to do something."

She's impressed. That was a dangerous move. "And what did Callix say?"

"Yes, of course. What other choice does he have?"

"I knew you had a heart in there somewhere." She taps him on the chest. "I'm proud of you, Phee."

"It's that bloody boyfriend of yours that you should be proud of." He moves away, embarrassed by her flattery.

"You've changed your mind about him, have you?" She smiles gently.

Phoenix lets out a long sigh. "He's so annoyingly likeable! Honestly, Wren. I've tried so hard to hate that guy, but the way he stood up to Dad in the ballroom was impressive. Never have I been able to do that myself. Not in my whole life. I could see he was prepared to die for his cause. He was more concerned about Kian's mom than he was about himself."

Wren nods, acknowledging that every word of that was true. Apart from one thing…

"He's not my boyfriend." Her voice is a whisper now. "He thinks I abandoned him for Cy."

"You were being held back," says Phoenix.

"He doesn't know that."

"I decided if he could do it, then so should I." Phoenix pulls back his shoulders and draws in a breath. "What Dad was doing in there was wrong. So wrong. The state of this garden is proof of that. I couldn't stand by and watch that. Those days are done."

"So, you took the people to the lab," says Wren. "You led Cy's men to their deaths."

"I didn't know they were going to kill them." The way he's looking at her shows her he's genuine. "Although, I wasn't especially sorry they did. The rest of it happened just as I said. Taco and Thrash came running up just as the people stormed inside."

"Flamethrower barrels don't just explode, Phee." Wren puts a hand on his arm, willing him to tell her everything.

He looks to the ground, remaining silent.

"You killed them, didn't you?"

Phoenix takes a few steps away and his hands fly to his temples. "If Dad ever finds out—"

"He's not going to find out!" She races to his side.

"I took the flamethrowers from Karlos and T-Bone. Wasn't like they needed them anymore."

"You didn't burn the other two alive, did you?" Wren asks. As much as she despises Cy's men, she wouldn't wish that kind of death on anyone.

Phoenix shakes his head slowly. "I hit them over the back of the head while they were trying to burn down the door. Taco first. Thrash second. They didn't see it coming. Never expected to go out in the exact same way they'd taken countless people before. Then I burnt the evidence. That's how their flamethrowers exploded. It was foolish. I almost killed myself in the process."

She can't argue with him there. He should've known better and removed their weapons before he torched them. But then again, she can't imagine he was thinking straight. Phoenix may be tough, but he's no killer. That wouldn't have been easy for him.

"Do you think Dad meant what he said?" Phoenix asks, his eyes filling with stubborn tears. "About us being pathetic, I mean. Like our mom."

"I think he meant it," she says, without any doubt. "And you know what? I don't think I should stop calling him Cy. I reckon it's about time you stopped calling him *Dad*. He hasn't earned that title. Because he was right when he said we're not like him. We're better than him, Phee."

"You are."

"Today, you proved that you are, too."

Phoenix pulls her into his arms and gives her a hug. They're not the arms she wants wrapped around her right now, but she buries her face in his chest, not caring how filthy he is and lets her tears fall.

This morning she had hope. This morning she had Dex.

Now, she has nothing but despair.

"What are we going to do?" Phoenix asks, breaking away.

"I only have one idea left," she says. "I don't know if it will work, but it's worth a shot."

"It'll work," says Phoenix.

"How do you know that?" She pushes him in the chest, laughing. "You don't even know what it is."

"Because it has to work," he says, refusing to return her smile. "It has to."

Wren takes in a deep breath. He's right. This could be their last shot.

She only wishes she had his confidence.

NOVA

ova clambers onto the beam despite her legs feeling shaky, Flick right behind her. It's wide and thick and sturdy looking.

Except it feels anything but that.

A breeze drifts over her, wafting the smell of moist vegetation as it tugs at her clothes. If she breathes deep enough there's the tang of decay, the mustiness that seems to permeate the crumbling buildings around them.

Right now, her breathing verges on panting as she takes several cautious steps. Flick is clutching her shirt like a lifeline as they watch the ground falling away beneath them.

"Worst idea ever," mutters Flick.

"Avis rescued us. She wouldn't go to all that trouble just to push us off." Nova clutches her stomach as if she's reassuring the baby within her, too.

"Remember how you only see the good in people? Who knows what's down there waiting for us."

Nova doesn't reply, because her imagination is answering that question and she doesn't like what she's seeing. More men like the one in the village. These ones with rocks and lengths of metal. Avis using them as payment for food or water.

She glances over her shoulder to find Avis regarding them in that unreadable way of hers. She nods. "Keep going. You're almost there."

Almost there to where? The beam juts out into nowhere but sky. And the further they walk, the higher they get. Only a few more feet and the crumbling pile the shaft of steel is resting on is no longer there. Gazing past her feet, Nova scans the vines and scrub that tangle over the rubble creating a mish mash of life and death.

And there's no way of telling which one they're about to join.

They're about one third of the way along when Avis calls out. "Stop!"

Nova and Flick freeze, glancing about wildly. Do polar grizzlies inhabit Fairbanks? Are men about to appear, scuttling over the debris like ants?

Avis approaches them and Nova can't help but shrink back. Avis seems to smile and scowl at once. "Still not used to the face, huh?"

Nova shakes her head. "Your scars tell me you've suffered more than we have." She slides her arm back to slip around Flick. "It's what suffering can do to a person that scares me."

The Outlands are proof that suffering teaches people survival comes first.

Avis stares at them for long moments, as unreadable as ever. "It should scare you," she states flatly.

Nova's heart rate spikes as Avis takes another step forward, her voluminous layers of netting making her big enough to be intimidating despite her short stature. But Avis squats down beside them, reaching over the edge of the beam.

She pulls away the vegetation, revealing that it's tied to more netting, this one much coarser than the one she's wearing. The vines and mesh have all been woven together so artfully it blends seamlessly with the mess of green around it.

Beneath it, a tunnel has been dug into the rubble, looking dark and dank. It's impossible to see where it leads.

"Quick," hisses Avis. "We can't be seen."

"You've got to be kidding me," mutters Flick. "This just keeps getting better and better."

Nova tightens her jaw. They've come this far, and it's not like they have any other options. "I'll go first."

She clambers down, sticking her feet into the narrow hole. It's not much wider than her, a human-sized pipeline leading into the unknown. Slithering in, Nova ignores the dirt and gravel that scrapes her skin. Her last glance up shows Flick chewing her nails nervously with Avis nodding encouragingly.

Why does this woman want them to do this so badly?

Nova can feel gravity tugging on her and, conscious that Flick is still out in the open with the possibility of the men looking for them, she moves down the tunnel. She's quickly surrounded by earth, moist dust feeling like it's coating her lungs. When the sunlight above is blocked as Flick makes her way to join her, Nova feels the panic take hold. It claws up her throat, gripping so hard it's almost impossible to breathe. She's not sure whether it's just the damp soil that's suffocating her, or all the decisions she's made that got her to this point.

Another short wriggle and suddenly the ground beneath her legs disappears. A short scream is wrenched from her when she tumbles down, free-falling for a breathless second.

Nova lands on something soft, her panicked brain too overwhelmed to register what it is. Her hands feel soft, prickly needles. Her nose tickles with the scent of pine. She looks down, realizing she landed on a bed of mangrove pine branches.

"Keep moving," shouts Avis from above. "We're right behind you."

Nova scuttles away before Flick lands on her, pushing

herself upright. She's in a small cave built of rubble. Holes in the roof let in shafts of light, illuminating the bare expanse. All that's here is the bed of pine that's been placed to catch people as they're spat out of the tunnel.

After a few seconds, Flick lands with a squeal and Nova helps her up, Flick clinging to her as she tries to get a sense of where they are.

Avis drops down a moment later, landing on her feet, her netting billowing then settling around her. She scans the area then nods. Reaching down, she tugs at the layers hanging off her, coming away with two lengths of fabric.

"Here, drape these over your heads."

"Like a veil?" Flick asks in horror.

Avis rolls her eyes. "Wear it how you like but covering the back of your head isn't going to help you much."

Nova does as she's told, the length of netting hanging over her face, the world now slightly blurred.

Not bothering to see if they're following her instructions, Avis walks to the other end of the man-made cave, shoving at a piece of metal. It scrapes back, creating a narrow opening that she slips through.

Grabbing Flick's hand, Nova follows her. She's getting tired of living in fear of what's coming next. The sooner they know, the sooner she can learn whether she's facing life or death.

Outside, the light blinds Nova for a moment. Shielding her eyes, she blinks rapidly as she takes in wherever Avis has brought them.

They're standing on cracked pavement in a street of some sort. Or what used to be a street. Just like they saw on the outskirts of Fairbanks, there are more hollow cars, more sloped buildings, more rampant greenery tangling through it all. But it now feels like they're in the heart of the destruction.

Chunks of concrete have dropped like meteors and partially embedded in the fractured ground. Some are overgrown with

moss and vines. Others look like they've only recently landed…
Nova looks up, feeling like more could drop at any second,
squinting through the netting. As she does so, insects swarm
around them, crawling over her, peppering the covering on her
face.

"Gross, gross, gross!" squeals Flick.

Nova swats them away, hearing her mother's voice listing all
the mosquito-borne diseases that killed millions as one whines
past her ear. But no matter how fast she flaps, bugs slapping
into her palms, there are more to replace the ones she just
whacked away.

Nova looks over to find Avis now covered in the swathes of
her own netting, almost indistinguishable beneath the fine
cloth.

"This place isn't safe," Nova points out.

"It sure as hell isn't," replies Avis. "You stay out here, you die."

She walks away, weaving her way through the rubble,
leaving Nova and Flick no choice but to follow. They circle the
chunks of building that have fallen, gravel crunching underfoot,
and Nova notices the beam high above. They seem to be
following it like the tip is a giant compass.

Avis takes a sharp right even though there's nothing but a
tall building there. It leans like so many of the others, a
sprawling mangrove pine looking like it's the only thing holding
it up. She indicates for Nova and Flick to join her.

"Please don't tell me we're going in there," pleads Flick
quietly.

"We've come this far," Nova mutters back. "Although, get
ready to run if we have to."

Cautiously, they join Avis, who darts away again the
moment they're close. She follows the wall of the building,
disappearing around the corner. Keeping her mouth closed
against the army of bugs around her, Nova follows with Flick.

They find Avis standing at a large expanse of metal built into a wall. She cups her hands around her mouth, mimicking the call of a raven again.

Long moments pass in tense silence as they seem to wait for something. When the sound of grinding gouges the air, Nova and Flick grasp each other. The metal wall starts to lift, creaking and groaning as it does.

"Come on," Avis waves her arm. "We're here."

We're here.

Except Nova and Flick have no idea where *here* is.

Or what it's going to mean for them.

They follow Avis as the ground dips, wherever they're heading appearing to be below the building. The moment they step through, the door lowers again, closing with a thud. Avis pulls back a curtain of the same netting she's swathed in and indicates for them to go in.

Her heart lodged high in her throat, Nova steps through, Flick glued to her side.

As her eyes adjust to the gloom, she discovers exactly where they've been brought.

Her hand claps to her mouth as she sees the number of faces staring at them. They crowd in, most smiling, all curious.

Every one of them…different.

Some have burns like Avis. Others are short, some missing an arm or a leg, some looking almost childlike despite being an adult. This is a place Dex would fit in seamlessly. If only he could see it. She knows he's always craved the idea of being normal, even though that's exactly how they've always thought of him

Avis smiles at them, something about her suddenly warm and relaxed. "We have visitors. This is Nova and Flick."

One girl, rounded and stocky, throws herself at Avis, clamping her in a hug. "Avis! I missed you!"

Avis's smile grows as she hugs the girl back, rocking from side to side. "Annabel. My very own welcoming committee." She pulls back, smoothing the girl's dark hair. "Have you got taller since I was gone?"

Annabel giggles in delight. "You only left a couple of hours ago, silly!" She turns back to look at Nova and Flick. "You found more..." she whispers, the sound not particularly quiet.

"I did," nods Avis. "I think they might be able to help me."

Annabel's eyes widen in her round face. "That would be wonderful." Turning, she scans them, her eyes lingering on Nova's then Flick's left hand. She turns back to Avis. "Can I?"

Avis's smile softens. "Of course."

Annabel walks toward them, her own swathe of netting wrapped around her stocky figure. She looks at Nova then Flick, her eyes deep and serious. "Welcome to Fairbanks." She pauses, then seems to make a decision. "And I'm sorry about your fingers."

Nova's chest blooms with warmth. "Thank you, Annabel. That's very sweet of you."

"Ah, yeah. Thanks," adds Flick.

"Now," Avis turns to the crowd. "Let's give these girls some space so they can settle in."

The people smile, several of them murmuring welcomes as they disperse. The area they're in is large, everything molded from cold cement, square columns lined up in regimented lines ahead. About forty people shuffle about, moving toward the odd pieces of furniture scattered around.

Avis smiles at them, the difference from the tense woman in the Outlands a stark contrast. "Let's get you something to eat and drink. I think a rest after that is called for. We have plenty of time to do the tour."

Overwhelmed and unsure what to make of this, Nova nods. "Thank you."

Avis is about to step forward when a young man limps over to her, dragging his left foot behind him. He glances at Nova then whispers in Avis's ear. Avis tenses. "Already?"

The young man nods and Avis thanks him. Turning back to the people in this cavernous area, she calls out. "Dharma, could you come here for a moment?"

A girl, probably Nova and Flick's age, hurries over, her red hair bright in the gloom of this man-made cave. "Yes, Avis?"

"Could you show these two to the sleeping quarters? And grab them something to eat and drink along the way, please."

"Of course," the girl nods solemnly.

Avis squeezes her arm. "Thank you." She frowns. "I have to make sure we're ready for when it rains again."

Avis is gone before Nova can ask what's going on. Flick grabs her hand, holding it tightly. "What is this place?" she murmurs, her voice hushed.

Dharma turns her big, serious eyes to them. "Fairbanks," she says simply.

"Yes, but—"

Flick doesn't get to finish because Dharma turns away. "This way. I'm sure you're hungry and tired."

They follow the girl, the columns counting their progression deeper into this new world. Several people smile widely and wave, most seeming to be content to be sitting around and chatting. The place is old and gray, but clean.

"This used to be a parking lot," explains Dharma over her shoulder. "The sleeping quarters are the level below. The kitchen area is over here."

She swings left where a mottled bunch of tables and chairs are littered around. Behind them, against the wall, is a haphazard looking kitchen. A tall, spindly man is moving around, clattering utensils and pans.

He angles his head as they approach, listening. "Ah Dharma, you've brought friends."

"Two new arrivals, Clint. They need something to eat and drink."

"Good thing I just made up a batch, then." He turns back,

where cups and plates are lined up in neat rows, grabbing a tray from his left without even glancing at it. Clint has obviously spent a lot of time in this makeshift kitchen.

Turning back, he holds out the tray with four cups. "Dinner and drinks, ladies."

Nova reaches over, smiling at him only to pause. The man's blank eyes are staring above her head. No wonder everything is so structured in the kitchen—Clint's blind.

Nova injects the smile into her voice as she passes Flick two of the cups, one with liquid and the other with some kind of food. "Thank you for your generosity."

Clint grins. "Avis is the woman you want to thank. None of us would be here without her."

Dharma leads them away, although they haven't got far when Flick stops, staring into one of her cups in horror. "Sweet Terra! Are those cockroaches?"

Nova glances down, eyes widening reflexively when she sees the cup she'd thought held food is filled with brown, shiny bugs. Cockroaches.

"They've been roasted," Dharma explains. "Very prolific in Fairbanks, and very good for you."

"They still have their antennae!" Flick squeaks.

Nova grabs her arm, warning her to be quiet with a look. These people are sharing what they have. It's important that they're grateful.

Nova swallows. "I doubt they taste worse than pteropods." She smiles at Dharma. "We're truly thankful."

Dharma shrugs. "Like Clint said. We owe all this to Avis."

"She established this place," Nova comments, knowing it's more of a statement than a question.

"Yes. She wanted somewhere to escape with her children. But—" Dharma bites her lip, probably wondering if she said too much.

"But the Commander took them before she could," Nova

164

murmurs. Her hand caresses her abdomen. Her child hasn't been born and she can imagine the pain of Avis's loss.

Dharma nods. "While she's waiting for them to return, she opened her doors for anyone else who...didn't fit in."

Flick glances down at her left hand, the glaring gap of her missing finger unmistakable. "We weren't allowed to fit in where we come from," she whispers. "They wanted us to remember we weren't good enough."

"Difference is celebrated in Fairbanks." Dharma almost smiles as she says those words. "You'll be safe here."

She starts walking again, this time heading to an opening at the other end of the concrete space. "But there's time to see that after you've had a rest. The sleeping quarters are just down here."

The opening turns out to be a ramp, one that heads to a level below. The further they walk down, the more the light disappears. It feels like they're descending into a tomb.

Nova slows, running her hand over the cool, cement wall, surprised when she feels a rough bump. She looks closer. It's the root of the mangrove pine they saw growing up through the building.

The further they walk down the ramp, the more they protrude—thick, brown, gnarled surfaces breaking through the concrete. Dharma pauses, picking up what looks like a small, lit candle tucked in at the base of one of the roots.

She glances over her shoulder, holding up the candle. "They're made from a mix of sap and pine oil."

Nova's brows shoot up. Another use for the mangrove pine they hadn't known about. "That's very clever."

"Clint is the only one who doesn't need to use them down here." Dharma says the words so solemnly it's hard to know whether she just made a joke.

Nova smiles, wondering when Dharma lost the ability to do the same herself.

Dharma turns back, holding the candle up high as she descends further into the next level. From the dim bubble of light, Nova sees the roots have infiltrated even further down here. They jut through in all directions, creating mounds that snake around like tiny mountain ranges. Between, blankets have been tucked in wherever the space was large enough.

The mangrove pine has created little nooks that these people are using as beds.

Dharma weaves her way through, lighting strategically placed candles so they can see where they're going. It would be easy to trip over the roots that criss-cross everywhere.

"So, Clint can navigate this floor by memory?" asks Nova. "That's pretty impressive."

Dharma stops where a larger space has been spread with blankets. "Yes. And he insisted on taking the furthest sleeping area, too." She points to the makeshift bed. "This one is larger than many of the others. I figured you'd want to share."

Nova nods, grateful that Dharma has noticed Flick has been plastered to Nova's side since they arrived. "Thank you. This will be wonderful."

Nova's body suddenly sags, even the cups she's holding feeling too heavy. The night on the raft. The storm. Arriving at the village.

It's all starting to take its toll.

Nova's about to thank Dharma again for her kindness when Flick steps around her. "Do you mind me asking..." Nova feels herself tighten. They don't need to get these people offside. "There doesn't seem to be anything...different about you, Dharma."

Dharma takes a step back and Nova almost tells her she doesn't need to answer. Flick hasn't realized that some wounds aren't physical.

But Dharma pauses. "I was running away from my village. My father was trying to sell me...again." She shrugs. "I arrived here, passed the test, and the rest is history." She straightens as she turns away. "I'll let you sleep. You've had enough to process today. I'm sure many of your questions will be answered tomorrow."

She's gone before Nova can thank her again.

They're left in silence, the small circle of light dancing and flickering around them. Flick lowers herself onto the blankets with a groan. "I'm too tired to process what's just happened."

Nova places her cups on a flattened area of root, taking Flick's as she curls up. "You should have something to eat first."

Flick grimaces. "I can't. I'm not *that* hungry."

Her stomach blanching, Nova fishes one of the cockroaches out of her cup. At least they're less visible in the semi-darkness. "These people would probably think eating pods is gross." Bringing one up to her mouth Nova has to work not to shudder. "Look, I'll go first."

The moment the cockroach touches her tongue, Nova gags. She suppresses it as Flick watches her closely. She needs to do this for her baby. She needs to do this for Flick.

Nova tries not to think or feel. To ignore the tickle of antennae on the roof of her mouth. The crackle as she bites down. The crumbling of wings and legs and the flat, crunchy body. With a few quick chews, she's swallowed it.

"Actually, pods do taste worse," she says in surprise.

Flick looks down at the cup just as her stomach rumbles. "Pass me the cup with water," she says resolutely.

Silently, with faces almost as twisted as the roots around them, they finish their meal, washing it down the moment the cups with the cockroaches are empty.

Flick lies back, curling around herself like a child. Nova pulls up the blanket rumpled at her feet. "Get some rest now, Flick. It's been a big couple of days."

"Understatement," she mutters.

Nova smiles in the gloom, realizing this is the first time she's felt remotely safe since they arrived in the Outlands. Could they really have found a haven? Where their nine fingers are just one of the differences among many?

Despite the hope, her heart aches. Can any place be home without Kian?

She settles back against the root of the mangrove pine. She's exhausted, but sleep is going to be elusive for a while. Everything here feels too alien.

Flick shuffles deeper into her new bed. "You didn't tell me you were pregnant, Nova," she whispers, the hurt in her voice unmistakable.

Nova sighs, not wanting to add to the pain Flick is already carrying. "It was complicated. I think a part of me was too scared to say it aloud."

And then Flick lost her baby and it just didn't seem right to mention it...

"Kian's the father, isn't he?"

Another stab pierces Nova's chest. "He is."

"Yeah, that's complicated."

Flick settles further into the bedding. "Nova?" she asks, her voice thick with sleep. "I would've let my baby grow up here."

Nova doesn't answer immediately, and within seconds Flick's breathing is deep and regular, the sleep of someone whose mind just welcomed oblivion.

Wrapping her arms around her middle, Nova doubles over. So much has happened. So much loss. So much change.

She just wishes she didn't feel so alone.

When the sound of shuffling whispers through the dark, Nova straightens, instantly on alert. The fear that's been her companion since she climbed on the raft flares in her veins, showing it hadn't really left. It had been sitting, waiting.

Knowing it was too soon to relax.

A small blob of light materializes, followed by a hand carrying it. Nova has shot to her feet, ready to protect Flick, when she realizes it's Avis. She angles the light to illuminate her unscarred side, leaving the pits and valleys of her left side in shadow. "I wanted to check you'd settled in okay," she whispers.

Nova sits back down, her legs suddenly shaky. Her body's had enough of adrenalin spikes. "Your people have been wonderful, thank you."

Avis settles beside Nova on the root. "Everyone here knows what it's like to be vulnerable and scared. Like me, they want to do what they can so others don't have to live like that."

"You've built something special here, Avis. You should be proud."

Avis pauses, then straightens her spine. "Do you know why I brought you two here, Nova?"

"You brought us here because our hands are deformed and we had nothing."

Avis has created a haven for the vulnerable. It's the only thing that makes sense.

"I have people at many of the villages around here. They keep me posted about anyone who might need help."

Nova nods. That was certainly them. "But why would anyone choose to live out there when they could live here?"

"Various reasons. Some have family members they can't bear to leave. Others are determined to try to build a better life. To show the people there's another way to live. They're brave souls, all of them."

"Incredibly brave," agrees Nova.

Avis pulls in a breath, seeming to need to steady herself. "I also have them tell me straight away about anything urgent I should know about. You said back at the village that you knew...Wren."

Nova freezes. Wren is the Commander's daughter. The same man who took Avis's children and disfigured her.

And Avis has her informants keeping an eye out for information on her.

169

She looks Avis in the eye. "Wren came to...our village." Nova omits they're from Askala. She needs to know more before she shares that. "She's the toughest, smartest, fairest person I know. If the Commander did this to you and others, I don't believe she's anything like her father."

Avis deflates and smiles, the motion seeming contradictory. "I'm glad. Things can't have been easy for her." She leans forward. "And her brother, Phoenix?"

Phoenix is Wren's brother? Nova almost laughs. So much makes sense now. She really should have guessed. But...

"He can't be her brother," she says. "Phoenix's father is Ronan."

Avis leans in closer. "Ronan calls himself Cy these days. He's the Commander. Wren and Phoenix are twins. They're his only children."

Nova reels back. Ronan is the Commander? That's even more shocking than the idea of Wren and Phoenix being twins.

"I need you to tell me everything you can about both of them," says Avis.

Nova frowns. She glances at Flick, suddenly unsure whether she should be answering these questions. Is this woman wanting to hurt the Commander through his children? Her revenge because he took hers...

Have they been nothing but a pawn after all?

Nova peers at Avis in the gloom, trying to get a sense of what's motivating this woman. She won't be getting any more information about Wren from Nova. "Why all the questions, Avis?"

A single tear trickles down Avis's scarred, twisted cheek. "Because Phoenix is my son." She smiles the gentlest, proudest smile Nova has ever seen. "And Wren is my daughter."

KIAN

"*T*hat place looks more dangerous than the one we just left."

Kian grinds his teeth at Dean's words. His comments are one of the few things to break the silence as they head due west, the sun sharp and hot above, the ground scorched and bare beneath them.

The Remnants could've been lying, you know.

We'll be out of food tomorrow. Out of water the day after.

The raft's probably been stolen by now.

You do realize there's nothing these people could teach us.

Have you considered that Nova could already be d—

The last comment had been silenced by Kian's furious glare. Dean realized he went too far as Kian had taken a step toward him. Dean had stepped back as fury had blazed through Kian's veins, demanding he silence Dean.

But, with his hands clenched, Kian had turned away.

Energy fighting with Dean is energy wasted. And everything is focused on one thing right now.

Finding Nova. Alive.

"I mean, there's a reason people left the cities to live out in wastelands."

Kian ignores Dean, figuring he's just about perfected pretending he doesn't exist by now. Getting into the city is what has to happen next. And that doesn't seem to be as straightforward as he'd hoped...

An undulating wall of rubble faces them, a large beam arching out over it. If there's a gap, giving a glimpse into the decaying world inside, it's framed by the fractured cement and twisted metal. One of the leaning buildings is just to their right, seeming to defy gravity with its angle. Everything looks like it's about to collapse at any minute.

Shiloh places a hand on Kian's arm. "I think this time Dean might be right."

Kian's worried his teeth are about to crack, there's so much pressure building up in his jaw. Have they forgotten Nova's in there? That they have no idea what they might be doing to her?

Kian strides several steps one way then back. The frustration that's nearing boiling point may have to do with the fact that Dean actually *is* right.

Every entry he can see into the city is dangerous.

"We don't have a choice," Kian responds. "Inside the city is where we're going."

Finn shuffles his feet, flurries of charcoal dust rising up. "Getting in there alive would be preferable."

Eyeing the first gap, Kian plans the footholds he'll use to climb the rubble between him and the city. "As long as we're careful, we should be fine." He walks forward, gripping a slab of concrete as he slips his foot into a gap. "Maybe we can find something to eat in there."

The others quieten down. Maybe they figure this has been dangerous from the start. Maybe they remember why they came here in the first place.

Maybe the prospect of food has swayed them.

It doesn't matter. Kian's just relieved when they start clambering over the rubble with him.

This pile is only a few feet off the ground and Kian reaches the top easily. The remains of whatever building this was make an uneven path ahead, so he watches carefully where he places his feet. "Maybe follow me, then we know that path is safe."

All it will take is one slipped foot and a twisted ankle will be likely. Or worse.

But Dean comes to stand beside him, the chunk of cement he's standing on making him a head taller. "If I have to do this, I'll make my own way," he snarls.

Kian turns away, acknowledging that ignoring this sullen guy is going to get harder and harder.

Carefully, they make their way over the minefield of holes and protruding metal. "Only a yard or so," Kian calls over his shoulder, conscious he's keeping his voice down. It's like he's worried even a shout could shift the small hill they're standing on.

Beside him, Dean eyes a flat section of cement a couple of feet ahead. He's obviously thinking of jumping to it.

Kian extends his arm, finding him out of reach. "I wouldn't, Dean. You don't know how stable it is."

"Make your mind up, oh-great-leader," Dean growls. "Do you want to get into the city or not?"

A short leap and Dean lands on the slab. He throws Kian a triumphant look as it holds steady. "Probably the safest part in this whole city," he announces.

Kian lets out a breath. He may not like Dean, but he doesn't want to see him injured. He's about to turn back to the others to tell them they'll follow Dean when something catches his eye.

A wire, more of a gossamer thread, beside Dean's foot catches the light. He steps back, making room for the others. The wire stretches taught, angling around him rather than snapping.

Uneasiness slithers through Kian. That wire is the only thing that isn't fractured or detached here. Instinctively, he glances around. The wire disappears into the walls of rubble that rise on either side of them. Maybe it just got caught there...

But then there's a grinding sound from above.

Looking up, Kian freezes. The leaning building above them hasn't moved. But a slab of concrete on the roof has suddenly appeared.

And is sliding toward the edge. Toward them.

"Get back!" Kian roars.

Leaping forward, he lands beside Dean, who's finally looked up. His face is frozen in terror. Kian grabs his arm, jerking him back the way he came as he surges forward with all his might.

A second later the sound of cement slamming into cement blasts behind them.

Not stopping, and glad that Dean is now propelling his own momentum, they leap over the pile, gravel peppering their back. In front of them, Shiloh and Finn are madly running back the way they just came. It only takes seconds to traverse the yards they just covered.

Kian leaps off the mound, stumbling as he hits the ground. Dean lands beside him a moment later. Dust billows around them, thick and gray.

The silence almost feels alien after the roar of destruction they narrowly escaped. Kian looks around, breathing heavily despite the choking dust. Finn and Shiloh sit shell-shocked a few feet away. Dean is already pushing himself upright beside him.

Holy Terra, what just happened?

Standing, Kian turns back to stare mutely at the place they were almost crushed. The dust is still settling, but it's undeniable that where they were just standing is now covered by another foot of concrete.

Dean steps beside him. "Thanks," he mutters. "You just saved my—"

"It was instinct." Kian shrugs, not tearing his gaze away from the rubble. "Not sure I would've made the same choice if I had time to think."

"We both know that's a lie." He slaps Kian on the shoulder. "But I appreciate you pretending."

Kian takes a few steps forward, not liking the suspicion that's creeping up his spine. The wire that Dean's foot pushed...

"What are you looking at?" Dean asks.

"There was a wire beside your foot..." Kian's eyes scan the building the concrete fell from. Now that he knows what he's looking for, the rope that's been tucked up the side is unmistakable. It reaches right up to the top...where the slab was only minutes ago.

Dean follows his line of sight and he must see it, too, because he gasps. "Someone built that? It was freaking deliberate?"

Kian swallows. It was a booby trap.

Shiloh and Finn join them, silent as they take in the near brush with death. Suddenly, Shiloh gasps, her horrified gaze staring at the pile of rubble. It's shifted as the next layer of mangled building landed on it...uncovering several bones.

Human bones.

Shiloh stumbles backward even though they're already a distance away. The realization of how close they just came to being part of that decaying pile of concrete and human remains is plastered all over her face.

Dean shakes his head slowly. "They don't want anyone coming in."

"Which means they have something to hide," Kian growls. "They want us to run, but I'm not giving up. We'll find another way in."

"And you don't think someone else before you thought that? That they can outsmart them?" Dean demands. "The only

175

people who got out of here alive are the ones who walked away." He crosses his arms. "I'll wait here, thanks."

Kian nods as he turns to him. "I think that's best." He looks at Finn and Shiloh. "I'll let you know when I'm through."

Kian goes to take a step away but Dean grips his arm, his fingers digging in hard.

"This was never about Askala, was it? It's about you finding the girl you treated like crap. I'm not risking my life so you can say sorry and make yourself feel better."

"I'm not asking you to," Kian grinds out. "I'll do this part alone."

But Dean doesn't release him. "What if she's dead, Kian? Was this all worth it?"

Kian's instantly in Dean's face. "Nova. Isn't. Dead."

Dean doesn't back down, his eyes blazing. "And how many people are you going to risk to prove that?"

Kian's breath is heaving through his chest. Fury throbs hot and heavy in his veins. It's going to suck that he saved Dean just to pummel him, but he's had enough. Bringing the brother of Ronan on this mission was a mistake.

Dean must read Kian's intent, because he pushes his face closer, his breath like a furnace. "Do it."

It's all the invitation Kian needs.

Finn slips between them, swallowing nervously. "Ah, guys. I'm not sure this is very helpful right now," he squeaks.

Kian blinks, the red haze slowly lifting. He takes a step back, shaking his head. The Outlands are starting to get to him.

Dean pulls in a deep breath, muttering one word as his hands work like pistons by his side. "Coward."

Doing what he should've done a second ago, Kian ignores him. "There'll be another way in. It's just a matter of finding it."

Except no one moves.

Dean turns to the other two. "I say we head back. Promise food to as many Remnants as we can and take down Ronan."

"A mercenary army?" Kian asks incredulously.

"Look at what we've learned! My bet is these people are quite comfortable with violence, plus they're desperate. They'll sell their soul for a decent meal."

Kian shakes his head, not liking how Shiloh and Finn seem to be taking this suggestion seriously. "That's no doubt how Ronan came to power."

"Exactly. We beat him at his own game."

Except Kian isn't going back without Nova. He knows without a doubt that their success is dependent on finding her.

Without her, they repeat the same mistakes his ancestors made, including his father. Every one of them forgot humanity is their strength. That it's what will unite them.

Askala must be founded on love.

"You guys go back. I'll follow you when I can."

"What?" Shiloh asks in horror. "We can't go back without you."

"Felicia is out here, too." Or had they conveniently forgotten that? "I'm going to finish what I set out to do."

Shiloh steps forward. "Kian. Maybe it's time to let this go. You tried, you really did. No one can say you didn't love Nova."

Kian blanches at her use of the past tense. "Shiloh—"

"You can't forget who you are— the leader of Askala. Too many people are depending on you."

Kian glances at Finn, wondering if he agrees with this. Finn swallows. "If you die, what does that mean for us? For Askala?"

Kian takes a step back, feeling like he's been assaulted. The three of them stare at him—Dean with a scowl, Shiloh pleading, Finn nervously chewing the side of his thumb. Kian's denial dies in his throat.

Are they right?

Is he risking too much?

He could turn around now and do what he can to save Askala...

"They're Unbound, Kian," Shiloh whispers, her eyes pleading.

Those words end Kian's doubt. He won't fight for a world where that's a deciding factor.

He takes a step back, dropping his shoulders and lifting his chin. "I won't leave them behind. Not without knowing they could be saved."

It's time to show no one is unworthy.

That this is what Askala will be built on.

Kian turns to the rubble, eyeing the beam. It may not be a way in, but it'll at least give him a bird's eye view of this part of the city. He might be able to spot a way to enter.

Leaping onto the end that's gouged into the ground, he bounces a little. It seems sturdy enough.

"Kian, please don't," Shiloh begs.

"Let him be the hero," Dean mutters behind him. "I'm not hanging around to watch him die."

Two steps and Kian's already a few feet off the ground. The tip of the beam pierces the blue sky up ahead and he wonders how high it will be. At least it'll be his best bet to get a good look at this city. There has to be a way in.

Kian's about to take another step when some vegetation rustles to the right, a child appearing out of nowhere. He leaps onto the beam several feet ahead, dark haired and skinny, looking at Kian as if he's a lion.

He hears Shiloh gasp behind him, then Dean mutters "What the…".

"Hey, little guy," Kian says quietly and slowly. "Where did you come from?"

The little boy doesn't answer, instead taking a cautious step back.

Further up the beam.

Kian squats down. "I'm not going to hurt you, I promise. I just want to help."

The little boy shakes his head mutely, nimbly jumping back a few steps.

Kian's eyes fly open in horror. "No! Don't move." He works to moderate his tone. "It could be dangerous."

The little boy eyes him, probably wondering how much of a threat Kian is. Kian smiles gently despite the alarm that has his heart racing. "I won't touch you, just come back down."

Without warning, the child runs a few more steps up the beam, only stopping when he's halfway up. The sky becomes his background, a breeze tugging at his tattered clothing.

Kian scoots forward, keeping his squat position. The smaller he is, the less threatening he'll be. "Please, come back down. This isn't safe."

The boy watches Kian shift closer, his brows twitching a little as the gap between them shrinks. It's as if he doesn't expect Kian to follow him. Kian extends his hand again, now only a few feet in between them. "I don't want you to hurt yourself. Maybe we can find your mom or dad?"

The boy frowns as he takes a few more steps backward, not even looking down as he does so.

Kian shoots up to a standing position, fear starting to feel like a rock in his gut. The breeze picks up now they're higher up and Kian glances down. The rubble of the city is falling away. If the child were to slip, he'd seriously hurt himself. If he's lucky…

What's happened to this kid that he'd prefer to move further along a gangplank to nowhere rather than let a stranger help him?

The boy frowns. "Go away!" he shouts. "Stay away from me."

"If you come back down, I promise I'll leave you alone," Kian gently counters. There's no way he's leaving this child out on the beam.

Another few steps and the boy widens the distance between them.

Getting closer to the end of the beam.

"I said, go away! I don't want your help."

Kian shuffles forward a few steps, a trickle of sweat frantically zigzagging down his spine. "This is really dangerous, little guy. I have some water and food down there, why don't you come and check it out?"

"He's not listening!" shouts the boy and Kian glances around, wondering if he's talking to someone.

But they're high above the city now, and a quick glance down has Kian's gut capsizing. There's nothing but concrete littered with boulders to catch them. Up ahead, a mangrove pine has punched through a building, and they're almost high enough to see its roof.

Kian tries again. "Please—"

Except the boy does the one thing Kian didn't expect. He grins.

And walks straight to the edge of the beam.

"No!" Kian shouts as he launches forward.

He grabs the boy's arm, who looks up at him in surprise. He didn't think Kian would try to stop him. Incongruously, his grin grows.

And then he jumps, taking Kian with him.

Kian registers Shiloh's scream the moment his feet leave solid metal. His only contact with land. His only chance of surviving.

For breathless seconds, he's flying, slicing through the air.

And then they're falling.

Kian twists so it's his body that will strike the cement first.

He instinctively anticipates when the ground is about to hit them, knowing the fall will be brief. He squeezes his eyes shut, sending out the only words that he wants to think right now.

I love you, Nova.

I'm sorry you never knew I was coming for you.

When something slams into his back, Kian braces himself for the pain, hoping it will be short lived.

Hoping the child will survive.

Except he finds himself propelled into the air like he just hit elastic, quickly dropping again only to bounce once more. As the springing up and down reduces, Kian looks around.

He survived? How is that possible?

The boy clambers from his slack arms and Kian finds his fingers tangling in some sort of netting. He looks down. It's like he's landed in a giant, finely spun spider web!

The boy shoves his face close to Kian. "You tried to stop me!" he says in awe. "The men hardly ever do that."

Kian blinks as he shoves himself to a sitting position. "Only because I thought you were about to die!" He shouts the last words, adrenaline roaring through his veins.

The boy sits back, bouncing on the makeshift trampoline. He grins. "You passed the test."

The test? That was a test? Kian opens his mouth to say something, only to find there's nothing. How could that be a test?

Suddenly, others appear, seeming to materialize out of the cracked buildings surrounding them. Kian looks around. The netting has been stretched between anything they could attach it to—trees, edges of the crumbling structures, posts. The people shuffle forward, their smiles not feeling like they should be there.

How is it they look like a welcoming committee?

The boy scrambles over the netting, dropping on the ground, and Kian does the same. He lands lightly on his feet, enjoying the sense of stability the ground suddenly has. The moments of freefalling through the air aren't something he ever wants to experience again.

A woman steps forward, lowering a hood made of netting from her face. Kian has to hide the recoil that wrenches through him. The woman's face...he's never seen scarring like that. It's an undeniable stamp of pain and suffering that you want to draw away from, but can't help but be riveted by.

The boy appears by her side and they all look at him, still smiling. Still unnerving. Kian says the only words he can think of. "I come in peace."

The woman smiles. "I can see that." She angles the scarred side of her face away, Kian now seeing that it only distorts half of her features. "My name is Avis, welcome to Fairbanks. You'll be safe here."

Kian blinks, still trying to understand what's happened. "I have friends—"

Avis nods. "We'll send someone to collect them. There's a much…" She tilts her head as her eyes crinkle. "A much simpler way to enter Fairbanks."

"Thank you." He swallows, discovering how dry his mouth is. "My name's Kian. The others are Dean, Shiloh, and Finn."

"Is there anything we can say to your friends so they know we mean no harm?"

Kian considers the question, his lips twitching. "Tell Dean it seems I haven't had enough of his complaining yet."

"Of course." She glances over his shoulder. "Ah, some of the others are here."

There are more? Kian's about to turn around when he stills.

"Kian?"

Every shred of his being freezes. Her voice. How can he be hearing her voice?

Slowly, he turns. If this is a dream he doesn't want to shatter it.

It's Nova. A little thinner. A little wearier. Still breathtakingly beautiful.

Kian's body trembles with such ferocity he has to lock it into place. "Nova?" he whispers, his throat so crammed with hope it chokes the word.

She smiles, a graceful movement that dazzles him as if he's staring at the sun. "You came for me."

Too much distance is between them. And yet he's lost the ability to move.

Nova takes the first step. It's a small step, almost a hesitant one. Her blue eyes swim with tears.

Something breaks in Kian. The hold around his heart. The fear this isn't real. He strides forward, desperate to hold her again.

And then she's in his arms. They collapse around each other, clinging and grasping.

"You came for me." Nova whispers the words this time, the tears now a stream down her cheeks.

Kian clasps her face, reveling in the feeling of his skin caressing hers. "I'll always come for you, Nova. You own my heart."

Their lips touching is an inevitability. This is a kiss where more than mouths are melding.

Hearts are healing.

Souls are touching.

As Kian draws back, he sighs. Then smiles.

Finally, he's whole again.

DEX

The first thing to hit Dex when he opens his eyes is the overpowering smell of too many human bodies crammed into too small a space.

Wincing as he rolls onto his back, he stretches out on the hard floor and stares up at his old bunk above him. How did Wren manage to sleep under here?

The lab wasn't built to hold this many people at once. The room his father had slept in during the Provings has been taken over by two families. The secret room has half a dozen people in it. The bunkroom is crammed with bodies, fighting for a little bit of mattress space. Even the dining room is filled with the sounds of snoring.

When Dex had been unable to keep his eyes open for another moment, he'd wandered around looking for a quiet place to rest and found his father asleep in his old bunk. He'd offered to scoot over for him, but Dex had opted for the space Wren had once claimed as her own.

No matter how complicated his feelings are, he can't deny it'd felt good to sleep in her little hiding spot. A comfort almost.

For someone always watching her back, it must have felt reassuring for her to have been tucked away under here.

The sound of a baby crying out in the hallway has Dex pulling himself from under the bunk, his movements awkward and jerky as his ribs protest at the change in position. Getting himself to a stand, he decides that although he's definitely had better days, he's going to live. Well, for now, anyway.

It seems nothing can be taken for granted anymore.

Glancing back in the dim light from the fire exit sign, he sees his father has vacated the bed and it's now occupied by two women who are tucked together, fast asleep.

Stepping over other slumbering bodies, Dex picks his way across to the doorway, yawning widely.

It's always been hard to tell the time in the lab given the lack of windows, but right now he has no idea if it's the middle of the day or the night. Had he slept for one hour or twenty? Whatever it was, it wasn't enough.

He blinks in the brightness of the light in the hallway. People are huddled in groups and their heads snap around at the sound of Dex approaching.

"He's here," several people whisper at once.

Dex slows his steps. They've been waiting for him? He hadn't really realized what he'd been saying yes to when Kian had asked him to be leader in his absence.

"Good morning," he says, noticing the frowns on their faces. "Or afternoon. Or evening. I actually have no idea what time it is."

"None of us do." A woman throws him a smile that feels a little like a lifeline. "We think it's morning."

"We want to know what the plan is." A man with a thin face narrows his eyes at Dex. "How long will we be trapped in here? Our supplies won't last long. And then what do we do?"

Dex's heart rate spikes. This man is right. All Dex has managed to do by bringing them here is save them from one dangerous situation and throw them right into another. At least in the forest they could have hidden from Ronan and his men. In here, they're trapped.

"I'm not sure what we do," Dex answers as honestly as he can.

"You said you're our leader," another man growls. "You must have a plan."

"Nobody could have planned for this." Dex throws out his hand, shaking his head. "But we'll make one. We're safe for now. That's something. I'm not sure how many of us would've survived a night in the forest."

"All you've done is delay our demise."

Dex turns to see who spoke, but it's hard to tell amongst the growing sea of anxious faces.

"We're hungry," says Bea, who's standing a little off to the side. "The food supplies need to be rationed."

"Bound before Unbound," says a man holding a toddler on his hip.

"We're all Unbound now," Bea replies, her words full of resentment.

"The children need the food more than we do." The man kisses his son on the top of his head. "They should eat first."

"Your child can eat your ration if you like," another woman retorts. "But I plan on keeping mine."

"Everyone will be fed equally," says Dex. He may not have a clue what the plan actually is, but this much he knows for sure. The days of dividing the worth of the colony into two groups are long gone.

"It doesn't really matter," someone else says. "We're all going to be dead soon."

There are gasps and a few moans, but nobody disputes this. They all know it. The lab might be able to keep them safe for a few days, but ultimately staying here will be the end of them.

"I killed a man for you," says an Unbound stepping out of the shadows, his eyes lit with fury. "I've never killed a man before. But Callix said it was the only way. He never said there wasn't a plan."

Dex pauses. Perhaps honesty hadn't been the best idea in this situation after all. He should've pretended there was a plan to reassure the people. Because it seems like this man might be contemplating his second murder in as many days...

"Well..." The people close in on Dex, their scared faces turning to anger, the tension growing at the same rate their food supplies are dwindling. They're starting to look less like a crowd and more like a mob.

"There's a plan," says Dex's father, from the doorway of the computer room. "I just haven't had a chance to talk to my son about it yet. Now seems like a good time, doesn't it, Dex?"

"Excuse us for a moment." Dex extricates himself and walks gratefully toward his father.

"We need answers!" a man shouts. "We can't stay in here forever."

"We'll keep you posted as soon as we can," says Dex. "Just give us a moment. Everything's going to be okay."

His father shoots him a glare and Dex closes his mouth and follows him into the computer room.

Noticing the hatch to the downstairs room is closed, Dex goes to it. "Is anyone down there?"

His father nods. "They're asleep. Everyone's exhausted after yesterday. We can talk. Just be sure to keep your voice down."

"What about the radio?"

"It's missing," his father says.

"That's weird." Dex slides into his old chair and lets out a groan, pressing his hand to his ribs. He has no time to think about missing radios right now.

Despite his injuries, it feels good to be back in his chair. He can almost pretend it's like the old days and Wren's going to pop her head out of the hatch at any moment to complain about Phoenix lounging about on the mattress. To think of the places his brain had gone imagining what they might have been doing down there! It seems ridiculous now that he knows the true nature of their relationship. If only she'd trusted him at the time, she could have saved him a whole lot of angst.

"How badly injured are you?" his father asks, noticing the way he's holding his chest.

"It's my ribs mainly," he says. "A bit of bruising on my shoulders."

"And that gash under your eye." His father leans over to inspect it.

"Yeah and that. Bit of a broken heart, too, if I'm honest." It's this injury that has tears welling in Dex's eyes. He's not even sure why he just said that. Perhaps it's the overwhelming need to confide in someone. And without Kian or Nova here to talk to, there's really nobody else left except his dad.

"I wouldn't write Wren off just yet." His father pats him gently on the shoulder. "Phoenix came around. She might yet, too."

"How do you know Phoenix came around?" Dex asks, checking Wren's pendant is still hanging from his neck. "He said he was coming here to get you. And then he was ambushed. He wasn't exactly behaving like someone who'd come around. He punched me in the guts!"

His father waves his hand at him. "He had to look tough in front of the guards. That would've been just for show."

"Well, it bloody hurt." Dex lets go of the pendant to rub his ribs again, remembering the shooting pain of the blow Phoenix had landed on him.

"Think about it, Dex. Phoenix didn't need to come and get me. Ronan could easily have done that later. He came here to give you a fighting chance."

"Maybe." Dex shrugs. That's very possible. But they can't

know for sure. It's too dangerous right now to trust someone on a maybe.

"I noticed you've encrypted the database." His father points at the computers. "Good thinking, but do you have a portable copy of everything?"

"Why do I need to do that?" Dex asks.

His father smacks his forehead with his palm. "Because *everything* is on that database. Everything! Not just the history of Askala but it's the control center for all the chips. Nobody can get through a single door without these computers."

Dex nods, not following why this is such a problem.

"What if we need to get out of here?" his father asks. "What if we need to escape?"

"Oh." Dex blinks, understanding at last.

"You need to load everything onto this." His father points to a laptop that's set up on the desk and connected to the computer bank. It's one Dex hasn't seen before and he shuffles his chair over so he can take a better look.

"Where did you get this?" Dex clicks the shift key to bring the screen to life, impressed by the power of the machine.

"We've always had it. We just haven't needed it before now."

"So, this is the plan?" Dex asks. "Load the database onto this laptop and evacuate? Where exactly are we evacuating to?"

"That's not my plan." His father sinks into the other chair and shakes his head.

"Then what is?"

"I don't have a plan!"

"Dad! You said you had a plan!" Dex's hand flies to his temples, a sudden headache taking hold. "You told those people you had one. They're going to want to hear something from us. What are we going to say?"

His father shrugs. "How about we start by moving those files across?"

Dex lets out a sigh and punches the password into the

computer. This whole thing is one big disaster. The people are angry and they have a right to be. This place is feeling more like a tomb than a lab. And it has them all sealed inside.

"What's the password?" his father asks. "In case I need it."

Dex isn't sure why, but he hesitates. Then he quickly realizes that out of all the people on this sad dying planet who are his enemies, his father isn't one of them.

"You know the code," he says. "Mercy forever. No spaces and *forever* spelled with a numeral four."

The smile that spreads across his father's face is like a beacon of hope. It's proof that even in the darkest of places, there's light to be found.

"I never thought to try that one," he says. "I didn't think you'd..."

"I loved her, too, Dad." Dex kicks off the file transfer and frowns at the timer.

The smile falls from his father's face. "We're not the only ones, apparently."

"Ronan didn't love her," says Dex. "He didn't even really know her. Not the real her. She was only seventeen when he was banished."

His father nods, pressing his index fingers to his chin as he thinks about this.

"She loved you, Dad. And me. She didn't love him. Although, it's pretty weird seeing her name across that creep's chest, isn't it?"

"Very." His father pretends to gag, which makes Dex laugh. It's exactly how he feels.

As their laughter falls silent, they stare at each other for a few long moments, aware of the shift in their relationship. They've never joked around like this. Never worked together or needed each other like they do right now. It's the one positive to come out of this horrendous situation.

"This could take a while," says Dex, glancing at the timer counting down.

"We're not in a hurry. It's not like we can go anywhere."

"Then why are we doing this?" Dex nods toward the laptop.

"I told you. *Just in case.*" His father rolls his eyes. "Although, to be honest, I'm not sure how we can get out of here. Ronan will have his men keeping a close eye on us."

"Is that the plan then?" Dex asks. "We stay here and starve to death? Do you want to tell the others or should I?"

His father shakes his head. "We have a small store of food in the kitchen and a little more in the hidden room. We can ration that. And we're connected to fresh water from the lake. We have power from the solar panels, fresh air coming through the vents and we're totally secure. Nobody can get in."

"Which as you just pointed out, also means nobody can get out!" Dex lowers his voice when he realizes he's shouting. "What happens when we run out of food? We can't exactly just pop out and grab us a polar grizzly to barbeque in the hallway, can we?"

"No need to be sarcastic," his father says. "We just haven't had time to figure this out properly yet. We'll think of something. We always do."

"We need to figure it out now!" Dex goes to stand but when his ribs protest, he sits back down. "We're ruined, Dad. We have no hope without a miracle now. You saw the people out there. They're angry. And as their hunger builds, they're only going to get worse. And that's if Ronan doesn't find a way in here first. This could all be over well before we even have the chance to starve to death."

He waits for his father to argue, but instead his eyes fill with tears. "I know that, Dex. I know all of that. It's not going to help us to panic now. Let's just do what we need to do right now. If we put our heads together, we can figure out a way to get out of here. Even if we have to dig our way out."

Dex shakes his head. It would take them longer to do that than they have left. It's impossible. He knows it. His father knows it. The angry people outside that door know it. Ronan probably knows it, too. Forget the flamethrowers and threats of being cast into the forest. The biggest weapon being used against them right now is time itself. And there's no doubt it's running out.

Looking back at the laptop, Dex notices the timer is dropping faster than predicted. He hopes that's not an omen about how long they can survive in here.

A noise in the hallway has both Dex and his father out of their chairs and running to the door.

The man who'd killed one of the guards has the father of the toddler pressed up against the wall with his hands wrapped around his throat.

"Stop!" calls Dex, almost tripping over a woman sitting on the floor in his hurry to get to them. "Stop that!"

Dex grabs one of the man's hands, while his father takes the other and they haul him off his victim. The sharp movement sends needles of pain through Dex's middle.

"What the hell are you doing?" he asks, keeping hold of the man despite his pain.

"He had a jar of pickled aibika leaves under his shirt." The man says it like it's a crime punishable by death. "And he wasn't planning on sharing them."

"They were for my son!" the man protests, grabbing at his throat as he tries to steady his breathing. "He's hungry."

"We're all hungry." A woman waves a jar of pickled leaves. "But nobody else is hiding food."

Dex recognizes the jar from the stack that's kept in the secret room. The stack that nobody was supposed to touch.

"How do you know what anybody's hiding?" another woman asks. "Everyone needs to be searched."

Dex's father lets go of the man they're holding to take the jar of pickles. "It's time we moved all the food to the kitchen and figured out our rations. I'll add this to the inventory."

People are spilling into the hallway now, having been woken by the commotion and keen to find out what their future holds. The anxious murmuring between them rises in volume and bounces off the walls.

Dex holds up his hand. "Quiet," he calls, knowing he needs to say something. He just wishes he knew what. Where's Kian when he needs him? He'd know what to say at a time like this.

A hush rolls down the hallway like a wave.

Clearing his throat, Dex rocks up onto his toes, trying to get eye contact with as many people as possible.

"When I walked into the ballroom and saw you all sitting there in the back corner of the room, I thought you were the bravest people we have left here." A sea of faces blinks back at him, and he focuses on them one at a time as he speaks. "You stood up to Ronan. You refused to bow down to evil. You were the ones who gave me the strength to fight when it would have been so much easier to tell Ronan what he wanted to hear."

"He's not my Commander," someone calls from the other end of the hallway.

Dex shakes his head. "He's not mine, either. People are only following him out of fear."

"We're scared, too," a woman says.

"I know you're scared." Dex gives her an encouraging smile. "The truth is that I'm also scared. We'd be fools not to be. What's happening out there is about as serious as it gets."

"What's the plan?" a deep voice calls from the crowd.

Dex looks at the anxious sea of faces, tempted to make a promise he knows he can't keep. He could soothe their fears with a few short sentences. Tell them something that will calm them. But he knows he can't do that. That's not the kind of leader he is. If he can even call himself a leader at all.

"We don't have a plan," he says.

Anger ripples across the crowd and Dex holds up his hand.

"Ronan sent us to the forest to die. But thanks to my father we were brought here instead. We have enough food to keep us alive for a couple of weeks—on limited rations, of course."

"Try one week," says a voice over near the door to the dining hall.

It's Thea. She hadn't been with the group of people who'd come here with Dex. She must have been one of the ones to arrive earlier with his father.

"I didn't know you were here, Thea," Dex says, relieved there's someone here who he trusts. "We're very lucky to have you."

But she's shaking her head. "I can't help you without proper medical supplies."

Dex's shoulders slump.

"What's happened to you brave people?" he asks, trying to pick his mood back up. "Where are the men and women who stood up to Ronan? Take a look at yourselves. You're stealing. You're fighting. You're pointing fingers at each other. That's no way to overcome what's been thrown at us. We need to work as a team. We need to support each other. Otherwise, there's no hope. We may as well walk out that door and let Ronan's guards take us down. Or lie down on this floor and starve to death."

The eyes in the room widen as they take in what he's saying. They can see it, too. They can see the light that's shining in this darkest of times.

"There are a lot of us here," Dex says. "Not as many as Ronan has on the Oasis, but we're the bravest souls Askala has to offer. If we work together, we can do this. We can come up with a plan and we can save ourselves. All is *not* lost."

"He's right," Bea calls out, raising her fist in the air. "We can do this."

More fists are raised and people call out their support, determination and hope permeating the air.

"We can do this," they chant. "We can do this!"

The lights blink as if they too are feeding off this newfound energy.

"We can do this!" shouts Dex.

But no sooner as the words leave his mouth, the lab is plunged into darkness and the constant low hum of the ventilation system shuts down.

He blinks, trying to process what this means.

"They've cut our power!" Was that Aarov's voice?

"He's trying to flush us out." That sounded like Bea.

"What are we going to do now?" That was definitely Thea.

This time Dex is silent, his body still, his mind whirling as he tries to think of something he can say to make this better.

But he comes up blank. It's so dark he can't see his hand in front of his face. And soon the air is going to become even more stale as the oxygen they depend on is seeped from it.

Somewhere out there a woman begins to cry.

Dex wishes he could join her. He doesn't want to be a leader. Not before this happened and not now.

Because the truth he doesn't want to admit to is that when those lights flickered and died, so had some of his hope.

He's not so sure they can do this.

He startles as he feels something at his legs. Putting his hand down, he touches a soft mop of hair, realizing it's a small child. Tiny arms wrap around Dex's legs, as the child mistakes him in the dark for their father. The soft sound of whimpering floats up to Dex's ears.

He ruffles the child's hair, trying to provide the only comfort he can.

This isn't fair. None of it is. This child should have been guaranteed a safe future growing up in Askala. And what do they have now? Certain death?

He can't let that happen. Not when this child hasn't even had a chance to live.

Dex knows he has to try harder. There has to be a way out of this mess.

They *can* do this. They will.

WREN

*W*ren's walked the perimeter of the lab so many times she's surprised she hasn't worn a ditch into the hard ground.

Two doors. That's it. Two ways in and two ways out. And both being heavily guarded by Cy's men.

She can't figure out another way in. That lab was built to withstand the strongest snowstorms. Whatever it's made from is impenetrable. There's a reason it's one of the only structures on the planet to have survived global warming intact.

Who would have thought its strength would one day become its weakness.

Each time she passes the severed power cable that leads into the lab, she feels sick. It must be so dark inside. So bleak. So... frightening. How long can the oxygen last without the air vents? How long can the people hold onto their sanity?

Cy's men have dug a hole to expose the pipe that takes water from the lake to be pumped into the lab. Without power the water will already be flowing at a trickle. But that's not enough for Cy. At first, he demanded the water supply be cut altogether.

But then he'd had a better idea.

Wren has to hold her nose as she passes the putrid pile of rotten plankton that's been pulled from the pod pool and left out to fester. Plankton that should've provided food for the life-sustaining pods and is now being used to poison the water supply.

Cy's made no mistake about it. He wants them all dead. Every one of the poor humans taking refuge inside.

And that includes Dex.

Phoenix should've taken the people to the forest. Despite the polar grizzlies, they'd have been safer out there. But even Phoenix hadn't known the depths of evil their father would stoop to. He'd led them straight into a trap. And now Cy has them exactly where he wants them. In one way it's fitting that he's feeding them plankton. Because they're no different to the pods in the pool right now. Turning in circles. Trapped. Hungry. Alive, but destined to die.

"Little bird."

Wren spins around to find Cy standing behind her. The last time she'd seen him, he'd been throwing chairs at the wall in the ballroom and making threats against her.

But he's smiling at her now with genuine affection in his eyes. This isn't unlike her father. His moods are as unpredictable as the weather. One minute he's like an angry storm and the next a gentle breeze rolls over and he's full of warmth and sunshine. These sudden swings in his mood are part of the reason he's so dangerous. He's impossible to predict.

"Dad," she says, deciding to follow Phoenix's lead and remind this man who he is to her.

His brows shoot up, unused to her using this name for him.

"I'm sorry about yesterday," she says, desperate to keep him on side if her plan has any chance of working. Like she explained to Phoenix, she has one last chance to try something here. "It was wrong of me to disrespect you like that."

"You love him, don't you?" Pain streaks across Cy's face.

198

"Of course, I do. He's my brother."

"Not Phoenix." Cy screws up his brow. "Mercy's son."

"Oh." Wren hesitates, unsure how to answer this. She doesn't want to put Dex in any more danger than he already is. "Why don't we go for a walk?"

"A walk?" Cy seems genuinely confused by this.

Wren puts a hand on his arm, giving him her most innocent of smiles. "There's something I've been wanting to show you. It would mean a lot to me."

"You're avoiding my question."

"No. I'd just like to walk while we talk. If that's okay with you? I have a lot to tell you. And show you."

Cy glances at his men.

"They can handle this," she reassures. "Come on. You won't regret it. Let's go while things are quiet here."

"Fine." Cy loops an arm across her shoulders and Wren leads him around to the back of the lab, past more guards and down the path into the forest.

The canopy of trees swallows them and she becomes aware of how much he's trusting her right now. A man who is said to trust nobody. She could pull a knife from her belt and stab him right now.

But she knows she'd never get away with that. Cy's men would know who did it. And they'd take great pleasure in doing the same to her. After they did things far worse.

And there's another problem with that plan.

As much as she hates this man beside her, she also loves him. She can't help it. He's the only parent she's ever known. And when he's not being awful to her, he's kind. Loving. Protective. There's a part of her that feels safe when he's around. Dex may wonder what his mother saw in him, but Wren knows. Mercy saw all the good parts along with the bad. A man made of shades and contrasts. A man so sure of himself that he doesn't care what anyone else thinks.

"I do love him," says Wren, stepping over a branch across the path. "I feel just the same for him as you did for Mercy."

"He's no good for you." Cy lets his arm fall from her shoulders. "Just look at who his father is."

"Callix didn't want to banish you," she says. "And he didn't want to burn the bridge. He's not your enemy, Dad."

"You could have any man that you want from my army." He ignores her comment, clearly not liking her argument. "Take your pick. You need a strong man from the Outlands. One who can fight for you."

"I can fight for myself." Wren clenches her fists as she grits her teeth. "I don't need a man for that."

"Have I failed you, little bird?" Cy glances at her before returning his eyes to the path. "Have I raised you to believe you're capable of more than you are? Men are stronger. Braver. Smarter. Don't tell me you don't need a man by your side."

Wren draws in a breath, choosing her words carefully. "When I arrived here I killed a leatherskin with nothing but a small knife. Did you know that? And I rescued a girl from a polar grizzly. I managed just fine on my own."

He doesn't look at her this time, seeming to be deciding if he believes her.

"I did lots of things," she continues. "And do you know which man was by my side? Dex was there every step of the way. He might not have the muscles of your men, but he's stronger than any of them. Because he's brave. And he's smart. And he would lie down right now and die for me if he had to."

"Well, that's fortunate, isn't it?" Cy scoffs.

"Don't let him die in that lab, Dad." She's pleading now in a way she never has with Cy before. "Please, don't let him die. You have to get him out of there."

"I learned to live without Mercy." He shakes his head. "You can do the same. It's too late to let anyone out of there now."

"It's not too late." She tries to keep her voice level and calm, contrasting with the rage that's boiling in the pit of her stomach. "Please, Dad."

The path inclines and they walk in silence for a little while. She's running out of options here just as fast as Dex must be running out of oxygen. If she can't convince Cy to let Dex out of that lab, there's no way she can break him out. He's going to die and she just knows there's a part of her that's going to stop breathing right along with him.

"You're taking me to the cliffs." Cy points ahead.

Her shoulders drop, disappointed. She'd hoped this wasn't a place he'd explored as a child. "You know about the cliffs?"

Cy laughs. "There's nothing in Askala that you can show me. I've seen it all."

"It's been almost two decades since you saw it," she says. "A lot can change in that time. A lot *has* changed."

"Are you sure you're not planning on pushing me off?" He doesn't make eye contact when he asks this question and Wren takes that as a warning. This is him letting her know that although he loves her, he doesn't fully trust her. Nor is he frightened of her.

"What would I have to gain by doing that?" She shoots him a grin.

"All of this." He extends his hands out to his sides, indicating the forest. "Without me, you and Phoenix could rule the world. One day, you will."

"The world isn't a place to be ruled," she says before she can stop herself. "Askala tried that and look what happened."

"Then what's your suggestion?"

She shrugs. "I don't have one. But I know that moving forward with peace is smarter than ruling by fear."

"I'll go to the cliffs with you," he says, not giving her words a moment's consideration. "But I'd prefer to do it without the lecture. You have no idea what you're talking about."

Wren bites down on her tongue to stop herself from

pointing out that she was the one who'd passed her Proving, when he'd failed. He wouldn't see that as an indication that she's smarter than him. It would only make him mad.

They walk on and Wren can only hope she hasn't ruined her plan before it even had a chance to begin. She'd intended to keep him on side. But it's possible she's pushed too far. He could snap into one of his bad moods at any moment.

They break through the trees and walk toward the cliff and Wren's relieved that, for now, Cy's mood has remained calm. She can only hope that translates to how he's really feeling on the inside.

"You're not puffing, are you?" He studies her and she knows he's counting the intervals between each breath she takes. "I trained you better than that."

"Not puffing." She focuses on slowing her breathing as she stops well short of the edge of the cliff. "Just excited to be here with you. I've wanted to show you these cliffs since I first saw them in my Proving."

"What was the test? A race down to the bottom? You'd have loved that." He laughs, well aware of her fear of heights.

"Collecting raven eggs." She points to one of the nests, her chest tightening as she looks at the steep drop. "We had to make a chain to get them safely to the top. A raven was swooping us and it was savage."

"Bet you were up here at the top of the chain." This time Cy laughs so hard he snorts.

Color rushes to her face. She hates that he's right. "Someone had to be at the top. It was an important job. I had to keep the eggs safe and make sure they didn't break."

She doesn't add that they ended up getting stolen by Felicia anyway.

"Your fear is a weakness, Wren. We've talked about this. You have to get over it. Focus on what strengths you lack and fix them. That's what I did." He straightens his back and lifts his chin, clearly proud of the man he's become. It's just a shame he's always been blind to his true weaknesses, pouring his energy into making himself physically stronger instead of smarter or kinder.

"Have a look at the view." She points, trying to draw his attention to the forest below. "Isn't it incredible?"

Cy sweeps his gaze across the land. The trees seem darker today with viridescent hues of emerald and jade woven between streaks of verdant pine. The sky is a deep blue with wispy clouds laced across it like a series of pulled threads. Birds are swooping between the treetops, circling the sky and calling to each other, the sound of their squawking echoing across the vast stretch of lush canopy. How can the exact same view that she's seen before look so different each time her eyes get a chance to feast on it?

"Not a bad kingdom I have myself here, is it?" Cy pushes out his chest and nods, like he really believes that he owns all of this. None of them do. Not him. Not her. Not anybody.

"I took Phee up here when he arrived." She dares to take a step closer to the edge, trying to ignore the way her pulse rises, pleased that Cy follows her. "He was amazed at how much life there is out there. Of how the land is capable of recovering when we give it the chance. The Outlands could be like this, if only—"

"If only what?" He turns to glare at her, not at all the reaction she'd been hoping for. "If only we weren't starving to death out there? People before trees, Wren. Some things are more important than a few plants and creatures with wings."

With a shaking hand, she places her palm on his back.

Her plan hasn't worked. She'd been hoping that seeing the beauty of this land would be enough to penetrate that thick skull of his and convince him this planet is worth saving. She'd wanted him to realize that although there'd been flaws in the way Askala had been ruled, there were also many strengths. But his greed has blinded him to Earth's majestic beauty. All he sees are the opportunities Askala presents to him personally. He doesn't care about the trees, or the creatures who call it home.

All he cares about is himself.

She feels the sheen of sweat on his back under her hand and she steadies herself. All it would take is one unexpected shove and just like Fern he'd be sent flying with the same shocked look plastered to his face.

But for all the reasons she'd thought of earlier, she knows she can't do it.

Still, it's tempting.

"Go on, Wren," he says, looking straight ahead. "Do it. You know you want to."

She freezes, hating that he knows her so well. Yet, somehow, he loves her anyway.

Her hand softens and she slides it around his waist, dipping her head to rest on his chest.

"Don't be ridiculous," she says. "You're my father."

He loops his arm around her and she wonders if that's a sign of affection or if he has plans of his own. She hasn't exactly been making his life easy lately.

His grip tightens and it's as if his fist is wrapped around her beating heart. If she were to disappear, nobody would question him. Except Phoenix, and she doubts he'd get very far.

"You're scared of me." Cy's tone is tinged with regret and it has hope soaring in her chest. "Mercy was, too. She never told me that, but I knew it. Your mother was frightened as well. Women have always stayed with me out of fear."

"Always doesn't have to mean forever." She does her best to keep her voice level. "Always can become *used to*. You transformed yourself once. It's not too late to do it again. You can reclaim the name Ronan and start again. Be a different man. Still strong, still respected. But no longer feared."

He holds still and for the first time it seems he's thinking about what she had to say. Maybe her plan hasn't failed. Maybe, just maybe, he can be the father she's always wanted him to be and the whiter shades of his gray can shine through in the darkness.

"A deer!" he hisses in a failed whisper, letting go of her to point. "It's a deer! I can't believe it. Do you see it?"

Wren looks down to see the deer she'd spotted with Phoenix. It's in the same clearing with the fawn off in the shadows, never far from the mother it depends on for survival.

"She's beautiful, isn't she?" Wren's eyes fill with tears at the privilege of seeing this fragile animal, not once but twice. "Do you see what's possible now?"

He nods, his eyes wide and shining, not shifting from the deer as it works its magic on him. The trees may not have been enough to show him what can be achieved when the land is respected but it seems this mother and her baby can.

Cy reaches into the side of his pants and pulls out something that takes Wren a few moments to recognize.

It's one of the slingshots from her Proving. Perhaps the very same one she'd used to save Nova from the polar grizzly.

"No! Cy, no! What are you doing?" She lets out an angry sob as he plucks a stone from his pocket and lines up his shot. "Don't. You can't!"

His leg swoops out in a practiced move that knocks Wren from her feet. She lands hard on her backside so close to the cliff that one of her arms dangles over the edge. Scrambling to regain her balance, she gets up and throws herself at Cy in an attempt to bring him to the ground. It's the only thing she can do to give the deer a chance to flee.

But even as she's in the air hurtling toward him, she knows she's too late. The stone has left the slingshot and is zinging down to the trees.

She slams into Cy's legs and he stumbles, landing hard on the ground beside her.

"What have you done?" she screams, trying to disentangle herself from him. "What have you done?"

He's holding on tightly to her now, his fingers locked around her wrists, preventing her from following the trajectory of that potentially lethal stone.

"You want to see what I've done, do you?" He pins her to the ground and she winces as he bears down on her with his full weight.

"They're endangered," she says. "We thought they were extinct."

"Well, maybe they are now." He turns his face to look down to the clearing. "Because if I do say so myself, that was an excellent shot."

Wren wriggles, desperate to free herself. But she's locked tight between the hard ground and Cy's muscled frame. Giving in, she falls limps, letting her cries of protest morph into sobs of futility. She can't get away from Cy any more than she could have saved that deer. In fact, it's all her fault. If she hadn't brought him up here then this would never have happened.

"I've always wanted to know what venison tastes like." Cy crawls off her, keeping hold of her wrist.

She's never heard the word for deer meat before. She wishes the word had no need to exist.

Getting to her feet, she leans out to get a better look at the clearing. The mother deer is lying on the forest floor, perfectly still. Its baby is sniffing at her, nudging her with its nose, trying to rouse her from the sleep from which she'll never wake.

Cy lets go of her wrist to load his slingshot once more.

Wren stands passively beside him, watching.

Waiting.

With one small rock clutched tightly in her hand.

Just before Cy lets his slingshot loose, Wren flings the rock hard toward the baby deer, aiming for the thick hide of its rump, hoping her stone will find its mark before Cy's.

Cy curses and fires off his shot. Tucking the slingshot back in his pants in one quick movement, he grips her wrist once more and they watch as the two rocks sail through the air.

"Run!" Wren cries, hoping to scare the baby into motion. "Run!"

The deer looks up at her just as her rock skims across its hind leg and it kicks back, pulling away in time before Cy's rock sails past its head. It takes off, running into the undergrowth and Wren hopes with everything she has that it's old enough to survive out there alone.

At least now it has a chance. That has to count for something.

"You soft-hearted fool!" Cy drags her towards the edge of the cliff and finds a foothold just below.

She resists, pulling back, but he's twice her size. Possibly, triple her strength.

With her heart beating faster than it ever has before, she flings herself to the ground, clawing at the dirt as he forces her off the edge.

Cy loses his grip on her and scrambles down the steep rockface with gravity insisting that she follow. He stumbles and trips and she loses sight of him as her worst nightmare comes true. She'd rather fight a leatherskin than see the ground so far away from her. Ground that is coming up way too fast.

She tumbles, rolls, grapples with anything her fingernails can find, but there's nothing she can do except wince at each bump, yelp with each scratch and curse with every heartbeat between.

How could she have possibly thought that innocent creature had worked any magic on a man who clearly has no heart?

The ground starts to even out and Wren fights to gain control over the momentum that's propelling her toward the clearing.

But it's no use. She's moving too fast, leaving her no choice but to ride this out until the very end.

The bottom of the cliff is covered in soft grass and hitting it is a sweet relief. She comes to a stop almost as suddenly as she began and is left lying on her back, arms and legs splayed, chest rising and falling, heart hammering, and head spinning.

She's alive. Injured but not badly. Scared but not defeated.

And certain of one thing.

She is *done* with Cy.

He'll never be the father she's always wanted. Because he's not the man she thought he could be. He doesn't love her. There are no white shades in his gray.

Lifting her head from the grass, she sees Cy drooling over the body of that beautiful animal. She wonders at what precise moment it stopped being a deer and became venison. Most likely the same moment its heart failed to take another beat. Perhaps it was always venison to a man like Cy.

She adds the animal to the list of those she's failed.

It's too late for her to do anything about it.

But it's not too late for her to save Dex. She needs to try harder. She knows that now. She's failed him far too many times already.

And if she can't get him out of the lab, then she needs to find a way to get herself in.

This time she's not going to run from Dex. This time, she's going to run straight back into his arms.

Exactly where she belongs.

NOVA

a s sleep dissolves from Nova's consciousness, she realizes she's waking feeling rested and rejuvenated. And safe.

When she registers the heartbeat steadily thumping beneath her ear, she realizes why.

Jolting her head up, her gaze meets Kian's. His dark eyes caress her, so full of love that Nova's heart swells.

"Good morning," he murmurs softly. "Everyone else is gone, but you were sleeping so soundly…"

"Kian." She whispers his name, still not quite believing it.

He came for her. He left his beloved Askala to find her.

There wasn't enough time to talk in any depth with Avis and the others around. The excitement of six new people in less than two days was too much for the people of Fairbanks. Annabel had trailed them, peppering them with questions. There were people to meet, food to eat, sleeping quarters to sort out. Flick had graciously vacated the little nest she'd shared with Nova the night before, glaring at Kian as she stalked past and warning him that he better not hurt her best friend ever again. Shiloh had stared at Nova with a sadness that was hard to explain. Finn had smiled. Dean's glance had been hard and cold.

As it turned out, there were too many words that needed to be said. Questions, explanations...apologies. So, they barely said a thing. Their gazes, the hands that didn't release the other, the bodies that seemed to be glued together, had said it all.

I've found you and I'm not letting go.

Kian lifts a hand, his fingers brushing her cheek. Nova leans into the touch, his hand cupping her cheek. She wants to close her eyes and lose herself in the sensation, but she can't bring herself to look away. It's like her mind has been devouring every change that has happened since she left—the way his skin has darkened from copper to bronze, the way he holds his shoulders as if he now carries a new truth.

The way his eyes promise nothing will ever tear them apart again.

"I'm so sorry, Nova."

"Shh," she smiles. "We've both made mistakes."

But Kian shakes his head. "No, I made a mistake and it was the catalyst for a whole lot of other mistakes. I should never have let you go." He lifts her left hand, caressing it tenderly, never pausing or hesitating as he brushes over the stump of her missing finger. "I shouldn't have let Askala define you, me, or us."

An ache clutches at the back of Nova's throat, and she realizes she's holding back tears. She doesn't want to cry right now, even if they're bittersweet tears of happiness. This moment is nothing but pure joy.

Nova slips further up, her body grazing over Kian's in the most delicious way. "And yet it only made us stronger. It showed us what's important. I can't regret that."

Kian groans as his mouth descends on hers. Up until now, their kisses have been brief. Limited by an audience. Fleeting touches to confirm this is reality.

This kiss, though, is the culmination of weeks of separation. Of the fear they'd never find each other again.

A consummation of a love that was tested and yet triumphed.

Their lips meld, their bodies press tight. Kian's hands spear into Nova's hair as she clings to his shoulders. Heat builds and groans escape. Passion soars, pulses spike, mouths smile and sigh and savor.

Nova has never felt so...complete.

They pull apart, panting and smiling.

Nova leans in, wanting for this to never end, but she realizes there are more words. Words that are desperate to be said. She pulls in a steadying breath. "I'm pregnant, Kian. I don't know how, but I am."

Kian's eyes glow. "Dex and your mother told me—they were so worried about you. But hearing you say it..."

Gently, he flips them around, his fingers splaying over her abdomen. "This baby is proof, Nova. That love knows no bounds."

This time, there's no stopping the tear that spills down her cheek. "Our child," she whispers. "A miracle."

Kian leans down, laying a tender kiss where his hand just was. "You were born of love," he promises their unborn child. "No matter what comes, you'll be raised surrounded by love." Looking up, Kian's eyes blaze with the promise in his words. "I love you, Nova."

Nova feels like she could float away any moment. "I I—"

"Are you guys even awake yet?" Flick's half-shouted question has them jolting. "You do know breakfast is almost over, don't you?"

A breathless giggle escapes Nova as Kian rolls his eyes. "We should be getting up," she says, already mourning the little escape they had.

With a quick kiss, Kian pushes himself upright. "For the first time in a long time, I'm looking forward to facing the world." Holding his hand out to Nova, he grins. "Let's go eat some more bugs."

When Nova laughs, she realizes how alien it feels. How often has that sound bubbled up from within her since the Proving? Taking Kian's hand, she lets him haul her up. As he clasps her to him, she decides the past isn't where she wants to dwell right now.

She's with Kian. She's carrying his child. They're safe. And that's all that matters.

Flick's hands hike to her hips as she huffs. "About time. Annabel offered five times to look after"—she puts hefty emphasis on the last words—"your cups if you weren't going to get here in time."

Nova glances at Flick's empty hands. "And Annabel won?"

"I gave the cups to Dean for safekeeping. He refuses to eat the cockroaches, and everyone is scared of him."

Nova feels Kian tense and she wonders what brought Dean to the Outlands considering he seems so unhappy to be here. Another discussion they'll need to have.

They make their way out, weaving around the roots of the mangrove pine branching like a network of rivers and the beds that are tucked between them.

Up on the next level, Nova discovers the colony is already alive with movement. It's busier than it was yesterday, people seeming to move around with purpose. They're still a few yards away from the kitchen when there's a squeal of happiness.

"Nova! Kian! I missed you!"

Annabel comes barreling at them, throwing her stocky arms around them both as she hugs them enthusiastically. There's so much excitement quivering through her that Nova finds herself smiling.

"Good morning, Annabel. How wonderful to see you."

Annabel pulls back, grinning. "You slept in. That's good for the baby."

Nova flushes, pleasure at those words filling her with warmth. Talking out loud about the child she's carrying is something she hasn't allowed herself to do. "It is."

"I'll help you look after the baby, Nova. Just like Kian will."

So trusting, so sure of the goodness in this world. Impulsively, Nova gives Annabel another hug. "You have a beautiful heart, Annabel."

It's Annabel's turn to blush. "I wanted to eat your cockroaches," she confesses quietly.

Kian chuckles. "That's because Clint does such an amazing job roasting them."

Nova glances at him, impressed that he remembered Clint's name after their brief tour last night. She squeezes his hand. "So true. It's hard to say no when they're cooked like that."

Annabel's smile returns with gusto. She spins around, calling over her shoulder as she trots away. "I've gotta go. I have a lot to do today."

She heads to the other end of the parking lot where several other people are sitting. Kian glances at Nova, his eyebrows raised in question, but she shrugs. She doesn't know much more about Fairbanks than he does.

The tables scattered around Clint's kitchen are largely empty. She doesn't see Shiloh anywhere, but Dean is there, sitting alone. Looking to the left, Nova blinks twice. Dharma and Finn sit at another, talking animatedly. Dharma is almost... smiling.

Nova heads to Dean's table, not wanting to disturb whatever's happening there, but also wanting to get a sense of what having Dean here is going to mean. She feels Kian tense as he realizes her intent, but she doesn't change trajectory, tugging him down as she takes a seat.

"Good morning, Dean," she says warmly.

Dean glances at her, his eyes slightly narrowed. "Ah, Nova. The girl we risked our lives to come and save." He leans back, slanting a look at Kian. "And didn't need saving at all."

"Dean." Kian bites off the warning but before he can say any more, Nova jumps in.

"I'd like to thank you for everything you've done." She grasps Kian's hand under the table. "Our baby is going to have a future I'm truly looking forward to."

Dean straightens in surprise. He shifts his gaze to Kian for confirmation, only looking more shocked when Kian nods. "Well, I'll be…" he breathes.

"Our child will not be defined by Bound or Unbound," Kian states. "The way it should be."

Dean flops back, his mouth slightly agape. "Does good ol' Magnus know about this?"

Kian tenses again and before he can talk, Nova grabs one of the cups in the middle of the table. "You're not eating, Dean?"

Dean curls his lip. "Those things aren't coming anywhere near my mouth."

Nova shrugs. "They actually taste better than pods, and they don't stick to the roof of your mouth." She fishes one of the cockroaches out of the cup nearest to her and pops it in.

She can't help the grimace as the carapace crunches between her teeth, but she swallows without gagging. That's progress from last night.

Kian grabs one of the other cups. "Hey, if Annabel recommends them, I'm in."

Nova watches, a little fascinated, as Kian mimics her action. He doesn't look at the insect he picks up, he even closes his eyes as he puts it in his mouth. He chews the fastest she's ever seen.

A giggle escapes her and Kian's eyes fly open, their dark depths alight with amusement. He swallows and she passes him the cup of water. He drinks it down in three gulps. This time, Nova laughs out loud.

When Kian is looking at her again, he's grinning. "I missed that sound."

"Me, too." Nova leans toward him. "Thank you for bringing it back into my life."

Kian's face softens with tenderness. "I have some lost time to make up for."

They kiss, Nova reveling in the emotion that's weaving around them. There's so much of it, it's almost palpable. When they pull back, she turns to find Dean gone.

Kian glances at the table. "At least he took his cups."

"He'll come around," Nova assures him. "Things are very different here."

There's the sound of footsteps behind them. "Different how?"

Nova and Kian spin around to find Avis approaching them, her head angled as she smiles. "And different to where?"

Nova glances at Kian. Neither of them have mentioned they're from Askala.

That, technically, Kian's the leader of Askala.

Kian rises so he can pull out a chair for Avis. The brow on her unscarred side lifts as she takes a seat. Avis rearranges the folds of netting around her. "You know you don't need to answer that question. I already know you're from Askala."

"You do?" Nova asks in surprise.

Avis rolls her eyes. "No one is as well fed or dressed in the Outlands. Plus, now that Askala has fallen, it's logical people would be fleeing."

Askala has fallen. That's what the boy was calling out when she was in the village. Dread feels like icy tar in Nova's gut. "What do you mean, fallen?"

Kian weaves his fingers through hers. "Ronan arrived with a small army of Remnants." Pain laces his words. "He used force to secure his place as leader. I left before I saw what else he had planned."

"Oh, no," Nova gasps. "That's horrible."

Her mother is there. Everyone she cares for. Her hand flies to her stomach. *Maybe she got out just in time...*

Kian looks to Avis. "I came here for Nova, but also to get answers. Ronan has to be stopped."

Avis's hand clenches on the table. "That man has taken too much for too long."

Kian leans forward, his body tense with focus. "What do you know about him?"

"More than most."

Nova grips Kian's arm. "Kian, I'd like you to meet Wren's mother."

Kian's brows shoot for the stratosphere and Nova almost smiles. Now that she knows the truth, she can see the resemblance. The short stature and nimble body, the dark hair that refuses to be tamed.

The eyes that don't miss even the smallest detail.

Kian glances at Nova. "Ronan is Wren and Phoenix's father," he states quietly, his eyes widening as the pieces fall together.

Nova nods. "Ronan took them. Only by then, he was calling himself Cy."

"He stole them," Avis snarls. "They were just babies."

Nova reaches out to clasp Avis's clenched hand. It's vibrating with pain and anger. "You don't have to tell us if you don't want to."

Avis's eyes blaze. "This is his shame, not mine." She leans back, squeezing Nova's hand before drawing away. "You need to know."

Nova nods, waiting. Kian is tense beside her, probably realizing this won't be an easy story to hear.

Avis looks away, watching the people milling about. It's just as well Dean has left the table. "Cy arrived like you did. Out of nowhere, looking vibrant and healthy in a way we hadn't seen in the Outlands. He just strutted into our village like we were lucky to have him there."

Nova never met him, but she can imagine the scene Avis is painting. A young male, tall and no doubt charismatic. "You were drawn to him."

"We all were. My father, the chief of the village, believed he could help us somehow. Maybe show us some way to find food." Avis frowns. "And that's exactly what Cy promised."

"He was like a man possessed. The moment he learned of the city, he started scouring it. Sometimes he caught rabbits, but mostly he trained the men. He told them they needed to be strong for when they took what they deserved." Avis shudders. "And then he found a stash of flamethrowers."

Kian tenses. "That's what he used to threaten us in Askala. No one stood a chance."

Nova's heart aches thinking of everyone there, so frightened and confused. Askala wasn't built for war.

It's a place of peace.

"Well, neither did we, it turns out," responds Avis. "He found them somewhere in the city, along with enough fuel to terrorize us for as long as he needed. If someone didn't swear allegiance, they didn't survive. He razed entire villages until they looked no different to the burnt Outlands that surround us."

Avis glances at Nova's midriff. "By then I was pregnant, having fallen for his charms just like everyone else. When I gave birth to twins, I was…" Avis looks up, holding Nova's gaze. "I've never felt such joy. Phee, big and strapping, Wren, so small and fragile. They were my light in a world that was now little more than ash."

Nova doesn't say anything. It hurts to know this story doesn't have a happy ending.

"They were two when Cy started training them. He'd become the self-proclaimed Commander by then. He said if they could walk, they could train." Avis's voice cracks. "They were so little, so confused. They just wanted to please him, but he turned into someone harsh and cruel. He told them over and over that they now had a job. One thing to prepare for."

Avis doesn't need to say what that is. Ronan wanted to return to Askala a powerful leader. He wanted to return to Mercy.

Nova wonders what it will mean now that Ronan has learned Mercy is dead.

"The bastard," Kian mutters.

Avis doesn't seem to hear him. She's lost in the painful memories. "I knew I couldn't sit by and let it happen. I planned, packed what food and water I could scrounge together. I decided to run when everyone was asleep. But Wren woke when I moved her away from Phee. Cy realized what was happening. He took them." Avis brushes a tear from her scarred cheek. "And when I tried to stop him, he took a flamethrower to me."

Bile coats Nova's throat as tears prickle her eyes. Kian must sense her distress because he reaches out and strokes her back. She leans into him, conscious his comfort makes the horror of Avis's story bearable.

"As I lay on the dirt, screaming in pain he told me that if I ever tried to take the children, he'd kill Wren. He believed she was the weakest one. He said she was as replaceable as I was."

Avis's eyes flutter shut. "I ran. Skin melting, every nerve on fire, I ran." She opens them again, looking around the parking lot. "And I came here."

Nova sags like the weight of all the sadness in Avis's voice is too much. "I'm so sorry, Avis."

Kian leans forward, his jaw tense. "Wren isn't weak."

Avis's gaze flies to his, fierce despite the pain. "She never was."

Kian's lips twitch. "She drove me nuts when she arrived. She questioned everything, pointed out anything that wasn't fair." He shrugs. "She's a fighter...like her mother."

Nova's heart warms as Avis's eyes prick with tears. Those were the words she needed to hear.

"It's true," she adds. "Wren fought for what she believed is right. I always respected her for that."

Avis pulls in a shuddering breath, straightening. As Nova watches, she sees a woman who's endured great loss and has come out stronger on the other side. "Fairbanks became my haven, it only seemed right that it should be for others. If I couldn't save my children, then at least I could help others who are just as vulnerable."

"You've helped a lot of people," Nova states. "That took courage."

An empty cup slams on the table, making them all jump. "What takes courage is eating those things," growls Dean.

Avis jerks back so hard her chair scrapes across the floor. Her eyes are wide as she stares at him in horror.

Nova reaches out to place a calming hand on her arms. "Avis, it's Dean."

The brother who looks just like Ronan. After reliving those traumatic memories, it would be difficult to see someone who resembles him so much.

Dean steps back, his lips a thin line. "Believe me, I want him dead as much as you do."

Avis looks away. "I'll believe that when I see your word is more trustworthy than his."

Nova watches as Dean stalks away, his shoulders tight with anger. Only time will show if he can be trusted...

KIAN

*A*vis stands, almost looking like she's shaking off the past. "Actually, before you tell me about this Askala that Cy was so desperate to have, let me show you the rest of Fairbanks."

Kian rises as Avis turns away, understanding her need to change the topic. Even if Avis didn't resemble Wren, once he knew the truth, it quickly became apparent they're related. This woman hasn't let the world define or limit her. She's fought for what she believes is right.

He just hopes Wren does the same.

Nova stands, too, and the moment she does, Kian tucks her into his side. She should never have left there.

He should never have let her go.

He brushes his lips over the crown of her head, breathing in deeply, filling himself with her essence. He has a lot of wrongs to make right.

Finding Nova was only the beginning.

Nova slips her hand into his, gripping it tightly, and Kian's whole body smiles. Finding Nova was the start of fixing this.

Avis walks ahead and Kian and Nova follow. He can understand that Avis needs to ground herself in the future she built rather than the past that took so much from her. She leads them to the back corner where several people are sitting, Annabel among them.

As they approach, Kian sees that Annabel is intensely focused on whatever she's doing with her hands, the pink of her tongue sticking out from the corner of her mouth. He quickly realizes she's weaving, a small square loom sitting in her lap, lengths of netting folded around her.

Avis leans over toward Kian and Nova, speaking quietly. "The netting that keeps the insects away was the first thing we needed to create if we were going to live in Fairbanks. We discovered that the tannin from the pine needles could be boiled down and mixed with anything we could shred to make a strong thread." She points to the layers wrapped around her. "Now we can move around the city without worrying about the mosquito-borne diseases that killed so many."

A young man, one leg stretched straight with his foot angling out oddly, is sitting next to Annabel. He shows her the fabric he's working on and Annabel murmurs something to him, pointing at it. He nods and grins, starting up again.

Avis smiles, pride softening her features. "Annabel took to weaving like she was born to it. She oversees all the netting we produce."

Kian can't help the shock he feels. Someone like Annabel would never have a role in Askala, let alone a leadership one. Shame burns low in his gut at the stark contrast between the colonies.

Avis grins at Kian. "And the tighter the weave, the stronger the elasticity."

Which is what he must've landed on when he leaped off the beam, trying to save the little boy.

Avis steps back, indicating she doesn't want to disturb the weavers. The moment they're out of earshot, Kian knows he needs answers. Those terrifying moments when he was weightless, gravity spearing him to the ground, won't be fading any time soon.

The boy said it was a test… "That's a pretty extreme way to welcome someone to Fairbanks."

Avis shrugs. "I have a responsibility to protect the people who've come here. What better way to ensure each person who wants to enter is willing to sacrifice for others?"

Kian's arm tightens around Nova's shoulder. "Except you believe you're going to die when you jump off that thing."

"You passed, Kian, as have others. But there have been plenty of people who followed Luca up the beam and just watched him fall, walking away as they shook their heads. How do you think they'll treat the others here?"

Nova tightens her grip on Kian's waist. "Before we were born, when the bridge still existed, there was a test to enter Askala. Except…"

Nova doesn't finish the sentence, but it doesn't matter. Avis does it for her. "People died when they failed. It was well known no one came back when they entered the bridge." She impales Kian with her gaze. "Which do you think is kinder?"

Kian doesn't respond. He can't. Avis is right. Askala has done a lot under the guise of kindness. But if his father were here, he'd be pointing out they did it for something bigger than themselves.

They were doing it for Earth.

Somehow, Kian has to find a way to reconcile that.

"Avis!" comes a high-pitched wail filled with indignation. "They won't let me go!"

Kian jolts with surprise when he sees the little boy he followed up the beam. Luca. The boy who jumped off it like he was wearing a parachute.

Avis squats down. "Luca, you know you can't go."

"But I've grown. I'm big enough now."

"You have grown," Avis says, tucking his shirt into his pants. "But not enough. The city is too dangerous."

Luca scowls. "The city doesn't scare me."

"That's what worries me," Avis chuckles as she straightens. "Nothing scares you, Luca."

Dharma appears, several others with her, and Kian notices Finn is among them. They're all swathed in layers of netting. "Sorry, Avis. We tried to sneak off without him noticing."

Luca crosses his arms. "You tripped a wire I set up by the main entrance. You're not going without me."

Probably similar to the wire that triggered the slab of concrete almost falling on Kian and the others.

Avis places a hand on Luca's shoulder. "Soon Luca, but not today. And they're only collecting water, anyway."

Kian notices the medley of containers the people are carrying, Finn helping Dharma carry a particularly large bucket as they each hold a handle.

Luca pouts, his lower lip trembling. The poor boy looks devastated.

Kian turns to Avis. "Jumping off that beam has got to be the scariest thing I've ever done. I can't believe people put their hand up for that job."

Avis's eyes twinkle. "We don't have many volunteers."

"Only me." Luca jabs a thumb into his chest. "None of the adults want to do it."

"You have a very important job then, Luca," Kian says, injecting his voice with respect. "You keep Fairbanks safe."

Luca puffs up at Kian's words. "Avis says my mama would be proud."

Kian grins. "I bet she would be. You're doing a job no one else can do."

"It must keep you very busy." Nova nods sagely.

Luca turns to Avis, chewing his lip. "I don't have time to collect water. I've got guard duty."

Without waiting, Luca darts off. Avis watches him go, her face sad but tender. "His mother left him at the edge of the city, nothing but a baby wrapped in rags. She either hoped someone would find him, or she simply wanted to leave him somewhere she couldn't hear his cries."

Nova's intake of breath is quiet, but Kian hears it. It tugs at his heart. She's no doubt thinking of their own baby. Of what a mother would have to go through to leave her child like that. Kian presses a kiss to her hair, telling her without words she never has to worry she'll face that.

The others turn to leave, too, adjusting their netting as they reach the door so it covers their faces. Kian notes one woman is missing a hand, just like Dex, although the amputation has occurred much further up her arm. The container she's carrying has a length of rope attached that's looped over her shoulder. She's contributing to the colony, anyway, and judging by her smile, she's enjoying it.

Dex probably would've felt much differently about his stump if he'd grown up in Fairbanks.

"They all have something to do," Nova muses as they watch them slip through the netting that keeps the parking lot relatively insect free.

Avis nods. "Everyone has a role at Fairbanks."

This time, the shame laps at Kian's cheeks. He fought so hard for what Askala stood for. The same society that relegated Nova and so many like her as having no use. If Dex had been Unbound, what sort of life would he have led?

Nova presses a hand to his chest. "You left that behind, Kian. Unlike those before you, you realized it was wrong."

Kian isn't surprised that Nova knew exactly what he was thinking. He lifts her hand to his lips. "Largely, because I lost you. What my heart knew and what my brain told me was true no longer aligned." In fact, they were at war with each other.

"And you listened to your heart. That's what counts."

Tenderly, Kian kisses Nova's fingertips. This girl is his hope and his salvation. He was right that he couldn't move forward without her.

Avis clears her throat. "Shall we continue?"

Grinning, Kian pulls away. "Lead the way, Avis."

This time, Avis heads to the ramp that will take them to the level above. It opens out into what must've been the foyer of the building they're beneath. Now, it's overtaken by the trunk of the mangrove pine that's dominated the manmade tower of decay. Branches jut out at regular intervals, breaking walls and shattering windows as the pine reaches up so high Kian can't see the top.

He eyes the crumbling walls and smashed glass. "Is this place safe?"

"Nowhere is safe anymore, Kian," Avis replies. "We're out of harm's way as much as we can be here."

Knowing there's little reassurance in Avis's words doesn't make Kian feel any more comfortable. He keeps Nova close as they walk around the massive girth of the pine tree.

They've only made it a quarter of the way when they come across more people of Fairbanks. They each have a basket on their hip as they squat or kneel down at the base of the trunk, rifling through the debris accumulated there.

One elderly man, his face broad and flat, crows with excitement as he grabs something. He holds up his prize for others to see—a cockroach. There are cheers and claps as he places it in his basket before he bends over, looking for more.

"This is where much of our food comes from. The bugs, but also the seeds of the mangrove pine."

Nova angles her head. "I thought they were poisonous."

Kian remembers the soup he and Nova made as children, trying to help while they waited for the pod numbers to build up again. He shudders at the memory of the violent nausea it caused.

"They are," Avis agrees. "If you don't bake them then peel off the flesh of the seed."

Nova looks up at Kian. "That would've been good to know."

Kian grins. "It sure would've been."

There's another cheer and handful of claps and Avis smiles. "It's the cockroaches that provide most of our food, though."

Kian watches as these people painstakingly pick through the litter. "Have you thought about breeding them?"

Avis glances at him. "We tried several times, but were unsuccessful. Breeding them would mean a regular protein supply for a lot less effort."

Kian scratches his chin. "It's a matter of figuring out what their optimal conditions are. Obviously they need somewhere to hide." He glances around, noting the warmth and humidity. "Somewhere warm and moist." Squatting down, Kian scans the litter around him. "What do they eat?"

"The adults will eat anything they find. That we could take care of. It's once the eggs hatched that we kept losing them." Avis shrugs. "The nymphs always died."

Kian thinks of the pteropods and how his mother studied their life cycle, discovering all the factors that affected their numbers—food, water, their environment.

"I can't believe I'm saying this"—for some reason breeding cockroaches doesn't feel as impressive as breeding pods—"but I suspect it's simply a matter of setting up some testing populations. You adjust a different variable in each population, you start getting some answers."

Avis nods thoughtfully. "That makes sense." She looks at Kian, her eyes assessing. "Everyone has a purpose in Fairbanks."

Kian doesn't point out he won't be here that long. Askala needs him. But teaching someone else how to do something like this is pretty straightforward. He's confident they could start breeding their primary food source much sooner than they think.

Nova pulls away as she peers more closely at the trunk of the tree. "Are those footholds?"

"Ah, yes. Luca dug those in." Avis states. "He uses the tree as his lookout sometimes."

Nova cranes her neck as she tries to catch sight of the top. "It's very high."

"You can see for miles from up there. It's been very useful."

Someone calls out for Avis and she excuses herself. Nova takes a few steps one way then the other, her eyes still skyward. "It really is quite high."

Something in Nova's tone has Kian pausing. "I doubt Luca thinks of safety first."

Nova lifts a hand to her hip, angling her head as she stands beside the tree. "It seems the protectiveness hasn't changed."

Kian raises a brow. "I can't see that it will, either."

"I'm not the scared, weak girl I was, Kian."

"You were never weak." Kian shakes his head to emphasize the point. "And you're the bravest person I know."

Nova stood up for the Unbound in a way he'd never seen before. She left the only place she'd ever known because she believed it would keep their baby safe.

"Then it would make sense that I'd climb this tree."

Kian's eyes widen, not quite sure he heard her right. "Pardon?"

But Nova isn't standing before him anymore. She's already scaled the first few footholds to grip onto the lowest branch.

"Hey!" he calls out, rushing to follow her.

Nimbly, Nova clambers up to the next branch, giggling. It's a sound so full of delight that Kian finds himself grinning. "Wait up."

Nova climbs several more branches, twisting and hauling her way up before she stops. She wraps her arms around the narrowing trunk as she stands on a branch. Her eyes dance with amusement. "Do you remember the last time we did this, Kian?"

They would've been about fourteen, maybe fifteen. A game had turned vertical as Nova had tried to escape him. He'd finally caught her, high up in the boughs. They'd stood there, like this, arms wrapped around the trunk, gazing at their newfound view.

Askala was magnificent, verdant and alive. A glorious testament of everything their colony was working toward.

But Nova had been far more captivating, practically glowing with happiness.

They'd leaned forward, the air thick with green and pine. They'd almost kissed...

Except they'd jerked back at the last moment, guilt flushing their cheeks. That part of their love was forbidden.

Not until they passed their Proving.

"I remember," Kian whispers hoarsely.

It was a beautiful, breathless moment. One that was severed by the laws he never questioned.

Kian leans his chest against the trunk, his hands coming up to cup Nova's face. "I should've seen it, back then."

"Neither of us did." Nova's blue eyes captivate him all over again. "This time we can do it differently," she breathes.

This time, there's no pulling back. There's no denying the hearts that want to beat as one. Kian kisses Nova.

Or maybe Nova kisses Kian.

It doesn't matter. Their lips brush, a chaste kiss. A blending of breaths. A sweet rewriting of history.

Nova's hand brushes his cheek. "I love you, Kian."

Kian's heart soars. How he's ached to hear those words. They set something free within him. He smiles when all he wants to do is laugh. He holds still although all he wants to do is dance. He whispers the words back even though he wants to shout them.

"I love you, too, Nova. I loved you before I knew what love was."

Nova's smile is dazzling. "Let's go to the top," she whispers excitedly.

Kian grins. "I'm already on top of the world."

Nova's laughter trills through the branches, sending Kian's heart chasing after it. With a quick press of her lips against his, she scampers up higher. Kian follows her, conscious of the world disappearing beneath them, watching each foothold Nova places.

Rationally, he knows he and Nova grew up celebrating nature. Climbing trees came as naturally as swimming in the lake or running through the forest.

But his heart knows keeping Nova safe is necessary for it to remain whole. He will always be her safety net.

The branches become more tightly packed the higher they climb, but suddenly, the building falls away and sunlight explodes around them. The pine continues up, having left behind the walls it fractured long ago, shading them as they have an unobstructed view of the Outlands.

"Oh, Kian." Nova's voice is full of the desolation they're looking over.

Miles and miles, horizon to horizon, of...black desert.

Kian swallows the bile that's razing his throat. Vast tracts of land aren't supposed to look like this. They're supposed to have some sign of life.

But all that breaks this charcoal world is the odd town scattered like rubbish. Everywhere else is death. Dead tree stumps. Dead soil. Even the air seems to hang over it all, dead.

Kian and Nova grasp one another, instinctively needing the support of the other. Kian points to the left. Even a village, the only attempt at color in this ashen landscape, has been burned.

"Ronan," he states flatly.

Nova shakes her head. "It's so sad."

"This is what we take back to Askala, Nova. We know what

he's capable of. What could happen if we don't stop him. We have to warn the others."

Nova's hand goes limp in his. "What? Go back?"

Something in Kian stills. "Of course we have to go back. Askala needs us."

"Kian." Nova's voice holds a note Kian wishes he wasn't hearing. "I'm not leaving Fairbanks."

Their hands fall apart and Kian has to grip the trunk of the mangrove pine. "But..."

Nova's eyes plead with his. "Surely, you have to see this is the safest place to raise our child."

The breeze whips Nova's golden hair across her face, but the truth shines from her eyes. Askala is at war. The Outlands are full of violence and degradation.

Fairbanks is a haven for those who need it most.

The closeness they've been reveling in disintegrates. Suddenly, the distance between them feels like it's growing, yawning as wide as the horizons they were just gazing at.

And Kian is the only one who can bring them back together.

The realization hits him hard, feeling like it could knock him right off the branch. The choice he's going to have to make comes at him at the same speed the ground would.

The same choice he was forced to make after their Proving.

Nova.

Or Askala.

Finding it, he pulls on the familiar weight as a most unfamiliar sight greets him.

Light. A glorious slither of it that grows the more he pulls on the hatch.

He blinks, wondering if he's seeing things. Is it possible to imagine light in the same way a thirsty man sees a mirage in the desert?

But when the hatch folds back to reveal the not-so-secret-anymore room, several sets of eyes blink up at him, their faces glowing from some kind of light source they've found.

"Who's up there?" someone calls. "Is that you Marieke?"

"It's Dex."

He swings his leg over to the ladder and the room below plunges into darkness once more.

"What's going on?" he asks as he steps down, rung by rung. "What happened to the light?"

Reaching the bottom, he stands with his hand in front of his face and his maimed arm crossed in front of his chest. The sounds of breathing are the only indication he didn't imagine the startled faces that'd stared up at him before the light source had been extinguished.

"Is anyone going to tell me what's going on?" he asks. "Can you turn that torch back on, please?"

Silence.

Then, eventually, a female voice pipes up. "It wasn't a torch."

"Well, whatever it was, then." He shakes his head, not having time for semantics. "Turn it back on."

Nothing happens.

Dex sighs. "The good news is that I've cleared my busy schedule today and I'm able to wait for you to turn that light back on."

Still nothing.

"Come on, guys!" Dex almost groans now. "We're supposed

to work as a team here. You can show me what you were doing. Nobody's going to be in trouble."

Then he sees it. A soft rectangle of light.

It takes him a few moments to figure out what he's looking at, his eyes are so unaccustomed to having to focus on anything.

"That's my laptop," he gasps, heading for the light source and snatching it out of someone's hands.

It's still on the password screen, which is a relief. This laptop contains all their security data and more. All extremely dangerous in the wrong person's hands. But he quickly realizes it wasn't the data anybody here was after.

It was the light. Light that will quickly extinguish as the battery runs out. And with no means of charging it, that would render the laptop as good as useless.

He slams the lid closed and the precious light vanishes along with all the joy in the room.

"How long did you have this turned on?" he asks, with no idea of what kind of battery life the laptop might be expected to have.

"Not that long," a man says.

"A minute?" he asks. "An hour? All night?"

"An hour," says a woman and Dex's heart sinks. Most likely she'll be under-exaggerating, aware they shouldn't have turned it on at all. He can only hope it's retained enough power for whatever emergency they might encounter. Should they live long enough to experience the luxury of having another emergency, of course.

"You're never to touch this again." Dex tucks it under his arm and climbs up a few rungs of the ladder. "This laptop could make the difference between life and death if we need it. Do you understand? If it weren't so important I'd be the first one here letting you run it down flat."

"We just wanted some light," a child says. "We were scared. The light brought back the happy."

Dex pauses on the ladder, not finding it easy to balance a laptop and navigate the rungs. If the laptop slips out from under his arm he may as well have let these people run the battery flat. Let them hold onto their happy for a little longer.

"We're all scared," he says to the child, softening his voice. "But just remember that this place is exactly the same as it was yesterday when the lights were still on. Nothing has changed. We just can't see it right now."

"It's like your hand," the child calls up to him. "You still do everything that everyone else does. It's like your hand is still there. But we just can't see it."

"The light will come back," says Dex, continuing up the ladder. "My hand won't."

He doesn't mean to sound so harsh, but the comment has taken him by surprise. Sometimes it really does feel like his hand is still there, like he's retained some kind of early memory of its existence.

That's one benefit of being plunged into darkness like this. He can't see his stump. The lack of light has put him on an even playing field with the other people trapped in here. He can almost pretend it's still there.

His father told him once of a boy he knew who was blind. No allowances were made for him in his Proving, no matter how smart or kind he might have been. He had a defect. One that Askala wasn't keen on replicating. But is sight any more important than having two hands? Who's to say which so-called defect should be bred out and which should be allowed to stay?

Dex climbs back up into the room above remembering Ronan's vow to find out who killed his mother and wondering if he's made any progress. That's one of the few regrets Dex has in life. He should've tried harder to figure this out for himself, no matter the pain it causes him to think about it. He needs to know who did this to him. And why. But for now, that's going to have to wait.

He feels his way to the desk, putting the laptop in a bottom drawer and covering it in papers. Hopefully in the darkness that's enough of a deterrent. It's not practical to consider carrying it around here with him. He should never have left it lying out on the desk like that. It was only lucky the encrypted files had finished downloading before the power had gone out. His father had been right to push him to get that job done.

With his stomach growling for food, Dex shuffles down the hallway toward the dining hall. All he's eaten since the power went out is a spoonful of something sticky and sweet. It might have been a pickled pepper but he's not sure. It could just as easily have been some kind of melon. He'd never realized before how dependent his tastebuds are on his eyes.

As he gets closer, he can hear his father's voice over the others. He's talking in a failed whisper. It's hard to hear exactly what he's saying, but whatever it is, he's not happy about it.

Dex quietens his steps. Keeping his hand on the wall, he feels his way to the dining room, coming to a stop in the doorway.

Nobody knows he's here and their hushed conversation continues. It's like he's become an invisible man. They all have.

"No, Thea," his father says. "It's too dangerous. You don't know what it is you're asking."

"I do know." There's a thump on the table and Dex imagines Thea banging her fist in frustration. "I'll just walk out with my hands up and declare my allegiance to the Commander. I have to get out. What if Nova's returned and I'm stuck in here? I have to help her. Please, Callix."

"I'm going with her," growls a male voice. "Has to be better than starving to death."

"And me," says a woman. "I can't stay in here another moment. I've always hated the dark. Plus, the air is getting stuffy. It's making me tired. We're suffocating in here."

"The lab isn't airtight," says Dex's father. "Granted, not much fresh air is getting in without the vents, but we should be fine for a while yet. And we still have a little food."

"What about the water?" Thea asks. "It has a strange smell to it. I'm not sure we should be drinking it."

"That's why we filled those flasks when we first got trapped in here." Dex's father is doing his best to keep his voice level, but Dex can feel his frustration.

"They won't last forever," the man grumbles.

"The Commander is flushing us out," says the woman. "And you can consider me flushed. I want out of here. You need to open the door. Otherwise, you're just as bad as him keeping us trapped in here."

"I have to get to Nova," Thea sobs. "She needs me. I can feel it."

Dex's heart breaks for her. Nova is Thea's whole world. It wasn't just Kian who lost her when she became Unbound. Thea's been fast sliding downhill ever since her daughter stepped out on that stage with only nine fingers. It's no wonder that this hell they're trapped in is tipping her over the edge.

"We can't open the doors," his father says in a whisper, no doubt hoping more people won't hear and come running. This could easily turn into a riot.

There's the shuffling of feet and a gasp.

"Take your hands off me!" Dex's father hisses. "Get back."

"We won't get back," the man responds. "Not until you let us out of here."

"Don't hurt him," pleads Thea. "There are other ways. I just wanted you to let me out. I didn't want this."

Dex lunges forward, arms outstretched, not entirely sure what he's grabbing for.

"Get off him," he shouts, touching a warm body but no idea whose. "He can't help you if you hurt him."

The scuffle seems to settle and Dex pulls back.

"Is that you, Dex?" Thea asks.

Dex nods, then realizing that's a useless gesture, he speaks up. "It's me. Any complaints anyone has, you can direct them my way."

"I overheard Callix telling Aarov he has a way to open the front door," says Thea. It seems Dex hasn't been the only one to listen into conversations from doorways. "But he won't do it. I have to get out. I need to get to Nova."

"Nova's gone," he says. "You know that."

"I don't know that," she sobs. "And neither do you. She could have come back. Maybe she was only hiding from us. I need to get out of here so I can look for her. I already lost her father. I can't lose her, too."

"We're done, Dex," the man says, sounding awfully close to Dex's face. "You need to tell your father to let us out. That's what a true leader would do. Listen to his people."

"Have they let go of you, Dad?" Dex's concern for his father exceeds any desire to help someone trying to get their way by using force.

"I'm okay, son." His father's voice is shaking and Dex has no choice but to take him at his word. He's a strong man.

"Is it true?" Dex asks. "Can you open the door?"

His father had told them security screens on the doors were impossible to open without power. Dex hadn't thought to question him.

"There's a way," his father says. "But it's too dangerous. Ronan might storm his way through as soon as the door is open. Letting Thea out puts every other person here at risk."

"We're already at risk," she says. "My daughter is at even greater risk.

"What makes you so sure Ronan's going to accept your apology?" he asks. "He already has too many mouths to feed. If he hadn't realized that before, he'll have realized it by now."

"I'm useful to him," she says. "I can go back to the infirmary."

"And repair all the black eyes and broken bones that he causes?" asks Dex. "Is that really the kind of man you want to work for?"

"I don't care about anything except my daughter." Thea's voice is level and calm. She's really given this some thought. Is it right of them to keep her here against her will? As a former High Bound she's already proven she's one of the smartest people on this doomed island.

"He might kill you," says Callix. "Despite what it says across his chest, that man knows no mercy."

"I have nothing left without my daughter," sobs Thea. "Even if Ronan kills me, it doesn't matter. My life is already over."

"Can we just get on with this?" the man grumbles. "We've wasted enough time already. Open the damn door, Callix."

"Open it," says Dex, reaching for Thea and drawing her into a hug. "Open the door for her. If she wants to get out, then I think we need to let her."

"What about the risk to everyone else in here?" his father asks.

"How about we ask them how they feel about that?" Dex rubs Thea's back, wishing he could take away her pain, but knowing he can't. Nova is lucky to have a mother like this.

Without waiting for his father's response, Dex leads Thea out into the hallway.

"Can I have everyone's attention, please?" Dex raises his voice above the frenzied talking that's broken out. It seems his father's fears were well-founded. They clearly heard the commotion and are discussing the pros and cons of leaving the lab with Thea.

He waits for the murmuring to die down and clears his throat.

"Thea has decided she'd like to leave. She plans to beg Ronan for forgiveness and pledge her allegiance in the hope he'll allow her to join the others on the Oasis."

A ripple of chatter stretches down the hallway.

"But," he says, as loudly as he can. "There's a good chance Ronan won't offer her the forgiveness that she desires. He's not known for his kindness. Deciding to leave here is a serious risk. It's very likely it will be the last decision Thea ever makes."

"He'll burn her alive!" someone shouts. "He'll break every bone in her body."

"But maybe he won't," comes a small voice not far from Dex.

"Let her go!" someone else says.

"There's also a risk that if we open the door for Thea that Ronan's men will storm the lab. It could put us all at risk."

He pauses to give the people time to think about this.

"Your fears about food and oxygen in here are valid," he says. "We can't survive for long, but we're doing our best."

"Let us out!" someone calls out. "I'll take my chances out there. He wins!"

"I can't get you to raise your hands in the dark," Dex says. "So, I want you to clap your hands as your vote. Please clap now if you vote for keeping the door sealed and everyone safely inside."

The sound of a dozen people clapping echoes off the walls. It's hard to know if that will be enough. There will be many people who'll likely be reluctant to vote at all. Thankfully, Dex doesn't need to vote. Clapping's never been his specialty...

"And now please clap if you'd like to allow Thea to leave the building, taking whoever wants to go with her."

He frowns as the clapping begins. Winces as the clapping raises in volume. And groans as it thunders down the hallway.

The vote is clear. The people have spoken. And as their leader, he's compelled to listen.

"Okay then," he says. "The door will be opened. Please make your decision. If you'd like to leave, then remain in this hallway. If you'd like to stay, then please seek shelter in one of the rooms. You'd be wise to hide yourself. I cannot guarantee your safety once that door is open."

240

"You can't guarantee it now," comes the same deep voice that had threatened his father in the dining hall.

"What's your name?" Dex asks. "The man who spoke just now."

"Vangel," comes the reply. "Why?"

"Because I want you to look after Thea out there," says Dex. "Promise me you'll take care of her, Vangel."

"I can take care of myself," says Thea.

"Never hurts to have a backup," Dex points out.

"Are you sure this is a good idea?"

Dex spins around at the sound of his father's voice. He reaches out his hand making contact with his arm.

"No, I'm not sure," he says. "But it's what the people want. We can't trap them in here against their will."

"Well, for the record, I think it's a bad idea," his father says.

"Then maybe you shouldn't have mentioned the doors to Aarov." Dex rolls his eyes in the safety of the darkness. It was his father who got them into this mess.

"Let's do it then." It's his father who grabs his arm now and leads him in the direction of the front door to the lab. "You're the boss."

"How will you do it?" Dex asks. "I can't see how this is possible without power."

"You'll see." His father comes to a stop and shuffles with something. "Or rather, you'll hear."

Dex would laugh if the situation weren't so serious.

"I'll open the door for one minute and one minute only," his father calls down the hallway. "If you've decided to go then you'd better be ready. I'm not opening it a second time."

There's more shuffling and Dex stands with his back against the wall.

"Good luck out there," he says, wishing he could see Thea's face. "Be careful. Do what you have to do. And remember to look after Thea, Vangel."

There's a crackling noise and then the lights blink back on and the ventilation system hums back into life.

Dex blinks rapidly, his eyes stinging from the sudden assault on his senses. His father is crouched by the front door with a small black box connected to some cables.

"You have a solar generator?" Dex's jaw falls open as he breathes in the freshest air that's ever entered his lungs.

But his father has no interest in explaining himself right now. "Get ready!" he shouts. "One minute starts now."

There's a clunk as the front door slides open and the security door begins to lift.

"Get moving!" his father shouts. "Crawl under. What are you waiting for? Fifty seconds to go!"

Dex squints back at the line of people in front of the door, surprised at how many of them there are. Over twenty people have decided to take their chances with Ronan, having decided that Dex is unable to protect them. That has to be more than half the people in here.

Thea shoots him an apologetic glance and gets to the floor in front of the opening.

But Vangel shoves her out of the way, squeezing himself out first as the screen lifts a little more.

Thea scrambles to regain her traction on the floor just as a flash of light and heat shoot under the door. There's a rumble and the sound of Vangel screaming the kind of scream only a dying man can manage.

"Flamethrower!" Dex darts forward and grabs the back of Thea's dress and hauls her backward, his damaged ribs screaming at him as agony slices through his core.

His father hits a button and the security screen pauses, changes direction, and comes crashing down once more.

But the screen can't get all the way to the floor. The tip of a flamethrower has been wedged underneath and is pointing right at them.

"Get back!" Dex pushes the people away, just as a giant flame leaps out the end of the barrel. The intensity of the heat feels like the sun has crashed to the Earth. The people turn their heads and shield their faces. Some are screaming, some are running down the hallway, others are frozen as if the heat has melted their feet to the floor.

Dex's father is inching his way toward the door, getting as close as he dares.

"Take the controls, Aarov," he instructs, and his loyal friend is by his side in an instant, ready to do what's needed.

The flame flickers and dies and Dex's father moves in.

"Now, Aarov!" he calls.

The screen lifts just an inch and Dex's father kicks the barrel of the flamethrower, sending it flying back. Another blast of light and heat comes shooting under the screen but Aarov has it closing again, this time managing to get it fully sealed.

He closes the inner door and pulls a plug and the power goes down with a slow hum as darkness cocoons them once more.

Dex feels his legs turn weak and he sinks to the floor. Thea grabs hold of him and throws her arms around him. Here in the darkness for just one moment he pretends she's his mother. Who knows…maybe she's also pretending he's her child.

Whatever it is, he holds her as tightly as his protesting ribs will allow him.

"It's okay," he says to her, even though it really isn't.

"You saved my life," she replies.

"No, I didn't." He doesn't bother to hold back his tears as he speaks. "I almost killed you. I should never have agreed to let you go."

But his father speaks before she has a chance to answer. "Now we all know why we can't open that door again. It's a death sentence."

"Can we turn the lights on again?" someone else asks. "Please, you have a generator. We all saw it."

"No!" It's Dex who shouts this word, understanding exactly why this isn't a good idea. It's no different to the laptop. "We must save the power for an emergency."

"And this isn't an emergency?" a woman asks, incredulous.

"Not yet," says Dex, the horror of these words sliding over him. "I'm afraid that as bad as this is, we're only just getting started."

WREN

*W*ren paces her cabin like a caged beast. She has to get to Dex. She should never have left him in the first place. They're no different to Nova and Kian. They belong together. And it's clear he can't get to her. Would he even want to if he could?

She reaches the end of the cabin and pivots to change direction, marching toward the other wall.

Of course, he would want to. Wouldn't he?

She stops at the other end of the cabin and thinks about that kiss. Her stomach pulls into a tight knot and she groans. Surely, he remembers it in the same way she does?

Intense. Passionate. Desperate. Emotional. Full of promise and empty of regret.

There's a quiet knock at her door moments before it slides open.

"Phoenix," she says, smiling to see her twin. She'd be happy to see anyone right now, as long as it's not Cy. He's forbidden her from leaving the Oasis, and it's been quite some work avoiding him in this confined space.

Phoenix is carrying something wrapped in a piece of hemp and sets it down on her table.

"Is it food?" she asks when he doesn't explain. Her stomach has been grumbling all morning but she hasn't wanted to venture out just in case she runs into Cy. It's getting too hard to pretend she's on his side.

"It's a gift." Phoenix runs his hand over his cropped hair. "I'll warn you though. I stole it."

She laughs as she goes to the package. "Sounds intriguing. And who did you steal this mysterious object from?"

"Callix." He grins.

She stops, her hands freezing on the hemp wrapping. "I don't understand."

"You will." He nods for her to open it.

She unfolds the hemp and as it falls away she sees the radio from the secret room.

"What the hell, Phoenix! How did you get this?"

"I swiped it when I went to see Callix before the lockdown. Thought it might come in handy."

She shakes her head as she runs her fingertips over the device. "Does it work from out here?"

Phoenix nods with a strange look on his face as he sits down on the edge of her bed. "Yeah, it works if you get close enough to the lab. I haven't had much of a chance to use it though."

"Heard anything interesting?" She picks up the radio and carries it with her, sitting beside him on the bed.

"Nothing much." He looks at the floor as he speaks, something he's done since he was a boy whenever he tells a lie.

"Phoenix. You tell me what you're hiding right now!" Her voice is stern, even though her eyes are shining with amusement.

"You broke the poor guy's heart," he says.

"He said that?"

Phoenix nods. "Told you he had it bad."

"Hang on." She shuffles on the bed, trying to get this story right. "Tell me his exact words. What did he say and who was he talking to?"

"I only listened for a minute!" Phoenix throws his palms up. "He was talking to Callix about his injuries. Said something about his broken heart being the thing that hurt the most."

"And what did Callix say?" Her eyes are wide as the pain she's caused Dex ricochets back to her own broken heart.

"Don't know." Phoenix shrugs. "I was too busy throwing up to hear anything else."

"Does this thing work two ways?" Wren asks, studying the dials. "We've only ever used it to listen in to the lab, not the other way around."

Phoenix shrugs again. "No idea."

"Why would you steal it?" Her finger rests on a switch she's fairly certain would enable this device to transmit sound in the other direction.

"Souvenir," he says.

She rolls her eyes.

"I just thought it might come in handy," he says. "Dad always taught us to plan ahead."

"Not when the plan goes against his own plans." She throws an arm around Phoenix's shoulders. "You're a genius, do you know that?"

"Been told that once or twice before," he laughs.

Wren hugs the radio to her chest, desperately hoping this might give her the chance to talk to Dex one more time.

"You're lucky, little bird." Phoenix reaches for her hand and squeezes it. "Nobody's ever loved me like that."

"They will one day. I know they will." She's surprised to have heard him admit that. His normally brash exterior doesn't allow for too many feelings to escape. "You're quite the catch."

"Yeah, I thought so too when Blondie caught me out in the

ocean. Except it seems she'd already been caught by someone else."

Wren nods. "Yeah, that was a losing battle if I ever saw one. There'll be someone else, though. Be patient. I never thought anyone would ever love me until I met Dex."

"Do you think our mom loved us?" Phoenix asks.

She rocks back at the sharp turn this conversation just took.

"She's dead, Phee. You know that."

"Yeah but I mean before she died. Do you think she loved us then?"

"Not likely." Wren leaps from the bed, still clutching the radio that she has no plans of letting go of any time soon. "If our mom loved us she wouldn't have left us for dead like that to run off with another man."

"I suppose so." Phoenix's voice is full of disbelief. He's always had a harder time accepting the heartless way their mother treated them.

"What kind of mother leaves her children with a man like Cy to raise them?" she asks.

"A scared one?" He blinks at Wren as she paces to the door and back.

"Then our mother was a coward." She looks Phoenix directly in the eye. "We weren't enough for her. You weren't enough and neither was I. She ran away with another man. If Cy was so awful to her, don't you think she would've taken us with her?"

Phoenix looks to the floor. "I just thought that may—"

"If she'd stayed with us maybe she wouldn't be dead." Wren isn't willing to listen to any more excuses for the woman who birthed them. "Cy would have protected her like he protected us. Which makes her a fool as well as a coward."

Phoenix lets out a long sigh and throws up his hands. "Sorry I asked."

"I'm sorry, Phee." She stops her pacing to throw him an apologetic look. "I just have a lot on my mind right now. Like, rescuing the living instead of speculating about people who left us behind."

She turns the dial on the radio, but all that comes back is a faint crackle.

"What does that mean?" she asks, hoping she has all the buttons set correctly.

"You're too far away from the lab. When I had it working I was outside in the garden."

"Oh great!" It takes all her willpower not to scream. "You give me this radio, knowing full well I can't use it. Why would you do that?"

Phoenix rolls his eyes as he produces the knife from the back of his pants. "Since when has a guard or two ever stopped you? Escape plan, Wren. What's your escape plan?"

"What are you suggesting?" She raises an eyebrow at him, impressed by his rebellious attitude.

"I'm not suggesting anything. Just wondering what happened to my fearless sister."

Wren pulls back her shoulders and takes the knife from Phoenix, tucking it into the back of her own trousers. It doesn't sit as snugly against her skin with her hemp clothing as it had with Phoenix's leather waistband, but it'll do.

"You know why I really took that radio, don't you?" he asks.

She shakes her head.

"I thought you might end up stuck in the lab somehow."

"Maybe I will. At least, I'm going to try my best to get stuck in there."

"It's dangerous, Wren. I'm not sure it's a good idea."

"Then why are you encouraging me?" She pats the radio and looks at him.

"Because you need to do this. What you've found with Dex is something I've always wanted and never had. The closest I've ever had to that is with you. Kind of sad, really, given you're my sister. But it's true. You give me hope for the future, little bird."

Wren smiles as she shakes her head at him. "If only all the people out there who think you're this big tough guy could see you now. Your heart is like a big squishy pteropod."

He pulls a face. "What? Bitter and hard to find?"

"No. Precious and valuable. It will be a lucky girl who will be on the receiving end of all that love you have to give."

"Okay," he laughs. "I'm feeling nauseous again."

Wren gives him an efficient nod, wraps the radio back up into the hemp cloth and ties it so it forms a sling around her shoulder. She goes to the door. Then deciding she doesn't care how nauseous Phoenix is, she doubles back and gives him a hug.

He stands, still hugging her in return, lifting her feet off the ground as he stretches to his full height.

"You mean the world to me, Phee," she says, fearing this may be the last time she sees him.

"You're not going to die, Wren," he replies, knowing exactly what she's thinking.

Letting go, she gives him a light punch on the shoulder and goes back to the door.

"Oh, Wren," he says as she presses her chip to the sensor. "If you do manage to get into the lab, make sure you look behind the bookshelf. The one with the jars of food on it."

She tilts her head. "Why?"

"I left something there for you." He winks at her. "Now, hurry up. Don't keep lover boy waiting. His poor widdle heart is bwoken."

"I'll bwake your heart in a minute," she mumbles as she marches out the door. "Or your nose."

She makes her way quickly through the corridors, avoiding the door to the gangplank that had four of Cy's men guarding it the last time she checked.

Instead, she heads for the upper deck. It's got to be an easier way to get off this godforsaken ship.

She climbs the staircase quietly, with no idea what she's

facing or what her plan is to get past Cy's men and off this ship. Some things are hard to plan for. Especially when she has no idea what she's about to face.

The deck is quiet when she steps out. It's late afternoon and there's a cool breeze sweeping across the worn timber boards. Unbelievably, she can't see anyone.

Treading slowly and carefully, she makes her way toward the ladder.

"Is it my birthday?" a rough voice growls from the shadows.

Wren spins around, her hand fluttering toward her back. She doesn't want to reveal she has a knife just yet. The element of surprise can be an equally sharp weapon if used correctly.

One of Cy's men is ambling toward her. She knows this one. He's taller than the others, his beard always filthier and his leer always slightly more threatening. This was the man who killed Dorian in the ballroom, something he's probably already forgotten about given the number of men he's killed.

"Ah...Garbin," she says, wishing Phoenix were here to remind her of this oaf's name.

"Close enough, love." He saunters closer. "But it's Garbo."

"How...lovely." Wren takes another step to the ladder, weighing up her options. If she scrambles down, Garbo will either follow her or raise the alert. Neither of which are appealing options. Much better if she can deal with him first.

"Where you off to?" He's so close to her now that she can smell his putrid body odor.

"Nowhere." She smiles as innocently as she can. "Just going crazy on this ship. I wanted to go for a walk. I won't be long."

"The Commander said not to let you go anywhere." He picks at some kind of crumb stuck in the coarse hair of his beard and flicks it away. "No matter what excuse you came up with."

"Oh, he didn't mean that." Wren forces out a laugh. "He's just being overprotective. You know how he is."

"The Commander always means what he says." Garbo doesn't

join her in laughing. Instead, he shifts his gaze to her chest and leaves it there. "Wanna know something else he said to me?"

"Sure." Wren readjusts her makeshift bag on her shoulder, wondering how long this is going to take.

He licks his bottom lip, still staring at her chest. "He said you'll be my woman one day."

Wren blanches at the prospect. There is no way *that* is ever going to happen. She'd leap to her death from this deck before she'd agree to that.

"Interesting," she says.

"Only a matter of time." He drags his eyes from her chest to her face, like it's some kind of effort. "And when that time comes, you're going to give me what I've been waiting for. Every. Single. Day. No more teasing me walking around the Outlands in those tight leather pants. You're not going to need them for what I have in mind."

"Why wait?" Wren reaches out with her left hand and strokes his revolting beard, trailing her fingertips down to his broad chest and undoing his top button.

His eyes pop wide open and he lets out a stream of foul-smelling breath.

"I knew you wanted it." A droplet of saliva flies from his mouth and hits her on the cheek. "They all do. And I've got the good stuff right here."

He lifts her hand from his chest and presses it to his groin.

Wren doesn't struggle. Instead, she draws in a deep breath, steadying herself. When she acts, she's going to need to move quickly.

"You're a big man, aren't you?" She smiles at him, squeezing him firmly as she slowly reaches behind her back with her right hand, slipping the knife from her waistband.

"That's it, girl. You know the way to a man's heart." Garbo groans, letting his eyelids flutter closed for only a moment.

But a moment is all she needs.

Wren grips him hard with her left hand, just as she brings her right hand swinging around her body, driving the long blade into his chest until only the handle remains exposed.

Garbo's mouth opens, his eyes blinking at her in shock as the realization hits him that his seconds are numbered.

"I know exactly the way to a man's heart," she sneers, twisting the knife and enjoying the sound of his strangled moan. "It's on the left side between the third and fourth rib."

He falls backward, hitting the ground and cracking his head on the hard boards. An injury that would have really hurt if he weren't already dead.

She leans over him, withdrawing the knife and wiping it clean on his trousers.

"Is that what you were waiting for?" Tucking the knife back in place, she swings herself down the ladder.

She needs to move quickly. It won't take long for Garbo's body to be found. Usually Cy's men work in pairs so wherever it is that his partner has gone, it won't take him long to return. Unless the death of those four men outside the labs has had an impact on how Cy can rotate his guards. Whatever the case, it certainly worked in her favor just now.

She scrambles down the ladder and runs to the lab, moving quickly and quietly, heading through the trees and threading her way around to the rear of the building where the courtyard is.

Peering through the trees, she sees one of Cy's men positioned at each of the gates. It's no wonder he doesn't have many soldiers in the Oasis right now. They're all down here.

Cy's men are yawning, glancing at the sky at regular intervals to check the time, no doubt counting down the hours until their replacements arrive.

Wren gathers some stones and fills her pockets with them,

wishing Phoenix had thought to steal Cy's slingshot along with the radio.

She positions herself at the base of the tree that has the branch overhanging the courtyard. The same one she'd once used to escape Dex to avoid letting him see a note Cy had sent her. How foolish she'd been to think Cy had any secret worth keeping.

Studying the two guards closely, she steadies her breathing and waits for her moment.

It doesn't take long. Another guard, who seems to be tasked with walking the perimeter of the lab, ambles up to them. He stops to talk to the first guard, and the second guard wanders over to join in the chat. Cy wouldn't be at all happy if he could see that.

Wren scales the tree and climbs along the branch, her movements lightning fast.

Trying not to look down, she's grateful the wall is no higher. This is most definitely her limit.

She pauses, assessing her position. The leaves thin out from here and it's going to be difficult to get onto the wall without being seen, no matter how fast she moves.

Reaching into her pocket, she withdraws a handful of stones and flings them into the trees in front of the guards.

Without waiting to see their reaction, she moves, praying this was enough to divert their attention for a precious few seconds.

She leaps from the branch to the top of the wall and jumps down, landing in a crouch and rolling to diffuse the impact on her joints.

But she lands on her back with the radio wedged underneath her and she lets out a quiet yelp. That's going to leave quite the bruise.

Freezing, she waits and listens, but it seems her diversion

had done its job. Those guards will be scratching their heads all night trying to figure out what happened.

Getting herself up, she moves to the edge of the courtyard as far away from the gates as she can manage. With any luck, the noise of the screeching birds coming in to roost will be enough to muffle the sound of the radio.

She slips her bag from over her shoulder and unwraps the hemp cloth. Thankfully, it's survived the rough treatment of the fall.

She turns the dial and holds it to her ear.

Nothing.

Then turning another dial she holds it to her mouth.

"Dex!" she hisses. "Can you hear me? Dex!"

Still nothing.

"Dex!" she calls again, tapping the side of the radio, wondering if she's gone to all this effort for nothing. "Dex!"

The radio crackles. "What was that?" says a woman. "Who's there?"

Yes! Wren quickly adjusts the volume down, hoping that wasn't too loud, her heart thumping with excitement.

"I need Dex," she whispers. "Tell him Wren needs to talk to him. Can you get him for me?"

"It's a trick," says a man. "Turn that thing off."

"No!" Wren squeezes the radio tightly. "I'm here to help you. Get Dex. Please, get him."

The radio goes silent and Wren waits, aware of the fast rhythm of her heart as she listens for the sound of the voice of the guy she'd just killed a man to get to.

"Wren, is that you?"

There it is. There *he* is. Dex. Her Dex.

"It's me!" she whispers, hoping he can hear her. "I'm outside. I came back for you. You have to let me in."

There's a pause, and Wren has no idea whether that's a good

thing. "No, Wren. Just…no. Enough's enough. Your trick won't work."

She swallows, wanting to throw the radio at the wall but continuing to grip it tight.

"It's not a trick, Dex. It's me. Wren. I'm here. Please. Let me in."

"How do I know you're not being forced to say this? Ronan could be standing right beside you."

"He's not. I'm alone. Trust me, Dex. I'd never lie to you."

"I know how you lie, Wren. You leave things out. You mislead. You manipulate your words. They're all lies to me."

Tears burst from Wren's eyes and run down her cheeks. What he's saying is true. She does do that. But never will she do it again. Well, not to Dex. Never to him.

"Dex, I'm sorry. I'm so sorry. I should never have left you. It was a mistake. Please, you have to let me in. I can help you."

"How can you help us?" he asks, ignoring her apology.

"I don't know. That's the truth. I'm not misleading you. I'm not leaving anything out. But I promise I can help you. I know I can."

"Wren, it's too late. The last time we opened the door your men killed one of our men. I can't open that door even if I wanted to."

"He wasn't my man!" She works hard to keep her voice down, wanting to scream the words instead of whispering them. "And you can open the door. I know you can. I'm alone out here. I'm in the courtyard. I promise you I'm by myself."

"Answer my earlier question," he says. "How do I know you're not being forced to say this?"

"Dex." She pauses, trying to find the right words. "You know me. You know me better than just about anyone. We've spent time together. Real time. And we've seen each other in good times and bad. And on any of those occasions did you ever once see me being forced into doing anything?"

Now it's his turn to pause. He pauses for so long she worries the battery in the radio has gone flat.

"I'm telling you the truth, Dex. I'm asking you to trust me. Please. Let me in. I can help you."

"Why do you want to help me?" he asks, although surely he must already know. "Why would you want to come in here?"

"Because I love you, Dex." She needs to remind him exactly how she feels. "I love every crazy, annoying, loyal, brave, stubborn part of you. I want another one of those kisses. I want another hundred of them. I want them now and I want them when we have gray hair and backs as bent as your ridiculous sense of humor. Let me in. Please, trust me."

He pauses for even longer this time. So long that this time she taps the side of the radio again, convinced it's no longer functioning.

"I'm turning the radio off, Wren." His voice is devoid of emotion and it breaks her heart. "I need to talk to my people."

The radio goes dead and Wren collapses to the ground, cradling it to her chest. It's a poor substitute for Dex but knowing that his voice just came to her through it is enough to make her want to hold onto it forever.

He has to let her in. He just has to. Not only does she have nowhere else to go, she also has nowhere else she wants to go. But his voice just now was so cold. Like the words she'd poured out to him meant nothing.

When Cy finds Garbo's body, it will take him all of about two seconds to figure out who killed him. If Dex doesn't let her into the lab, then she may as well just lie down out here and die. It will be all over for her.

She knows now how Nova must've felt when Kian pushed her away. It's no wonder she ran to the Outlands. Wren would run to the moon if that were an option.

She wonders what he's saying to his people right now. She wouldn't blame him if he refuses to let her in. All she can hope is that whatever's passed between them up until now has been enough.

It's getting cooler now. Still warm, but not like it was when she'd stepped out onto the upper deck. Picking herself up, Wren goes to the door and presses her palms against the metal screen that's sealing it closed.

"Let me in, Dex," she says in a failed whisper as she leans her forehead on the screen.

She's so close to him, but still so far.

The minutes tick by and Wren's anguish turns to fear. Garbo must surely have been found by now. People are going to be looking for her. And anybody who knows anything about her, is going to know the first place to look.

Lifting her head from the screen, she fights back another flood of tears.

It seems Dex's silence is his answer. He doesn't trust her. She ran away from him one too many times.

With nowhere else to go, and nowhere else she wants to be, Wren sits down in front of the door with her knees pulled up and her back against the wall.

She'll wait all night if she has to.

A noise startles her, and her head whips around.

Is it possible that Dex has changed his mind?

NOVA

*T*he words have gone again.

As Nova wanders through the parking lot, she realizes how much just the brief moments when she and Kian were connected again lifted her.

She felt like all her parts were aligned once more. Her heart. Her soul.

Her destiny.

But up the top of the tree, they discovered they're yearning for a different future.

Kian wants to return to Askala.

Nova wants to raise their child in safety and peace.

Without realizing it, Nova finds herself at the base of the mangrove pine again. It had started raining last night as they'd climbed back down in silence. It's like Mother Nature was mourning the loss of alignment between them.

It had been so brief. So beautiful.

The bark of the pine is slick and dark with moisture. The rain stopped early this morning, leaving everything in the sleeping quarters damp and cool after the water managed to trickle all the way down to the roots. Nova and Kian had clasped each other close in their little nest.

Although neither of them knew what to say, their bodies communicated what their hearts ached for.

To never let go.

This morning when they'd woken up, they hadn't stayed in bed like the day before. They'd gotten up with the others, eaten a breakfast of flat bread made from the ground seeds of the mangrove pine. Then Kian had left, talking to Avis about what they'd need to start experimenting with breeding the cockroaches.

Nova hadn't seen him all day, but then again, it's possible she's avoiding him. If they don't talk, they don't need to find the words to say goodbye. She hadn't seen much of the others, either. Shiloh is keeping herself scarce. Finn is permanently attached to Dharma's side. Dean had set off straight after breakfast to explore more of Fairbanks, and all Flick seems to want to do is sleep.

Nova slips her foot into the first foothold, testing it. Her shoe wedges in, firm despite the slickness. The need to climb is strong. She's not sure whether she's running away from the decision she needs to make, or whether she's running toward the place she last felt connected to Kian, but it doesn't matter.

She climbs the mangrove pine, the drops of water around her sparkling like diamonds in the afternoon light. Each time she brushes one, it melds and dissolves, wetting her clothes and hair.

Her hands are stained with tannin and the damp bark is packed under her fingernails as she reaches the top. She pants, feeling the same exhilaration she did yesterday. She and Kian used to climb trees all the time in Askala. It was a way to escape, to literally rise above the restrictions and responsibilities imposed on them.

They could just be...together. Surrounded by nature. And their love.

Now, Nova has the scent of pine and the sensation of rough bark against her palms...but no Kian.

"If you're trying to hide, you just sounded like a polar grizzly climbing up here."

Nova startles so hard she grips the tree. "Luca!"

The boy grins, water droplets caught in his wild mop of hair and darkening his lashes. "Surprise!"

Nova relaxes as she smiles. She indicates for Luca to scoot along the branch, then settles in next to him. "Avis said you come up here sometimes."

"It's the best lookout in the place. If anyone is coming close to Fairbanks, then we'll see them." Determination fills Luca's voice, his gaze sharp as he scans the horizon. Somehow, it makes him look older and younger all at once.

Nova looks around. Even after the rain, the Outlands haven't been washed clean. Everywhere is still coated with ash, as if it's been painted with such permanence it won't ever go away. "Looks all clear at the moment."

Luca nods, drops sprinkling onto his shoulders. "They don't come after rain. They're less desperate for water, and the road is too muddy." Luca grins as he looks at Nova. "And Fairbanks gets too dangerous."

Nova's heart flutters. "Too dangerous?"

"Yep. The buildings are more likely to collapse," he says with relish.

Alarmed, Nova looks through the branches at the crumbling building the pine has speared straight through the middle of. "But—"

Luca waves a hand dismissively, his own nails chipped and brown. "We're as safe as we can be. Avis says the tree actually makes the building more stable—I'm pretty sure it's the only thing holding it together."

Safe as we can be.

That's what Avis said. It's all Nova can ask for her baby considering the world they live in. Surely Kian can see that?

Askala needs us, Nova. Kian's words, so full of passion and conviction, weigh heavily on her mind.

They hold the heaviness of truth.

Stopping herself from getting stuck in the useless loop that's stolen her ability to know what to do next, Nova angles her head. "If there isn't anyone coming, what are you doing up here?"

Luca's dark eyes glint, reminding her of Kian. "You're a smart one, aren't you?"

Nova grins, suddenly realizing Askala stopped defining her the moment she left it. Maybe even before that. "I used to love climbing trees. My guess is you like it up here."

Luca turns back to stare at the horizon where the sun is progressively sinking below it. "It's the best. All that"— he waves his arm at the desolation around them then glares at the town Nova and the others escaped from—"just reminds me…"

"Reminds you of what?" Nova asks, wondering why he's hesitating to finish the sentence.

Luca shrugs. "How lucky I am that my mama left me to be found."

Nova almost reaches out to hug him, but she stops herself. There's an independence about Luca that feels as if he's fought hard to establish. "She must've loved you very much to do that, Luca."

Luca shrugs again. "That's what Avis says. One day I'm going to ask her."

Nova's brows lift a little. The determination in Luca's voice tells her it's probably something he'll do one day. If his mama is still alive. "We're both very lucky to have found Fairbanks."

Luca looks down, peering through the branches as if he can see the colony below. "I get to feel safe."

Something in Nova unwinds. "Feeling safe is something every person should have, Luca."

Especially a child.

If only Kian were here to hear this. He'd understand where she's coming from.

Why she can't leave.

Suddenly, Luca leaps to his feet, acting as if he's standing on a broad beam rather than a narrow branch. "Yeah, and I get to do that because Avis was brave enough to find this place."

A safe haven. In possibly the unsafest place on Earth.

Luca grins again. "And I'm going to be just like Avis. I'm going to fight for what I believe in."

Just like Kian.

The words have sliced through Nova's mind before she can stop them, almost making her gasp. Without people fighting for Askala, the haven it was supposed to be will die along with everything else out there.

Luca has skipped around her before Nova gets a chance to move. The boy seems to climb and jump as if they're only a few feet off the ground.

"Anyway," he says brightly. "I'm gonna go set up another tripwire 'cause the others will go out trying to snare rabbits tomorrow. They come out after the rain just like the roaches do. And this time, I'm going with them."

Nova hides her smile. Avis is going to struggle keeping this one within the crumbling walls of this building. Does she realize Luca's fierce need to protect their colony stems from his wise little soul understanding Fairbanks needs to be fought for?

Her smile dying, Nova grips the trunk as she prepares to stand. "I'll come with you."

"Nah, you stay." Luca's boyish gaze twinkles. "Something special is about to happen."

Something special?

He's gone before Nova can reply, and she imagines his lithe little body shimmying down the trunk as if it's a pole.

Nova looks around, wondering what he was talking about. Evening is almost here, the sky above the wasteland around them losing light almost as fast as she's losing the ability to know what the right choice is.

The sky turns from gold to dusk, time passing as Nova comes no closer to a decision. It feels like she's being forced to choose between her child and Askala.

One life balanced against those of many...

There's a rustling behind her and Nova smiles as the branches below her part. Maybe Luca brought back some cockroaches for them to share as they watch the sunset. She's sure even in the Outlands, those could be stunning.

The smile freezes when she sees it's not Luca.

Kian hoists himself up the remaining feet, finding a branch slightly below to stand on. His eyes are somber as they meet hers. "Hey."

"Hey," Nova breathes.

How her heart aches to touch him. For twenty-four hours she was free to do that in the way she's always dreamed of. Yearned to.

A day is too brief to compress everything she feels for him into.

Kian stares at her for long moments. "I was looking for you."

Nova nods, not surprised he found her. He always has.

Maybe after all of this their hearts will have a chance to come back together again.

Nova chokes on a sob, her hand flying to her mouth. Surely, everything they've been through can't have come to this.

Kian's arms are around her as the sobs wrack her shoulders. "Nova..." His voice is full of the agony tearing through her. "We need to talk."

But now the tears have started, they're a flood, each one carrying the pain of everything she's endured.

The Proving. The Announcement. Losing her finger.

Losing Kian.

Leaving Askala. Discovering the Outlands.

Flick losing her baby.

The violence in those men's eyes. Wondering if she was going to survive any of this.

Losing Thom.

Then finding Fairbanks. Then Kian finding her. The hope that this could end well for them.

Now losing Kian again.

"I know." Kian strokes her hair. "I know."

He doesn't try to stop the torrent of tears, simply holding her and acknowledging the pain. It allows the deluge to cascade out, unfettered. It almost feels like…a relief.

As the tears begin to ebb, Kian pulls back, only to pause. "Look," he says. His voice is quiet, full of reverence.

Nova looks up and blinks away the tears blurring her vision. "Oh my…"

The sky is black apart from a narrow band of light over the land, the last sliver of day. It's what's above that steals Nova's breath. Dancing across the night are bands of light, shimmering and fragile. Ribbons of green have been woven through the sky.

"It's beautiful," Nova breathes.

"I'd heard about the northern lights," Kian whispers, as if he's worried he'll fracture the moment. "But it felt like they were as extinct as everything else."

The ribbons slowly ebb and flow, in shades of spring and rainforest and sea, misty and ethereal. The edges glimmer as if they're alive, energy pulsing and throbbing in streams.

"It's a serpent of light." Kian's voice is hushed, the words almost a prayer.

Mother Nature at her most breathtaking. At her most precious.

Nova rests her head on his shoulder. "I'm glad we got to see this together," she sighs. She won't be forgetting this moment any time soon.

Kian's hand rises and his thumb and finger gently grasp her chin. Her eyes come up to meet his.

"This is why I was looking for you, Nova. I wanted to let you know I've decided."

She frowns. "You've decided?"

"We're going to be sharing a whole lot more of these northern light shows together. I'm not going anywhere."

Shock has Nova bolting up straight. Did she just hear him right? Surely, she has to be dreaming.

Kian's face softens as a smile graces his face. "I'm staying. Here. With you."

Joy soars through Nova and she has to grip onto the branch because it feels like she could float away any moment. "You're… staying?"

Kian nods. "Here. With you."

Although he repeats the words, Nova wants to hear them again. And again. And again.

Staying. Here. With her.

But as quickly as the joy mushrooms through Nova, it comes crashing down. "You can't. Askala needs you."

Askala is a part of Kian. He was born to defend it. To champion it.

But Kian is already shaking his head. "I've realized something, Nova. There is no Askala without love." He shrugs. "Without you, I'm half a man. A shadow I barely like." His hands splay across her belly, warm and sure. "You were right. Our child deserves to be safe. This is our future."

Nova bites her trembling lip, but the quiver simply spreads through her. They shake the tears that are clinging to her lashes and tumble down her cheeks. It never occurred to her that Kian would choose her.

This time, something else sings through her veins. Lifting her. Shedding the last of the uncertainty.

It's like the moment Kian released her of having to make a choice, she was free to make the decision she needs to. She finally knows what she has to do. In fact, she's never been so sure as she is in this moment.

She cups Kian's face, her heart echoing everything she sees there—the promise, the love. The raw, honest truth. Their love is the foundation for all of this.

"Kian—"

But her words are cut off by a shuddering ripping through the tree. No. Below the tree. Or is it everything around the tree?

Kian lunges forward, plastering Nova against the trunk as he wraps himself around her. The tremors increase, a strange creaking and rumbling filling the air.

Nova clings to him. "What's going on?" This time she has to shout.

The creaking has gone. The rumbling is growing exponentially louder.

"I don't know," Kian shouts back. "It's like an earthquake!"

He's right. It feels like the very air is shaking.

Suddenly, with a shriek of twisted metal, the roof of the building that's to their left drops. Crashes. Disappears through the branches like it's been sucked down. Nova screams as a cloud of dust billows around them. The roar of the collapsing walls swallows them, battering against Nova's eardrums.

Kian holds her tight, pressing her hard into the trunk. Nova buries her head against the rough bark, the terrifying sound feeling like a monster determined to devour them.

The tree shudders, the branches shaking and quivering around them. Droplets shower down as if it's raining.

"Hold on!" Kian shouts, the fragility of their situation evident in his voice.

They're at the top of a towering tree. The world is collapsing around them. What if the mangrove pine topples?

Nova grips the trunk with all her might. Wet and terrified, she focuses on Kian's harsh breathing in her ear. It's the sound of life.

Unlike the sound of destruction that's surging like a tidal wave around them.

The roaring stops almost as suddenly as it erupted. There's cement crumbling and shifting, but little else. The contrast feels too sharp, almost as if it can't be trusted. Surely, whatever just happened isn't finished?

Nova unclenches her hands and opens her eyes one at a time.

The tree is covered in dust, the branches still quivering like it's afraid this isn't over. But there's no more rumbling. No more disappearing roof or walls.

Slowly, Kian pulls back, scanning the area with wide, alert eyes. Dust cakes his hair, the moisture turning it to mud. "I don't think it was an earthquake."

Nova looks around, shudders rippling through her body. "You don't?"

"No. The other buildings around us are intact."

Nova's eyes widen. "That means..." She glances to her right. Half the building is still intact.

Kian's jaw clenches. "Part of this one collapsed."

Sweet Terra, they need to check on the others.

Kian nods as if she said the words out loud. "I'll go first. We need to be careful."

Nova nods frantically. Avis. Flick. Annabel. Luca. All the others. They were all down there!

The climb down is slipperier than it was on the way up. The water trapped between the needles has been unleashed, the deluge wetting everything. Plus, this time, there's an urgency.

A hope no one's been hurt. Or worse...

Kian still takes it slowly, watching Nova climb down just as much as where he's putting his foot next. Nova's heart batters her ribs, thinking of the way Luca climbed down in minutes.

Luca...

Finally, the ground becomes visible, but now, it's much higher than it was before. Fractured rubble has buried the floor that was there when Nova climbed up. It blankets as far as she can see, an uneven, rolling canvas that they're going to have to negotiate.

Gingerly, Kian steps onto the nearest concrete piece, putting weight on it. When it holds firm, he holds a hand up to Nova. "We just need to go slow."

Nova nods, even though her mind screams for them to hurry. The others need their help!

Picking their way through the minefield of what used to be floors and walls is slow. Twice, the concrete shifts and there's a heart-thudding leap, hoping the chunk they're going to land on is safer than the one they left. Each time, they land without injury.

Each time, they squeeze each other's hands in relief.

The rubble angles down, most of the destruction having fallen away from the mangrove pine as the building peeled away. Nova hopes it means the colony has been spared from being crushed.

Unless the parking lot collapsed.

As they make their way across what used to be the foyer, the base of the mangrove pine no longer visible, they find the rubble continues to spill down the ramp like a tsunami of debris.

"Avis!" Nova calls desperately. "Can anyone hear me?"

She's met with silence, any sound muffled by the dust

clinging to the air. The worry on Kian's face echoes the tightness in Nova's chest.

Please…

The air is grimy with dust, making it hard to see. But as Nova and Kian make their way forward, they discover much of the parking lot is unchanged. The square columns remain intact, the roof is where it should be—above them.

Finally, noise pierces the dusty air. Cries and groans and the odd frantic shout.

Relief fills Nova. Cries mean functioning lungs and bodies. It's better than silence.

The first person they come across is Clint, not far from where the wave of rubble has spilled its last chunk of debris. Nova falls to her knees beside him. "Clint, it's me, Nova. Are you okay?"

He sits on the ground, nursing a gash on his head as blood seeps through his fingers. "Someone put some cement where it wasn't before," he jokes around a cough.

Nova presses his hand more firmly against the wound even though he winces. "Just keep up the pressure. I'm going to check on the others, okay?"

Clint nods. "I'm thinking I'll just sit here for the moment."

Nova pats his hand. "I'll come and check on you. I'd say we'll need your help soon."

Seeing the flicker of a smile she was hoping for, Nova grabs Kian's hand so they can move on.

A few more steps and people rushing about become visible. Annabel spots them and barrels forward, gripping them in a hug. "Avis did a headcount. She's been looking for you!"

Nova hugs her back, relieved that everyone seems safe. "We're fine. The others? Are they okay?"

Before Annabel can answer, Flick rushes over, her curls limp and covered in dust. "Nova! Were you trying to give me a heart attack?"

"Sorry, we were—"

Annabel is scanning frantically, her face still panicked. "Have you seen Luca? He's the only one left to find."

"Luca?" Nova has to work to keep the alarm from her voice. "He said he was going to set up a tripwire..."

Annabel gasps. "Oh no!"

Not sure what that means, Nova's gaze tears to the door Luca would've been at, diligently setting up his little trap so he wouldn't get left behind. The wall has collapsed, reduced to a pile of gunmetal-gray rubble.

"No," Nova moans.

Kian is already running toward it, Nova close behind. They skid to a stop when they reach it.

The pile is almost waist high, the slabs of concrete varying in size. Some would fit in your palm.

Others are the size of a table.

And Luca could be under one of them.

Nova falls to her knees, already scrabbling to clear it away, but Kian grabs her shoulder. "We need to be careful. We don't want it to shift."

Crushing Luca even more.

A sob escapes her throat. He was supposed to be safe.

"What's she doing?"

Nova spins around at the voice—a bright, young voice full of incredulity.

Luca's voice.

He's standing beside Kian, his hands on his hips, his hair now caked and gray. "She knows I can make more wire, doesn't she?"

Kian's gaze catches Nova's. Shock. Relief. Exasperation. A flicker of humor. They all combine as his lips twitch. "She was looking for you."

"For me?" Luca snorts. "I'm faster than any stupid wall trying to squash me."

Nova's shoulders sag. Then tremble. Then shake with laughter. "I'm glad you're okay, Luca."

"Of course I'm okay." He eyes Nova where she sits, still at the edge of the debris. "Do you need a hand up?"

Nova smiles shakily. Her knees still feel like sap. Kian takes a step forward, extending his hand, but Luca darts around him to do the same. "Here, I'll help you."

Touched, Nova takes his small hand, letting him think he's hauling her up. Despite his size, she's surprised at his strength, even if his frown shows how much he's straining.

Once she's standing, Nova dusts herself off. "Thanks, Luca. I—"

The air is knocked straight out of Nova as Luca throws himself at her. His fierce little arms wrap tight around her. "I'm glad you're okay, too," he muffles into her shirt.

She hugs him tightly back, her throat feeling thick. Protectiveness wells within her, telling her she's made the right choice about what she has to do next.

She looks up to find Avis there, her eyes full of relief as she watches them. She nods at Nova, a silent thank you.

Nova dips her head back. It was Avis's courage that gave Luca a chance at life in the first place.

Luca draws back, his eyes blinking rapidly. "I...ah..."

Nova's heart aches. Luca looks lost, and that's not something he'd be comfortable feeling. "Would you go check on Clint for me? He hurt his head and we need to make sure someone is looking after him."

Luca draws his shoulders back, his face recovering its usual confidence. "I'm on it."

He's gone before Nova can thank him and Kian is back by her side. She folds into him gratefully. The adrenaline has well and truly worn off.

Avis joins them, her face drawn. "Everyone's accounted for."

Nova feels Kian's body relax. "That's good." Kian looks around at those moving through the parking lot—some look dazed, others are holding one another, two people are crying. "We were lucky."

"We were," Avis sighs as she looks at the rubble beside them. "At least we'll be able to clean this up in a few days."

Kian's arm tenses around Nova's waist. "Unless the other half of the building falls," he says quietly.

Fear spears through Nova anew. The parking lot isn't likely to survive another collapse.

Avis's shoulders sag, suggesting she's already thought of this. "The rain has been steadily weakening the building. We'll look for somewhere else. In the meantime, we'll do what we can here."

Kian nods. "We'll start the cleanup in the morning and take it from there," he states, his voice hard with determination.

Nova lifts her hand to rest on his chest, pulling away a little. A part of her can't believe she's about to say this. "Once we've cleaned up, we need to go back."

Kian's mouth opens in shock. "Go back? Where?"

"To Askala."

When the words are out, Nova feels something unwind within her. It unclenches from her heart, replaced with the calmness that comes from the knowledge this is what they need to do.

That it's the right thing to do.

Strangely, Avis doesn't look surprised. She nods in understanding. "I was hoping you'd say that."

Nova doesn't have time to ask what that means, because Kian spins around and grips her shoulders.

"Are you sure?" he asks, trying to contain his hope.

Nova nods, her heart more than sure. "We need to build a safe place for everyone."

Including Luca. And Flick and Annabel and Clint. And every other soul who will be the future of this planet.

Including their baby.

KIAN

The ocean, red and sulfurous, is calm as Kian scans it in the dawn light. He draws the acrid scent deep into his lungs. It's the only smell he's ever known when it comes to the sea.

Brushing his hair from his eyes, he wonders if they'll ever find a new normal. One where the ocean is as blue as the sky. Where people can swim in it, play in it, eat from it. Where it's not humanity winning at the cost of Mother Nature.

And not Mother Nature proving they could never win that war.

Nova passes him the food and water, this time even less than they brought when they arrived, and Kian smiles. When he told Nova he'd stay in Fairbanks with her, he meant it. He tried to do this on his own, and only made more of a mess of things. He's realized if he can't lead with his heart, he can't lead at all.

But it turns out she wants this, too. To fight for balance. For peace.

For their child's future.

He should've guessed. His strong, brave, passionate Nova. She's a warrior whether she realizes it or not.

Nova bites her lip as she passes him the bottles of water. "I think we're all set."

He looks at his crew, most of them not who he expected to be on this raft.

Avis had come to them the morning after part of the building collapsed. "You don't need to stay for the cleanup. It's more important that you return to Askala as soon as possible."

Kian had to stop himself from instantly agreeing. The moment he knew they were returning his heart had started tugging at him to get moving, desperate to return. "Are you sure? We could stay for a day or so."

But Avis had shaken her head. "No. This is important." She'd narrowed her eyes and set her jaw. "And I'm going with you."

He'd been surprised but Nova had just nodded. "You want to see Wren and Phoenix."

"Yes, I do." Avis had crossed her arms. "And make sure Cy sees justice for everything he's done."

Kian had nodded. Her knowledge of their mutual enemy could prove useful. "You're welcome to come with us."

Of course, then Luca had appeared, his chin tilted just as stubbornly as Avis's. "I'm coming, too."

They'd been saved from that argument because Finn had approached them, Dharma by his side. He'd shuffled even more than usual, his gangly body looking like it wanted to fold in half and disappear.

"Ah...Kian...I, ah..." Dharma had cleared her throat, almost as if she was doing it for him. Finn had straightened. "I'd like to stay, if that's okay with you."

Kian had been surprised for the second time in as many minutes. "Of course, Finn. I'd never force you to come."

He'd flopped in relief. "It's just that I..." He'd glanced at Dharma then looked back. "I'm happy here."

Nova had gripped his hand then. She knew it was hard for

Kian to hear that someone could find more happiness here than back in Askala. Especially a Bound.

Kian had nodded. "Good luck."

Finn grinned, looking happy in a way Kian hadn't seen before. "I'm pretty sure you'll need it more."

Kian does a last visual check. The tide is running out. There's a tailwind. The conditions couldn't be more perfect. At least they won't be needing any of their luck yet.

The others come to stand beside him. Nova on his right, Avis on his left. Beyond her stands Shiloh, still as silent as she's been since they arrived at Fairbanks. Kian knows she's been avoiding him, and he figured the best thing to do is respect that. It can't be easy for her to see him with Nova...

Next to Nova is Felicia, a gritty frown plastered on her face, Nova's self-appointed guardian angel. He doubts Felicia's keen to return to Askala, but no matter how much Nova argued she should stay, Felicia refused. Nova wasn't leaving without her, and that was that.

And then there's Dean, hovering in the back, his frown far more ferocious. Kian looks away. That's been Dean's expression since they arrived. Possibly since he was born. If it weren't for his strong rowing arms, Kian would've regretted having brought him.

Another deep breath of sulfurous brine and Kian bends over, placing his hands on the raft they'd left up on the rocks. "Let's get this thing into the water."

Everyone does the same and the raft scrapes over the sand, the logs gouging deep ruts. Several shoves and the water lifts the other end. "Everyone get on. Dean and I will push it the rest of the way."

Nova, Shiloh, Avis and Felicia clamber on, spreading themselves out so the raft remains balanced. Keeping his head down, Kian pushes again, his muscles straining. The raft moves, inch by inch, and the ocean slowly takes on the weight on the other side.

The water is at Kian's knees when he jumps on. The sooner they get rowing, the sooner they arrive back in Askala.

And discover what destruction Ronan has wreaked.

Nova glances over his shoulder. "Kian."

He looks up to find Dean hasn't moved. He's standing by the edge of the water, his clothes and body dry.

Not liking what this means, Kian jumps in and wades back, gritting his teeth as his skin starts to prickle. It will be red by the time he makes his way back to the raft again.

Planting himself in front of Dean, Kian can't help the scowl. "Did you forget something?"

Dean's frown is the darkest Kian has seen so far. "I'm not coming."

"And you chose now to tell me?"

Dean shrugs. "Figured it would keep the argument short and sweet."

Kian's hands clench at his sides. After the way Dean has acted this whole trip, why is he surprised by this? "Remember how you promised you'd work hard? Or are promises something you throw away as easily as your responsibilities?"

Even Ronan kept his word.

Dean glares at him. "I'm staying so I can get a Remnant army together. I'll bring them over as soon as I can."

"We don't need an army, Dean. We need to get to Askala."

"I know my brother," Dean bites through gritted teeth. "You'll need an army."

"Kian!"

Kian spins around at the worry in Nova's voice. The raft is floating away, the tide and wind doing what he'd hoped.

Dammit! Dean knew they wouldn't have time to have this conversation. He knew he'd be able to get away with this. No doubt so he can run away and disappear into the Outlands, trying to forge a life just like his brother did.

It would've been his plan all along.

Kian jams a finger into Dean's chest. "I'll give you till the new moon."

He spins away before Dean can answer, striding into the ocean. The water hits his chest by the time he gets to the raft. Hauling himself up, Kian looks back to shore. Just as he suspected, Dean's gone.

"That's probably the last we'll see of him," mutters Kian, a small part of him relieved.

He picks up an oar, noting Nova is already gripping hers on the other side of the raft. A quick nod and they spear them into the water. They've just completed the first stroke when Avis gasps.

"Luca!"

What? Kian and Nova spin around and a cry escapes Nova.

A small body is running into the water, droplets splashing high into the air as he waves his arms frantically.

"Get back, Luca!" Kian roars. "Get out of the water!"

But Luca ignores him, still barreling forward. He pitches over as a wave hits his knees and Avis gasps again. "Luca can't swim."

Breath held, Kian waits for Luca to resurface. His eyes would be stinging by now, his young skin burning. He'll realize he needs to turn around.

Except when Luca's head bobs up, he pushes forward again. His arms flail wildly as he tries to maintain his momentum.

Kian dives into the water, not even bothering to close his eyes. He surfaces, blinking rapidly as he tries to locate Luca. It takes a heart-stopping moment to find him because Luca is no longer making a pretense at swimming. Luca is desperately working to stay afloat.

Striking out with long strokes, Kian kicks with all his might, getting to Luca in time his only goal.

"Kian!" Luca's frightened voice calls out only to be cut off by a wave.

Doubling his effort, Kian swims as fast as he can. Luca calling out was a good thing, but he won't be able to hold his head above water for much longer.

When he reaches Luca, the boy grasps him with the desperation of the drowning. Kian has to kick fast to keep them both afloat, but he hugs Luca hard.

"It's okay," he soothes between panting breaths. "I've got you."

Luca nods, his tight arms trembling around Kian's neck.

"I'm going to turn around. I want you to hold onto my back."

Luca nods again, seeming to have lost the ability to speak for now. Kian loosens the boy's death grip and spins around. Luca's arms are back to clinging to Kian's shoulders in a blink.

The swim back to the raft is slow but steady. Luca's panting breaths count out Kian's strokes as he focuses away from the stinging in his eyes.

They reach the raft and Kian turns so the others can lift Luca up. Once Kian knows he's safely out of the water, he hauls himself back on a second time, his muscles trembling after the frantic rescue.

Nova scuttles over to him, her eyes asking if he's all right. He nods, his chest still heaving from the exertion. "Is he okay?"

Nova moves back so Kian can see Luca squatting beside Avis.

He shakes the water from his hair. "Thanks for the invite," he grins.

Kian flops onto his back, staring up at the sky. "You've got to be kidding me."

There's a rocking of the raft and Luca's face appears above

him. "Too bad we can't go back. It would be a waste of energy and time to go against the wind *and* tide."

Kian shoves himself up, forcing Luca to rear back although he never loses his smile.

"That was dangerous, Luca. For you and me."

Luca only grins wider. "Kinda cool, huh?" He looks around. "You want me to row?"

Kian frowns at him. "No, I don't want you to row." Grabbing an oar himself, he notices Nova trying to hide a smile. "Go and sit somewhere quietly."

Luca salutes him. "Aye, aye captain!"

Scuttling like a crab, Luca heads to Nova, plonking himself beside her. He smiles at her like he's found where he's supposed to be. As the adrenaline wears off, Kian lets out a breath.

The kid's tenacious, he'll give him that. And loyal and brave.

And now Kian's responsibility.

"Let's row," Kian says, his voice far more moderate. He doesn't plan on letting anyone down, and that includes Luca.

The hours pass and the sun gets hotter the higher it climbs into the sky. Kian stays on his side of the raft as the others take turns on the opposite side. Although not Luca, no matter how much he asks.

As the day wears on, Kian sees Nova tire. Her shoulders droop, her face reddens beneath the shawl protecting her skin. Except he knows if he suggests she rest she'll refuse, even though Felicia has already dozed off, her head resting against Avis's shoulder.

Nova offers to take the oar from Shiloh, saying it's her turn, but Shiloh shakes her head.

"Have a rest and then you can take over."

Kian watches as Nova bites her lip and his heart swells. Shiloh's still taking care of Nova, despite everything that's passed between them.

Despite Nova being the one with Kian.

"For the baby," Shiloh urges.

Those are the words that tip Nova into agreeing. She nods, crawling to the center of the raft, but Kian pats the rough timber by his side. "I'll keep you warm," he jokes.

They're all sweating as the sun beats down without even the promise of shade. Hopefully the weather holds and they'll make it to Askala before their water runs out.

Nova smiles back, her face drawn and pale beneath the red as she makes her way toward him. Kian throws Shiloh a grateful look, glad Nova is giving her body a rest, but Shiloh's already focused on rowing again. Her jaw works like she's gritting her teeth. Kian goes to look away, uncomfortable with being the cause of her pain, when his gaze falls on Luca.

He's frowning as he fiddles with his shirt, suddenly looking small in the space Nova just left.

"Luca." Kian indicates for him to join them. "Come and help me keep Nova warm."

Luca's face lights up. He doesn't need to be asked twice, his nimble body zipping over the space between them.

Nova's already laid down, her back against Kian's leg, and she opens her arms. Her eyes flutter closed as Luca tucks into her front and she curls around him protectively. "Mm," she murmurs quietly. "All warm."

Nova's asleep within minutes, Luca dozing off right after her.

Kian focuses on keeping his rowing steady. As Nova and Luca's even breathing keeps in rhythm to his rowing, he starts to consider what they might be about to face. Each pull through the water brings them closer to Askala.

They've seen the violence that happens in the Outlands. It's hard to imagine it existing in Askala, but Kian knows it's the only way Ronan would be able to exert dominance. He thinks of his parents, his siblings, of Dex.

Please let them be okay.

Please don't let them be too late.

Avis shuffles to the front of the raft, and Kian's mind turns to Wren.

She was sent as a spy. She was raised to undermine Askala. To be part of its downfall.

And yet the connections she built went deep. Has her heart won out just like Kian's?

"Kian," Avis whispers. "There." She points and he follows the line of her arm.

The sun is behind them as Kian gazes at the sliver of land visible on the horizon.

Askala.

He glances down, seeing Nova's still asleep, her face soft and relaxed. Her arm wraps protectively around Luca and Kian realizes he's awake.

And yet hasn't moved. Either not wanting to disturb Nova or not wanting the moments of being held to end.

Fear elevates Kian's pulse at the same time as determination settles in his gut. He glances at Avis. "What do you think we're going to see when we get there?"

Avis looks back at him steadily. "That depends. Will the people of Askala do what Cy asks?"

Kian thinks of his father. Of his mother. Of Dex. None of them would align with Ronan and what he stands for. No matter what he threatened. "Not all of them."

Avis looks away, setting her gaze on the horizon as if that will get them there faster. "Then Cy will burn it to the ground."

DEX

*D*ex slams his hand on the door to the courtyard, the sound of his palm slapping the metallic surface echoing around the room. As soon as he'd turned off the radio, he'd headed here, needing a moment before he approaches his father. A moment to figure out if this is the kind of situation where he should be thinking with his head or his heart.

Wren is on the other side of this door.

She came for him.

Or had she run from her father?

This whole thing could be a trap. It's impossible to know.

But she's there. Right there. So close. So far.

The girl who's so right and so wrong, yet no matter how hard he tries, she's in his head. His heart. Every cell of his being.

He wants her by his side. Because without her, he can't breathe.

Or is that just the lack of oxygen in here?

Lurching away from the door, Dex heads down the hallway with his hand extended in front of him and his feet shuffling in a habit he hopes he doesn't hold onto if he ever gets out of the lab. He must look quite ridiculous.

"Callix!" he calls, knowing there's no point in a place this crowded calling out the name *Dad*. "Callix!"

"Over here!" comes the reply from the direction of the dining room.

Dex apologizes to three people on his way to his father's side as he crashes into them.

"You need to open the back door," says Dex, grabbing his father on the sleeve.

"Have you lost your mind?" his father shoots back. "Dex, what's going on?"

"Wren," he says. "She's there. She wants me to open the door."

"Don't trust her!" a man calls from behind them. "She's the Commander's daughter."

"Let me talk to my father," Dex snaps, immediately regretting his tone. He'd done so well to keep his cool until now. It really shouldn't be a surprise it's Wren's return that has him so wound up.

"How do you know she's there?" his father asks, leading him into the dining hall. "The cameras haven't worked since the power went down."

"She has the radio. The one that went missing."

"How did she get that?" His father's voice is laced with incredulity.

"I don't know. We didn't exactly get to have a long conversation."

"It was long enough for her to tell you she loves you."

Dex spins around. "Is that you, Thea?"

"It is. And I think you should let her in. She wasn't lying. I could hear it in her voice."

Dex wonders how many other people had been listening in. Eavesdropping has become a favorite pastime in this place lately. It's impossible to know at any given moment who might be lurking nearby.

285

"It could be a trick," his father says.

"I asked her that." Dex's hand flies to the pendant around his neck. A pendant that's become a symbol of the bond he has with Wren. "She swore it wasn't a trick."

"And you believe her?"

He swallows, nodding in the dark before he answers. "I do."

"She said she could help us," says Thea. "If anyone can get us out of here, it will be Wren. It's got to be worth a shot."

Silence fills the air as Dex waits for his father to think about this.

"It's not a good idea," he finally answers.

"And what is a good idea?" asks Dex. "To wilt away in here? This place is doomed. Open it right now."

"I see." His father is clearly annoyed at having been handed out an order. "So, let me get this straight. You think this place is doomed, yet you want the girl you love to come in here? Not very heroic."

"If she wants to come in here, she doesn't see it as hopeless," Dex says. "We need to trust her. She has a different way of looking at the world. You saw that in the Proving. She solved problems that none of us knew how to tackle, simply because she wasn't trapped by the cages we've built around our minds. She thinks she can find us a way out of here and I believe her."

There's a murmur and he wonders just how many people are listening in this time.

"Let her in," says a man, who sounds suspiciously like the same one who only just moments ago was shouting for him not to trust Wren. "We have no other options. It's worth the risk."

The murmur raises to a dull roar as the people debate which side they find themselves on. But Dex is determined that this time the decision won't be going to a vote. He can't risk a negative outcome. He couldn't accept it or abide by it. He's already decided he's going to open that door whether he does it with permission or by deceit.

"Dex, this could be a huge mistake," his father says. "You have the lives of all these people at stake. If Wren's lying to you then is that something you can live with?"

"If she's lying to me, it seems I won't have to live with it for long," he replies. "Now, open the door."

If he knew how to open it himself, he would. It's the only reason he's standing here having this conversation.

"Callix, listen to him," says Thea. "We have to do something. We can't keep going as we are. That's certain death. At least if we let Wren in then we have a chance. I think everyone here would like that."

A warm hum of agreement fills the room, and hope soars in Dex's chest.

"Aarov!" his father calls. "Where are you?"

"I'm standing right behind you," says Aarov. "And for what it's worth, I think Dex is right. We need to try something different if we're going to find a way out of this mess."

Dex clears his throat, ready to project his voice. "The decision has been made. We're letting Wren into the lab so she can help us find a way out. You put trust in me as your leader and I trust her. If anyone feels strongly against this idea of opening the back door to let Wren in, then you need to speak now."

"I don't th—"

Whoever chose to speak is cut off abruptly and Dex imagines a hand's been clamped over their mouth. He hates that he's pleased not to have to hear the complaint.

"We're frightened," a woman calls out. "We're not ready to die."

Dex thinks immediately of his mother. She hadn't been ready to die either. But still, she had. Is it better to be ready and embrace the death that comes to you, or is it better to be unprepared and have your life taken without warning?

Right now, both those options suck.

"I'm not ready to die, either." Dex turns his face in the direction of the woman who spoke up. "Which is why our best chance is to let Wren in. She knows this lab. And she knows what's going on outside. If we have any hope of finding our way out, we need to let her in."

"Do it, then," says a man. "Before she comes to her senses and changes her mind. I know I would."

"Clear the way." His father grabs Dex by the sleeve and pulls him past the mass of bodies in the doorway and out to the corridor.

"How do we do this?" Dex asks, his heart thumping as he dares to believe that in a matter of moments, Wren will be back with him.

"The generator's by the front door," his father says. "I'm going to power up the lab from there. Aarov will open the security screen for you."

"I'm on it," says Aarov.

Dex heads back down the corridor to the rear door.

"Thank you, everyone," he says, over the hushed silence that's fallen over them. "Thank you for taking a chance. Nobody is hoping more than me that we don't regret it."

He gets to the door and waits.

Waits for the lights. Waits for the gentle hum of the ventilation system. Waits for the blast of fresh air when the screen slides open. Waits for the girl who stole his heart the first moment he saw her. The girl who just sent his stomach into a series of flips when she told him for the second time that she loves him. And he's never had the chance to say it to her in return.

The lights flash on without warning and his father's voice comes bellowing down from the other end of the corridor. "You have thirty seconds, Dex. Starting now."

Dex blinks in the light, willing himself to adjust to the harshness. But it's too much. He's been in the dark for too long now.

So, instead he closes his eyes, hating that the familiarity of the darkness is almost a comfort.

He puts his hand on the door as it slides open. He squints through the impossibly bright light to see the security screen begin to lift.

Trying to keep his eyes open, he crouches down, ready to pull Wren inside the minute there's a sign of her. His blinking slows just a little and he shakes his head, willing his eyes to hurry up and adjust.

A waft of fresh air hits him first as the gap under the screen widens and Dex draws in a deep breath. His whole body sighs in gratitude. He hadn't realized just how oxygen-deprived he'd become.

The screen lifts a little more and he knows this is the moment of truth. Either Wren will be alone as she promised, or she's fooled him for the very last time.

There's a movement so fast, he barely has time to react.

He rocks back, remembering the intense heat of the flamethrower the last time he waited for a door to open.

But instead, Wren comes flying through, rolling under the screen and launching herself at him.

Dex opens his arms as he falls backward, the screech of the security screen closing ringing in his ears.

He lands on his back, yelping as his tender ribs scream in pain. But it's a pain he can tolerate. Because it's a pain that's brought Wren into his arms.

He catches one glimpse of her beautiful face and crazy cropped hair that's growing back in every direction except down, before the lights extinguish and they're plunged into darkness.

He reaches for her, not caring about the blackness surrounding them. In fact, it's a blessing. It's like invisible walls have fallen around them, giving them the privacy this reunion deserves.

Drawing her face toward him, he senses her lips before he feels them.

A long moment of tortured anticipation hovers between them.

"I love you, too, Wren," he says, relieved to have finally been given the opportunity to say the words.

He goes to say more. To tell her exactly what she means to him, but her lips muffle that chance.

As she kisses him, he realizes that words aren't always needed. Sometimes actions can say so much more.

Her lips are as soft as he remembers. Just as sweet. Just as enticing.

He pulls her closer to him and kisses her harder, wondering if they're in danger of using up all the limited oxygen in the room.

"I hear kissing," someone shouts, laughing.

A cheer breaks out around them. There are whistles and applause and whoops of joy.

Dex pulls back, his hand tracing Wren's jaw as a wide smile spreads across his face.

Her arrival has made a difference already. She's lifted these people's spirits and given them back the hope they thought they'd lost forever.

The cheers die down and Dex hauls Wren to her feet.

"Gee, it's dark in here," she says.

He laughs gently.

"And no offense but it doesn't smell the best either." She sounds like she's holding her nose. "How are you people breathing?"

"Not very well," says Aarov. "Which is why we need your help. We have to get out of here."

"Who said that?" asks Wren.

"That was Aarov." Dex wraps an arm around Wren's waist,

not wanting to have any distance between them. "You'll get used to all the voices around here."

"No, I won't," says Wren. "Because we're going to get out of here."

"If it were that easy, don't you think we'd have done it by now," comes Dex's father's voice as he makes his way down the corridor.

"Callix!" says Wren. "Now, there's a voice I'll never forget. *May your Proving serve you well.* I sometimes hear you saying that in my sleep."

"And did it serve you well?" he asks.

"Not especially," she says. "But it did bring me Dex, so I can't complain."

"Have you seen Nova?" asks Thea. "This is her mother speaking. Has she returned to Askala?"

Dex feels Wren's spine straighten. "I'm sorry, Thea, but no. We haven't seen her since she left for the Outlands."

Thea's disappointment is palpable. If Dex knew exactly where she was, he'd go to her and offer her whatever comfort he could.

He jumps when there's a banging noise on the roof and turns his face upward even though there's nothing to see but blackness surrounded by more blackness.

There's more thumping. So much that it sounds almost like the roof is going to cave in.

"They're on the roof!" Aarov calls. "Turn the power on, Callix. If we were waiting for our emergency, we've got it now."

Dex tenses as he hears his father's footsteps pummeling back down the corridor, his grip on Wren tightening as he instantly regrets allowing her inside this death trap.

People are whimpering now, most likely clutching each other in the same way he's holding Wren.

"What are they doing?" he asks over the noise of the rising panic.

"I don't know," Wren says. "But Aarov's right. That's the sound of their boots on the roof. Cy must've come up with a new plan."

"What's that smell?" someone calls. "Can you smell that?"

The lights flick back on and Dex blinks, not finding it quite as blinding this time.

It looks like all fifty of them are in the hallway and in unison, they turn their faces upward to see the most terrifying sight Dex could ever imagine.

The air vents are no longer pumping fresh air into the lab.

They're pumping thick gray smoke.

WREN

*I*t's worse inside the lab than Wren had imagined. She's not sure anyone would be capable of picturing a hell like this.

It was a shock stepping into the blackness, the air thin and putrid with too many oxygen dependent bodies trapped in this small space. It had been darker than the Outlands on a night of a new moon until Callix had turned the generator on.

But the moment she'd landed on top of Dex and their lips had found each other's, the shock had evaporated, morphing into something closer to a feeling of relief. Or coming home. Because she doesn't belong in the Outlands anymore, nor does she belong in Askala. She only knows that she belongs with Dex.

Which would all be terrific if it weren't for the small—okay, make that huge—problem of the smoke pouring through the air vents.

Looking around at the faces surrounding her, she almost wishes for the lights to go down again. At least in the darkness, she couldn't see the way these people are looking at her. It's like they think she's their savior. Although, she did sort of imply that's exactly what she'd come here to do, so she supposes she deserves those desperate looks.

"Shut down the ventilation system!" Dex shouts. "It will slow the smoke."

"It's not isolated," Callix calls back. "To shut that, I have to shut the power."

"Then do it!"

"They're trying to set us on fire!" someone shouts.

"Don't panic," Callix calls back. "The lab is fireproof. Nothing can burn through the exterior. It's just a bit of smoke."

The lights blink off and Wren breathes out a sigh.

Right, think Wren, think. She has to come up with something.

"Get some wet cloth and stuff them in the vents," she says, knowing this isn't the solution but desperate to buy some time and keep these people busy. "Use towels, your shirts, sheets, anything that you can find. We have to keep this smoke out."

There's the shuffling of feet as people mobilize and figure out how to get the job done.

She wraps her arm tightly around Dex's waist.

"What's the real plan?" he asks. "How are we going to dig ourselves out of this hole?"

"Maybe that's it?" Her eyes spring open in the dark. "We can dig out from one of the walls in the secret room."

"Already thought of that," he says, jabbing a pin in her bubble of hope. "But that's as useless as opening one of the doors. Ronan's men will torch us the moment we pop our heads up. We're no match for twenty trained fighters."

"Fifteen," she says, hope igniting again. "Four died when you were brought to the lab. A fifth one died...just before."

"Better odds...But still not quite good enough."

She's glad he doesn't ask how the fifth one died. Garbo's death isn't a story she's ready to relive just yet.

An idea hits her, so clear she's amazed it took her this long to come up with it.

"Then how about…" She draws in a breath, trying to get her words right. "How about we open one of the doors? Just half-way. And we wait."

"Wait for what?" he asks. "To die?"

"No." She wonders if he can hear her rolling her eyes at him in the dark. "They'll expect someone to come out, but we won't. We'll be inside waiting for one of them to come in. That will take some time. Valuable time for fresh air to come in. Then when someone comes in, we're ready for him. We'll tackle him. Immobilize him. Get his flamethrower. Close the door before anyone else can enter."

"And then what?" She can hear the disbelief in his voice.

"And then we do it again with only fourteen to go. One at a time, we'll pick them off. Each time will be easier as we'll have one extra weapon. There must be fifty people in here. We can do this."

Dex remains silent as he thinks it over.

"It's a good plan, Dex," says Callix.

Wren spins around in the direction of his voice. She's not sure she'll ever get used to this darkness.

"It is," says Dex. "Any plan is better than a total lack of plan, which is what we had before Wren got here. Lucky we let her in, hey?"

Wren senses some resentment in his voice toward his father. Had Callix been against letting her inside?

"Phoenix is on the radio!" says a deep male voice. Aarov, perhaps? "Says he'll only talk to Wren! Hurry!"

Wren's heart thumps. She'd left the radio outside the door in the hope Phoenix would find it. After all, he said he'd stolen it in case he'd needed to communicate with her.

Her feet tap as she tries to figure out which direction the computer lab is in. All the commotion has her questioning which way she's even facing. She squeezes Dex's hand. "Can you take me there?"

He pulls on her hand and she follows, impressed at how confident he seems moving about.

They walk quickly, Wren trying to angle herself so she's behind Dex. It's impossible to shake the feeling she's about to slam straight into a wall.

She hears Dex mumble a few apologies, but they make it to the computer room.

"Wren! Wren! Wren! Can you hear me? Wren!"

Phoenix's voice over the radio is clear and familiar. It's almost like he's in the room.

"Phoenix!" she shouts. "I'm here. Talk to me! What's happening out there? We have smoke coming through the vents. We can hear Cy's men on the roof."

"Wren, you have to get out," he replies. "Now! I don't care what's going on in there. Get the hell out of there right now. That's an or—order."

The breaking of his voice sends a crack tearing through Wren's heart. She shared a womb with this guy. They've always been together. He knows her better than anyone. Even the guy she'd left him to stand beside.

"I can't leave," she says to him. "They need me in here."

"And I need you out here. I never should have given you that blasted radio! This is all my fault."

The radio crackles and Wren moves a little closer.

"It is not your fault, Phee. Don't blame yourself."

Silence.

"Phoenix?"

"Don't forget—"

The line turns to crackle and Wren puts her hand on the radio, tapping it with her fingertips.

"Phoenix? Phoenix?" Then turning to Dex. "What's happened? Where is he?"

"I don't know." Dex places his hands on her shoulders. "Maybe the radio battery ran out? Maybe someone came and he had to turn the radio off."

"Or maybe someone hurt him," she says, trying to face up to the most likely truth.

Dex drops a kiss on the top of Wren's head, squeezing her like he's trying to extract her anguish.

"The vents are all blocked," a woman calls from the doorway. "What do we do next? A few of our youngsters are starting to have breathing problems."

"We open the door," says Dex, taking Wren's hand and pulling her back toward the doorway.

"We what?" several people say at once.

"Attention, everyone," Dex calls over the din of worried people. "We have a plan. It's a risky one, but if we do it right, it will work. It's our only hope."

Wren tilts her head as he talks, wondering if this is really Dex whose hand she's holding. She's never heard him take charge like that. It's only then she realizes that somehow, in all of this, he's become their leader.

"We're going to open the front door," he says. "Just enough to let one man in before we close it. I need some volunteers to help disarm and secure him. To...to kill him if needed. Once we've disposed of him, we'll let another man in. We'll keep going as long as we have to. There are fifteen soldiers out there. We can't fight them when they're united, but we can take them on one by one. Who's with me?"

There's silence for a long few seconds, before a cheer erupts. Wren smiles, glad her idea hadn't been shot down before it'd been given a chance.

"We need to get organized," calls Dex, over the noise of the people as they settle to listen. "If you're not a fighter, then we need you out of the way. Please take refuge in the secret room downstairs and keep the hatch closed. We don't know if Ronan's aware of the room's existence. It could work in your favor if things go wrong. If you're prepared to fight, please fetch any weapon you can get your hands on and move toward the front door. Now!"

Wren checks that the knife is still sitting at her back, knowing there's a good chance she's going to have to take the lead with the attack. Saying you're prepared to kill a man is far different to actually doing it. Even a scumbag like Garbo hadn't been a pleasure to dispose of.

"You don't have to be the one to fight," says Dex, leaning down toward her.

"Are you kidding me?" She punches him gently in the ribs and feels him bend over as he yelps.

"Dex! Are you hurt? Is this what Cy did to you in the ballroom?"

"I'm fine." He snatches at her hand and drags her down the hallway. "We don't have time for this right now."

She nods even though he can't see her. Her following footsteps and closed lips should be enough to tell him that she agrees, no matter how much she wants to check on his injuries.

Knowing Dex is in pain refuels her anger. There's no way he's going to stop her from fighting. She doesn't care how protective he is. This was her idea. She's the best fighter here. She's going to take the lead.

"Is everyone here who wants to be here?" Dex asks. "Please say yes so I can get an idea of how many of you we have."

A series of yeses bounce from the walls. Wren's surprised to hear so many of them. She'd thought maybe half a dozen would volunteer, but it sounds like around twenty people. Possibly more.

"Some of you will have met Wren before," says Dex. "I once saw her kill a leatherskin with her bare hands."

"And a knife," she adds.

"Have you got any advice before we open the door?" he asks. "How should we approach this?"

Wren pulls back her shoulders, pleased that Dex is positioning her as the expert. "This isn't going to be easy," she says. "Cy's men are trained to fight. And they're good at it. But they won't be expecting the ambush when they get inside. That's where our advantage lies. The first to come in is likely to already be firing his flamethrower as he rolls under the screen. Do we have anything we can use to smother the flames?"

"How about a blanket?" says Thea.

"Thea?" Wren's surprised that she's volunteered to fight. "What are you doing here?"

"Fighting for our lives," she answers. "Fighting to get back to my daughter. But right at this minute, I'm off to collect as many blankets as I can find."

"Thank you, Thea," says Dex. "Good work."

"We'll throw the blankets over the flames," says Wren. "Then two by two, we attack. Priority one is to disarm him. Priority two is to demobilize him. Hitting him over the head with his own weapon is particularly effective. Knives work well, too. Whatever you choose to do, you must do it fast. If you give him time to think, our advantage is lost."

"If anyone wants to back out, now's your chance," adds Dex. "Because once that security screen lifts, it's too late. When the lights go on, assemble yourself into pairs and be ready."

"The generator's almost connected," says Callix. "As soon as Thea has the blankets, we're good to go."

Excitement thrums through Wren's veins as she lets go of Dex's hand and readies herself for the fight ahead. Fighting is what she knows. She's trained for this moment her whole life.

Dex pulls Wren back to him and presses his cheek to hers.

"Be careful," he whispers directly into her ear. "I just got you back. I'm not losing you again."

"You'll never lose me." She slides her cheek across the roughness of his and kisses him.

There's nowhere near the time to give him the kind of kiss she yearns for, so instead she injects as much feeling as she can into the few short seconds that she's pressed against him. If they ever manage to get out of this lab, she's going to do a lot more of this in the future. She fully intends to kiss him until he's in danger of his lips falling off.

"I've got the blankets," Thea shouts, her breathless voice travelling toward them.

Wren barely hears the hum of the generator as the lights switch on. She's too busy blinking and rubbing at her eyes as she tries to adjust to the brightness.

Looking around, she sees about a dozen people gathered. Fewer than she'd thought. Or perhaps some had second thoughts and retreated before it was too late.

She sizes them up, uncertain if this was the army she would have selected given the choice. But there's no point thinking this because this is the army she has.

Thea has placed a large pile of heavy blankets by the front door. She's already holding one, ready to throw at the first sign of a flamethrower.

Wren shifts her gaze to Dex, wanting to drink in the sight of him one more time.

He looks a mess. But he's her mess and her heart lurches to see him. His hair is sticking up in knots, his face is covered in the stubble she'd felt brushing against her cheek, and he has dark rings underneath his eyes.

His eyes lock on her and they nod at each other.

They're ready.

"Who's our first pair?" Callix asks.

"We are," Wren and Dex say in unison, not needing to ask each other if that was the plan.

Wren withdraws the knife from her waistband, tosses it in the air and catches it by the handle.

Dex goes to Aarov who's holding a smaller knife out for him to take.

Two knives versus a flamethrower. Wren can only hope this will go the way she wants it to.

Callix is staring at Dex, a frightened look on his face. It seems the man of steel has feelings after all. He's clearly worried about his son.

Dex goes to Callix and to Wren's surprise he kisses his father on the cheek.

"Open the door, Dad," he says as he pulls back.

Callix swallows, tears his eyes from Dex and presses some buttons on a keypad.

The door slides back.

Wren and Dex position themselves about a yard back from the door, with Thea off to the side, ready to pounce.

Callix presses another button and the security screen lifts. When it gets about three feet off the ground, it halts.

"Is that enough?" Callix asks.

"Perfect," says Wren, not lifting her eyes from the gap, no matter how much she wants to turn to look at Dex enjoying this fresh hit of oxygen.

As Wren expected, nothing happens at first. Cy and his men will be weighing up their options, trying to decide how to approach what must be an unexpected development.

"Hold steady," says Wren. "It's going to take a moment for them to realize we're not coming out. Don't throw the blanket until you see the actual weapon, Thea."

As if on cue, a burst of flame licks its way under the door, sweeping across from left to right, falling just short of where they stand.

"Hold!" Wren says, following her own advice as she maintains her position. Feet apart, knees bent slightly, knife firmly gripped and extended.

From the corner of her eye, she can see that Dex has mimicked her pose.

"Get read—"

A man rolls under the screen. Fast. He's on his feet before Thea's had a chance to throw her blanket. His flamethrower is pointed directly at Dex, thankfully devoid of fire right now. If Wren lunges at him now, Dex will be fried on the spot.

The security screen is already closing when Wren hears the familiar click of the trigger.

"Thea!" she screams.

The blanket comes flying at the soldier just as she sees the flame leap out of the end of the barrel. It smothers the flame and Wren is only a split second from making her move to slice the soldier's throat when the blanket catches fire. A huge whooshing sound fills her ears as the flame rapidly grows, catching the soldier's shirt and lighting him up like a candle.

It happens so quickly and dramatically Wren isn't sure if this move had been genius or a disaster.

The soldier falls to the floor, rolling as he tries to put out the flames. But he only entangles the blanket further around himself and the weapon, which is still spewing out flames. He's screaming the most terrifying sound Wren has ever heard.

Wren and Dex take a step back as Wren tries to figure out what has gone so horribly wrong.

Then it hits her.

Hemp. The blankets are made from hemp. They're not like the woolen blankets they use back home in the Outlands. She hadn't realized they'd be so much more flammable.

"Get back!" she shouts. "Our clothes will catch fire. It's the hemp. It burns."

The people back away, some screaming, others staring with wide eyes and open jaws.

The soldier is somehow succeeding at putting out the flames and Thea grabs another blanket and throws it over the top of him. It ignites and this time his hair catches fire.

"No more!" shouts Wren, unable to stand watching a man burn alive. "There are other ways."

Unbelievably, the soldier gets to his knees, howling in agony. He tries to turn around, desperate to get back outside. But the screen is now firmly closed and he collapses on the pile of blankets beside the door, turning them into a fireball.

The flames ignite, a huge burst of color and heat licking up to the ceiling. The soldier's cries fall silent as an awful smell fills the hallway. It's a little like the time Cy barbequed a polar grizzly. It makes her stomach turn over.

"We need to put out the fire!" Dex screams as he tears at his hair. "It's catching on the walls."

"I thought Callix said this place is fireproof," she says, panic starting to tear at her insides as her heart beats like it's outside her chest.

"The outside is," says Dex. "But not when the fire is coming from the inside."

"Fire needs oxygen." She's shouting now, trying to lift her voice over the roar of the flames.

"It does." Dex's arms fall to his side in a gesture that looks an awful lot like defeat. "Which means we're either going to burn to death or suffocate."

Someone throws a bucket of water over what's left of the soldier, but it's far too late. The flames are climbing the walls, gobbling up the ancient plaster like a leatherskin on a feeding frenzy.

The smoke builds and Wren puts her elbow over her mouth, trying to filter out the worst of it before it hits her lungs.

"Open the back door!" someone shouts. "Hurry, Callix. We have to get out of here."

"It's too late," Callix shouts back, just as the electricity buzzes and dies. "The control system's just gone up."

The sound of fire seems to rise a few notches as darkness descends, the eerie flickering of the flames the only source of light.

Dex hauls Wren away from the fire and her lungs are given a momentary reprieve.

He throws her against a wall, presses himself against her and kisses her.

Hard.

It's like it's the last kiss on Earth. Which for them it most likely is.

She drops her knife and reaches for the back of his head, her tears running down her cheeks and mingling with the kiss as they slide over her lips.

"You never should have come in here," Dex says, breaking away, his forehead leaning against hers. "I'm sorry."

"I'm not," she replies.

And she means it. She'd face death one hundred times over if it means being kissed like that.

Her plan failed. The lab is burning. Her future with Dex is coming to a catastrophic end.

All when she'd been certain they were just getting started.

There's no doubt the only thing that will save them now is a miracle. And they need it in the next few seconds.

That's not too much to ask for.

Is it?

THE END

Ready for the next installment?
Check out Book 4, RECKONING, now!
http://mybook.to/ReckoningThaw

BOOK FOUR - RECKONING

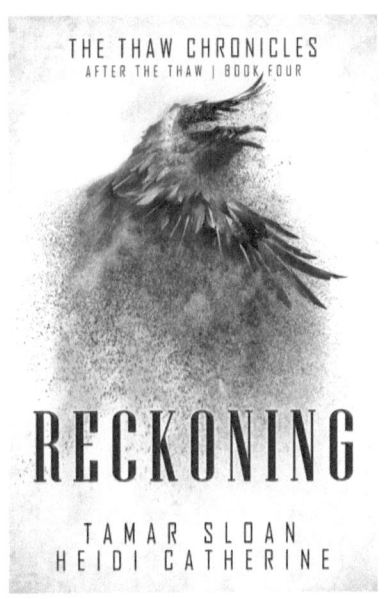

Only the chosen shall breed.

Nova. Kian. Dex. Wren.

Four teens reunited, only to discover their world has been torn apart.

Askala has been seized by a new order. A cruel army that rules
with greed and fear. An army that seems impossible to defeat.

Forced into the forest, the people struggle to survive using all they've learned from the harshness of the Outlands. Bound, Unbound and Remnant alike are going to have to create unity in a world founded on division if they are to win.

Will they discover a way to carve a better path for the future? A future about more than just fighting to survive. A future where all can thrive, not just the chosen few.

In the greatest battle for Askala yet, sides will be chosen and loyalty will be tested. Is it possible that love and intelligence were the key all along?

Lovers of Divergent, The Hunger Games, and The Maze Runner will be blown away by the breathtaking conclusion to After the Thaw from USA Today best-selling author Tamar Sloan and award-winning author Heidi Catherine.

Grab your copy now!
http://mybook.to/ReckoningThaw

WANT TO STAY IN TOUCH?

If you'd like to be the first for to hear all the news from Tamar and Heidi, be sure to sign up to our newsletter. Subscribers receive bonus content, early cover reveals and sneaky snippets of upcoming books. We'd love you to join us!

SIGN UP HERE:

https://sendfox.com/tamarandheidi

ABOUT THE AUTHORS

Tamar Sloan hasn't decided whether she's a psychologist who loves writing, or a writer with a lifelong fascination with psychology. She must have been someone pretty awesome in a previous life (past life regression indicated a Care Bear), because she gets to do both. When not reading, writing or working with teens, Tamar can be found with her husband and two children enjoying country life in their small slice of the Australian bush.

Heidi Catherine loves the way her books give her the opportunity to escape into worlds vastly different to her own life in the burbs. While she quite enjoys killing her characters (especially the awful ones), she promises she's far better behaved in real life. Other than writing and reading, Heidi's current obsessions include watching far too much reality TV with the excuse that it's research for her books.

MORE SERIES TO FALL IN LOVE WITH...

ALSO BY TAMAR SLOAN AND HEIDI CATHERINE

The Sovereign Code

Elemental Games

ALSO BY TAMAR SLOAN

Keepers of the Grail

Keepers of the Light

Keepers of the Chalice

Keepers of Excalibur

Zodiac Guardians

Descendants of the Gods

Prime Prophecy

ALSO BY HEIDI CATHERINE

The Kingdoms of Evernow

The Soulweaver